MEMORIES OF CÍBOLA

12/5/04

Para Rogelio y
Su Pardo —

Grandes Amigos
de Costa Rica.

Abrazos,

A. P.

University of New Mexico Press   Albuquerque

Abe M. Peña

Memories of Cíbola

Stories from
New Mexico
Villages

FOREWORD BY MARC SIMMONS

© 1997 by the University of New Mexico Press

All rights reserved. Third paperback printing, 1999

Library of Congress Cataloging-in-Publication Data

Peña, Abe M., 1926–

Memories of Cíbola: Stories from New Mexico Villages / Abe M. Peña / foreword by Marc
Simmons

1st ed. p. cm.

ISBN 0-8263-1773-1 (paperback)

1. Hispanic Americans—New Mexico—Folklore.
2. Tales—New Mexico
3. New Mexico—Social life and customs.
I. Title.
GR111.H57P46 1997

398.2′089680789—DC20   96-25288

CIP

Unless otherwise credited, all illustrations are reproduced
courtesy the author's private collection.

Designed by Sue Niewiarowski

I dedicate this book to Viola, my wife

and

*To our daughter Ramona, and her husband
Norman Alires, and our grandchildren
Andrea and Marco.*

*To our daughter Paula, and her husband
Michael Ladd, and our grandchildren
Maria, Michele and Paul Michael.*

*To our daughter Cecilia and
her husband Randy Salisbury.*

And to our son Marco José Peña.

Contents

Foreword

My friend Abelicio (Abe) M. Peña has a good ear for a story. I've heard him firsthand relate a number of them, and I've read a good many more that he has put down on paper. Reinforcing Abe Peña's story-telling ability is the rich reservoir he draws upon for his source material—the traditional Hispanic culture of west-central New Mexico and its generous supply of native wit and wisdom. He has a strong sense of history, too.

Growing up on an old-style sheep ranch near the village of San Mateo, Peña was given the opportunity to know personally the wonderful, quirky, always interesting people who spun out their lives in that beautiful but isolated and harsh land. Their unusual doings, which he observed, were filed away in the back of his mind for future reference.

In 1953–54 Peña traveled to Australia as a Fulbright scholar to study wool production at the University of New South Wales. When he came home again, it was to the job of foreman on one of New Mexico's largest sheep operations, the one owned by the Frank A Hubbell Company in Catron County.

That ranching enterprise, Peña has said, was still following the traditional system of using sheepherders on the range rather than unattended grazing inside netwire fences. Working closely with numbers of old-time herders, the foreman was able to collect and store away an additional body of lore associated with rural life and customs.

After returning to manage the family ranch at San Mateo for an extended period, Abe Peña received a call from the White

House offering him the directorship of the Peace Corps in Honduras. Peña and his family left for a new career in the foreign service in Latin America in 1972. He directed Peace Corps and USAID programs in several countries.

Upon his government retirement, in 1984, he and his wife Viola settled in Grants, just around the corner from his boyhood home at San Mateo. Since that time, Peña has devoted himself to ranching, public service, volunteer service with AARP, and to the ingathering and refinement of this splendid trove of tales.

The collection of folk histories that makes up his book contains examples so expressive that, I am convinced, they bear retelling again and again. In addition to the usual elements of humor and pathos, tragedy and triumph that one is accustomed to find in stories, these also contain the quiet truths as represented in the lives of the New Mexico paisanos of yesteryear.

The careers of some of Peña's out-of-the-way characters are often rocky, but they generally lead to pleasant pastures. And in the quickly glimpsed lives of individuals and families we see how these people made real the "American Dream" of each generation improving their lives.

The engaging men and women who walk so free through his pages seem infused with the elixir of southwestern air and landscape and with the tonic of their own vibrant cultural history. The majority are inherently decent; a few are flawed and would probably be rated as tragic figures. All have stories worth recording, as Abe Peña so ably proves.

The author himself, having actually lived the life that he describes, can address his subject with words authentic and vivid. He has captured the mood of a time now gone and the spirit of an earth-bound people who are fast fading from memory. I for one am gladdened that Abe Peña has saved these tales, and I have no hesitation in extending them my heartfelt recommendation.

—*Marc Simmons*

Preface

In December 1987 Joe Looney, a reporter with the *Grants Daily Beacon*, and I were having a cup of coffee at the Monte Carlo Cafe in Grants. He asked about traditional Hispanic Christmas plays or pageants, and I excitedly told him about Los Pastores, the shepherds' pageant performed in San Mateo and other Hispanic villages during the Christmas holidays. He said, "Abe, why don't you write that up for the *Beacon*?" I came home and wrote what was to be my first story, "Los Pastores." That began a relationship with the paper that continues to this day. Since then, the *Beacon* has published every story I've given them.

This book is a compilation of those and other stories about the daily lives of the people of northwestern New Mexico, especially the Hispanic people. The people communicated orally, and very little is left in writing. Much of the material for these stories came from listening to people tell their stories and from old-timers who shared their memories with me. Feedback on the stories when they were published was positive and encouraging.

Following are some of the comments that convinced me to continue writing and sharing the daily lives of our forebears. From Barbara Salazar, "Abe, I want you to know how much I enjoyed your story of Los Pastores in the *Beacon*. The way you described the shepherd Bartolo breaking into a jig when he saw the Christ child, gave me goose bumps and made me feel like breaking into a jig myself!" Frank Barela at Tommy's Phillips 66 continually reprimanded me when I stopped to gas up if there wasn't a story in that day's paper. Tactfully he reminded me that Elias Saavedra from San Rafael had stopped by and was not buying the *Beacon* that day because there wasn't a story in it.

The late Celito Jaramillo, a boyhood friend from San Mateo who lived in Grants and was homebound from a stroke, called me frequently to suggest I keep on writing, because he "enjoyed the stories" and was clipping them and sending copies to friends and relations outside the area.

Florencio Marquez, the barber on First Street, told me he saved all the stories and also sent copies to his sister Felicita and her family in California. Ted Allen, a friend and history buff, told me he wanted to be the first in line when I put the stories into a book.

Readers called seeking information about individuals in the stories and thanked me for writing about a relative, an acquaintance, or an ancestor. Calls came from Arizona, California, Colorado, Texas, and New Mexico. Schoolteachers began asking me to speak about local history to their classes. A teacher in Cubero had one of my stories tacked to the bulletin board. "I tack every story you write." Several children gathered around us and identified me from the *Beacon* picture with the title "From the Past." I could sense their excitement. They were ready to listen and I was ready to share my knowledge with them of the history of Hispanic northwestern New Mexico. I found that in general, the younger readers wanted to learn about their past and the older readers wanted to relive theirs. I also found that there was little written about the daily lives of our people.

People in the Spanish and Mexican colonial periods were struggling to survive, tending their small farms and livestock and focusing on the church, not on schools. Very few people could write, and most of what was written consisted of official land and court records, kept in Santa Fe by officials who came from Spain. There were also church records, kept by priests trained in Spain.

Little was written or has been published about life in villages, especially in west central New Mexico. This book provides a look into the life of the village. The people you meet are real people.

The stories fill a void and provide a window into the past, not only in Cíbola County, but in northern New Mexico and throughout the Southwest where Hispanic people settled with similar customs and traditions.

Memories of Cíbola: Stories from New Mexico Villages consists of six parts, each with a brief introduction, highlighting important locales in the region: Seboyeta, San Mateo, San Rafael, Grants, Navajoland, and Cíbola. Within each part are stories of people, culture, and customs. Because my ancestry stems from Seboyeta and San Mateo, part two in particular contains the most stories.

In addition to those that appeared in the *Beacon*, some of the stories were published in *Prime Time* in Albuquerque; some in *Enchantment*, the Rural Electrification Administration (REA) magazine distributed throughout rural New Mexico; some in *The Voice of the Southwest*, published by the Diocese of Gallup; some in *La Herencia del Norte*, published in Santa Fe; and some in *Noticias*, newsletter of the Hispano Genealogical Research Center of New Mexico.

This book is intended to teach everyone—from children in the primary grades, to the life-long learner—about the daily lives of the people of Cíbola and northwestern New Mexico. The stories in large part tell about the people who came from Spain to Mexico and their descendants, who traveled north to colonize this beautiful region of the United States, inhabited by American Indians and known today as America's Land of Enchantment.

Acknowledgments

I wish to acknowledge the *Cíbola County Beacon,* formerly the *Grants Daily Beacon,* which published many of the stories in this book over a period of eight years. There were several changes in publishers and editors over that time, but the newspaper's support never wavered.

Also my sister, Sister Lydia M. Peña, of the Sisters of Loretto and a university professor and author, who spent many hours of precious vacation time helping edit and reviewing the manuscript. And my brothers Bennie, Fermin and Eddie, and our younger sister Dorothy, for a lifetime of support. Also Lena Cisneros Sweeney, my sister-in-law, who spent many hours proof-reading.

I am dedicating this work to my wife, Viola (Fabiola) Cisneros Peña, and to our children, their spouses and our precious grandchildren. All were a source of inspiration to me. Viola listened patiently to every story at the breakfast table and offered suggestions for improvement and kept encouraging me. "You have to keep on writing, Abe. People are reading your stories in the *Beacon* and keep looking forward to the next one. That's what they're telling me wherever I go." She also checked the spelling of all Spanish words.

I also wish to note the help of Marilyn Mabery, a writer and friend, who read some of the stories and offered suggestions on grammar, composition, and overall presentation. Also Professors Patricio Rojas and Betty Habiger, who helped with the computer, saving the stories and putting them on floppy disks.

The late Fray Angélico Chávez, my mentor, whom I would meet at his "office" in Santa Fe—an ornate park bench on the Plaza—where I picked his brain.

Dr. Gerald Thomas, past president of New Mexico State University, and Mrs. Thomas have been loyal supporters through the years. The late Celito Jaramillo's keen memory led to some of the stories you'll be reading. He frequently called to relay information or a verse or two from a *corrido* he remembered.

I especially wish to acknowledge writer and historian Marc Simmons, who read some of the stories and encouraged me to share them with the University of New Mexico Press, which led to this book. Marc's timely notes of encouragement while I wrote, rewrote, and labored on the manuscript kept me going.

Finally I wish to acknowledge the help of the Almighty, my silent partner in this whole enterprise.

West-Central New Mexico

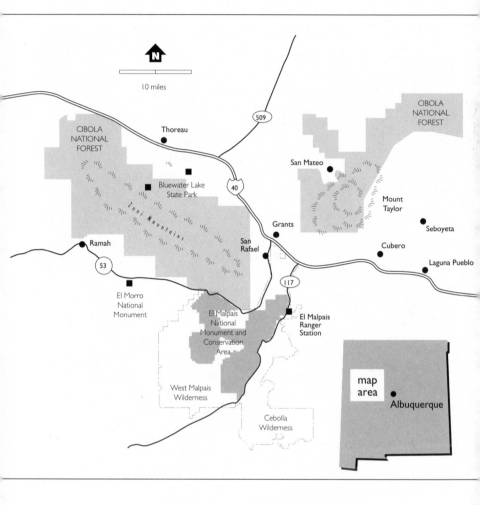

Map taken from Robinson, El Malpais.
Map drafted by Carol Cooperrider

In his Dictionary of New Mexico
and Southern Colorado Spanish,
Professor Rubén Cobos states that
Cíbola was the "sixteenth-century
Spanish name for Zuni and
all the lands which later (in 1583)
became known as Nueba Mexico."
The stories in this book
are one part of Cíbola's story.

PART ONE

The Mother Village

Seboyeta is considered the mother village to the Hispanic expansion west into the land of Cíbola.

Around March 1, 1800, cart wheels squeaked and groaned, as thirty settlers and their families slowly made their way west from Albuquerque-Atrisco on the Río Grande to settle "Cebolleta." It was one of the first Hispanic settlements west of the Río Grande, and the first one west of the Río Puerco.

In 1804 the village was attacked by Navajos and besieged for four days. When the Navajos could not penetrate the fortress village, they finally left. A short time later, fearing for the safety of their families, the settlers decided to leave and return to the Río Grande but were met by some thirty soldiers sent from Santa Fe with the promise of protection. They returned, and the village has not been abandoned since. Here are some of their stories.

Seboyeta

From Don Juan de Oñate, who carved his name on Inscription Rock at El Morro in 1605, to 1800 when Seboyeta was founded, little happened in western New Mexico. A Franciscan mission to the Navajos was started in Seboyeta in 1746, by Father Menchero, but within two years it was abandoned for lack of support or interest on the part of the nomadic Indians.

On January 23, 1800, Governor Fernando Chacón granted thirty bold colonists from the Albuquerque-Atrisco area a community land grant at "Cebolleta." Governor Chacón was very specific in his written instructions. He told them, "possession of said place is granted on condition that you form a regular settlement and not abandon it under any pretext." The original grant document with all the appropriate seals and stamps of the Spanish crown spells the name "Cevolleta," later spelled "Cebolleta" and today, "Seboyeta." The settlers took physical possession on March 16, 1800, from Don José Manuel Aragón, the alcalde and principal justice, acting on behalf of Governor Chacón. He wrote in his report, "The settlers today received the grant in community and the suertes individually and acknowledged same by throwing stones in the air, pulling weeds and shouting, God save the King, three times. Wherefore they hold and enjoy all the ownership over said tracts which I have distributed for such is the will of His Majesty the King."

King Charles IV reigned over New Mexico, Texas, Arizona, and California through his viceroyalty in Mexico City. Not forgetting their religious obligations, the colonists asked the alcalde if the Catholic church, yet to be built, could be named Nuestra Señora de Los Dolores, Our Lady of Sorrows (see Fig. 1). Their request was granted, and by 1820 the church was finished. It still stands today. As a child in the 1930s, I recall playing in the shadows of the magnificent structure. It seemed like a monumental cathedral at that time.

Upon receiving the grant, the colonists set about building a walled village to protect themselves from the Navajos (see Fig. 2). They worked feverishly to build a secure village, with the back of the houses having no windows and forming the outside wall about 10 feet high. Two entrances with circular adjacent guard towers were constructed. One faced south and the other faced east. The foot-thick wooden doors at both entrances were hand-hewn of ponderosa pine. I remember as a boy playing in the tower we called "el torreón." It had circular steps inside that led to peepholes with a good view to the east. The towers are gone now, but to this day one can see part of the old wall that surrounded this historic village.

The nearby Laguna Indians maintained peaceful relations with the Hispanic settlers. Navajos, on the other hand, felt the continued encroachment was not in their best interest. The assertion of their territorial rights led to conflict. In part it was the settlers' fault. They often organized raiding parties to the west over the mountains and kidnapped Navajo children, then ran for their lives to their walled village. Young maidens had a value of up to five hundred pesos in the Albuquerque-Alameda area. They were trained to serve as maids and servants, relieving the patrón's wife from domestic work. They also became nannies to the children, who grew to love them dearly.

In 1804 the Navajos attacked and laid siege to the walled village. During the battle they threw "hand grenades" made of pine pitch, in an attempt to burn the village. Of this encounter, Gary Tietjen, the author of *Encounter with the Frontier*, wrote,

> At one point in the battle, one brave woman, Doña Antonia Romero, climbed to a housetop to see if all was well and was horrified to see a Navajo had just climbed over the

wall. . . . He was in the act of drawing the bar of the great
wooden door, hewn from ponderosa pine, while swarms of
Navajos were waiting outside for the moment to break in.
Snatching a heavy stone metate Doña Antonia lifted it
above her head and brought it down with all her strength
on the head of the savage, killing him instantly. She thus
proved herself worthy of her courageous husband, Don
Domingo Baca. . . . In the hand to hand combat Baca had
seven lances driven into him. One cut across his stomach
so wide that his bowels fell out. Grabbing a pillow he tied it
around his abdomen and was able to continue fighting until the attack subsided. Afterwards he replaced his entrails
and sewed up his own wound.

In 1805 because of repeated encounters and constant threats
from the Navajos, a plea was sent to the governor in Santa Fe for
their release from the covenant "not to abandon the village under any pretext." Without a response, they decided to leave, and
on the way to Albuquerque, were met by thirty soldiers sent by
the governor to protect them. They returned to Seboyeta. As
relations with the Navajos improved and trouble subsided,
Seboyeta became the Mother Village from which settlers founded
San Mateo in 1862, San Rafael in 1865, and El Concho, in Arizona, in 1869.

Don Fermín

The church bells tolled, and the word went forth that Don Fermín
had died. It was late in the afternoon, a cold and windy eleventh
day of February, 1930. He was born August 30, 1870, in the
village of Seboyeta, to Rita Candelaria Márquez and José Rafael
Márquez. He died suddenly of pneumonia at age fifty-nine, in
the village of his birth.

As the bells rang, some of his neighbors, as was the custom,
started toward the Márquez home near the church, to pay their

respects to the widow, Doña Beneranda. Don Fermín, whom we called "Mi Pandín," was my maternal grandfather, and Doña Beneranda, whom we called "Mi Lala," was my grandmother. I was four years old when he passed away. His life and death are but a foggy blur in my mind. His passing was told and retold in the family for many years. Sometimes I wonder whether I really remember him at all, or merely recall stories I heard as I grew up.

In those days they took the coffin outdoors and took pictures with members of the family (see Fig. 3). The first known picture of me was taken with him. I am standing among several others of his grandchildren surrounding the coffin on the day of the funeral. In another picture Mi Lala is flanking the coffin, along with her daughters, Rita, Perfilia, Prudencia, Pablita (my mother) and Onofre. Anastacio, the only son, is standing at the head of the coffin.

A beautiful 18-carat gold ring encrusted with grape leaves, made for him by Casimiro Lucero, a talented goldsmith from San Rafael, was filed off his finger and passed on to his son, Anastacio. When Mi Tío Anastacio passed away in 1987, the ring went to his youngest son, Anastacio, Jr. In 1991 when my mother died, the last offspring of Don Fermín to pass away, Anastacio, Jr., came to her funeral and gave me our grandfather's gold ring, saying, "You are preserving the family history, and I want you to have it." I wear it today.

He was about 5 feet 9 inches tall, thin of build, with black hair, a medium complexion, and a very prominent mustache. He was an entrepreneur and built a successful merchandise and livestock enterprise. He had ranching properties at La Lagrimilla, east of Seboyeta, and in the summers grazed his sheep on La Sierra de San Mateo (Mount Taylor). When he started sheep ranching, he got some sheep, *al partido* (on shares), from Don Silvestre Mirabal, a large sheep rancher from San Rafael. Don Silvestre helped many young men get their start in the sheep business. He and Don Fermín became good friends, and so did their wives, who were related. Grandmother said she and Doña Lorencita spent many afternoons "quilting in a quiet room of the large house in San Rafael."

Mother used to tell the story of her father sleepwalking. "Mi
Lala told us she heard a wagon sometime past midnight going
down the road at a noisy trot. She noticed her husband was not
in bed and got up to see what was going on." Looking out the
window, she saw Don Fermín in his long johns in the moonlit
night, reins in hand, standing on the wagon and urging his horses
to go faster! She hurried to Uncle Demetrio, her son-in-law who
lived nearby, and gave instructions to "follow Fermín and bring
him back." He saddled his horse and gave chase. He caught up
with him on the road to La Lagrimilla, "going to check on my
sheep herds!"

Don Fermín liked to play poker. Mother told of *taures* (card
sharks) coming from Albuquerque and sometimes playing "for
two or three days around the clock." She told us of the night her
mother cried. She feared he was becoming addicted to cards and
losing a lot of money. Mother, about fourteen years old, went to
the room behind the store where they were playing. "I entered
the semidark room lit by a kerosene lantern. Crying, I ran to the
table and pulled the blanket off the table. Chips and cards flew in
every direction. Father followed me to the house without saying
a word."

Wallace Gunn from Laguna says, "I remember Don Fermín
very well. He had one of the first cars in Seboyeta, a Maxwell,"
and tells of the problems they had trying to keep those first cars
running. "There was an old blacksmith in Laguna who came with
the railroad and was a fair mechanic." Once he spotted Don Fermín
pulling his car with a team of horses towards the blacksmith shop
and said, "Here comes my best customer!" (see Fig. 4).

Don Fermín was a member of the Republican party and served
two terms as county commissioner in Valencia County. He was
serving on the commission when they built the old brick courthouse in Los Lunas, shortly after the turn of the century. I remember seeing his name on the bronze plaque at the entrance to
the courthouse. When they tore down the building in the 1960s
I tried to find the plaque, but with no success.

When Don Lizardo Salazar, my father's stepfather, and
Manuelita Peña Salazar, his mother, of San Mateo, asked by let-

ter for the hand of Pablita Márquez to marry their son Pablo Peña, on February 10, 1922, it read in part, "Nos dirijimos a ustedes con el fin de aserles saber que nuestro hijo, Pablo Peña nos a manifestado, que el desea y pide la mano de su adorada hija, la jovencita Pablita Márquez, para unirse con ella en la compañía conyugal del matrimonio" ("We address ourselves to you to let you know that our son, Pablo Peña, has manifested to us that he desires and asks for the hand in marriage of your beloved daughter, the young lady Pablita Márquez, to unite with her in holy matrimony"; see Fig. 5).

They were married on February 27, 1922, and launched an exemplary marriage, as well as starting a fine relationship between father-in-law and son-in-law in the world of business. Pablo Peña sought business advice from the more experienced man, sometimes by letter. We have two letters written by Don Fermín. One is dated in October and another in November of 1923, responding to Pablo's questions on business matters. The letterhead on the stationery, printed in bold type, reads: Fermin Marquez—Criador de Ovejas y Comerciente. The November letter begins, "Apreciable hijo, acabo de recivir tu carta en la misma me dices que están buenos tu y mi hija. Eso es lo que yo les deseo," etc. ("My Dear Son, I have just received your letter in which you tell me that you and my daughter are doing fine. That is what I desire for you," etc.). It is very evident they liked and had a lot of respect for each other (see Fig. 6).

When he died in 1930, he had lost most of his business to pay debts from cards. I still wear his ring with pride and reverence, a precious memento of my grandfather.

Mi Madre

Pablo put his foot out to trip Pablita on her way out from the dance hall in 1920. That gesture led to marriage in 1922!

Pablo Ortega Peña first met Pablita Chavez Márquez in 1917, at St. Vincent's Academy in Albuquerque, where she was a student (see Fig. 7). He and his father, Abelicio, had stopped to visit his sister Eufemia, also a student at the Academy. Eufemia, age twelve was a friend of Pablita, age thirteen, and introduced her to her father and her brother. Pablita used to say, "We visited in the parlor. We were all very proper and very formal." She added that "Don Abelicio was a large imposing man in a dark suit and Pablo, age eighteen, was a handsome young man, also in a suit." Then she would say, with a telling smile, "Pablo gave me *cuatro reales* when they were leaving. I never forgot him!"

Pablita was my mother. Her parents were merchants and stockgrowers in Seboyeta. They had purchased a home on Twelfth Street in Albuquerque to be close to better schooling for their children. Her father, Don Fermín Márquez, spent most of his time in Seboyeta tending to business, and her mother, Beneranda Chávez Márquez stayed in Albuquerque with the children, although she preferred life in the village. Mother said, "We rode the train from Laguna to Albuquerque. Sometimes my father, whom we called "Mi Pandín," took us in his car. He had one of the first cars in the village and the roads were terrible. We more or less followed the wagon tracks to Laguna and the railroad tracks to Albuquerque. *La cuesta* (the hill) between Paguate and Laguna was a monster. Sometimes we had to push the car going up hill, and sometimes walked when going down hill."

In her youth the camptenders came with the burros from the sheep camps to pick up groceries at Seboyeta. She had a favorite burro called "El Pardo," which she usually rode while the camptender loaded "las provisiones." She recalled that one time she kept asking for El Pardo and they told her, "That's it." It looked like El Pardo, but she wasn't sure. She didn't think it was, but finally, her friend Anita persuaded her. She mounted the burro and he pitched her over a 4 foot high adobe wall into a cornfield! In a fury she pulled a corn stalk and chased Anita, "For telling me a lie and laughing when the burro threw me!"

Pablita had four sisters and one brother: Perfilia, Rita, Prudencia, Onofre, and Anastacio. She used to say, "When we were young we did very little housework. We had servants. I didn't learn to cook until after I got married."

After the episode of the outstretched foot at the dance hall, the courtship picked up. Pablo often rode his horse over the mountain to Seboyeta. Pablita used to say, "In the beginning he was dating another Pabla from Moquino. She was a very pretty girl, but in the end . . . I got him!" Some letters found in Pablo's files show the true grit of this remarkable seventeen-year-old girl. In a letter dated January 29, 1922, she wrote in Spanish, "You say in your letter you cannot come in February. This is to inform you that if you do not come in February I can no longer wait for you. Therefore, if you want to marry me it has to be right away" (see Fig. 8).

Twelve days later, on February 10, Don Fermín and Doña Beneranda received a letter from Pablo's mother, Manuelita, and his stepfather, Lizardo Salazar, asking for Pablita's hand, after a most courteous introduction in polished Spanish. It was Pablo's handwriting! (See also pages 30–36.)

On February 27, 1922, seventeen days later, they were married by Father Robert Kalt, the legendary Padre Roberto, at Our Lady of Sorrows Catholic Church in Seboyeta. With an inheritance of 225 sheep and a modest house in San Mateo, they started a new life that bound them, for better or for worse, for sixty-four years.

Pablita was a friendly and caring neighbor, and she soon made many friends in San Mateo. She very quickly learned to do housework and became a noted cook and a meticulous housekeeper. Their first child, Benito (Bennie), named after his paternal grandmother Benita, was born in 1924. One day Pablo drove in with a load of firewood from La Mesa del Pino, and Bennie, a toddler, imitating his elders, found a little rock to put behind the wagon wheel. Somehow the horses moved, and the wheel caught his little head and hand. It cut him behind the ear and split a thumb and the wounds bled profusely. He recovered but gave his parents a scare.

I followed Bennie in 1926 and was named after my paternal grandfather, Abelicio. Fermín came next, named after our maternal grandfather, then Eduardo (Eddie), followed by Eloy, and after five boys came a little girl, named Lydia. Pablo was a great admirer of the professional singer Lydia Mendoza, who brought many pleasant moments to our isolated villages through radio and the Victrola during the Great Depression. I recall turning the crank on the old phonograph to keep the record going.

On December 4, 1934, when Lydia was born, Pablo took out his Colt 45 and fired several shots into the starry night. It was a happy night for the family and for the whole village, tucked in the shadows of majestic Mount Taylor.

Dorothy, the last one of my brothers and sisters, was also delivered by Doña Virginia. We loved Dorothy. It's fair to say we spoiled her, but still she turned out a beautiful person in every way. She was given the name Dorothy by her sponsors, which shows the trend away from Spanish names, and the proverbial American melting pot at work.

Pablita's other sisters married and went in different directions. Perfilia married Samuel García and moved to Belen, where they raised a family of seven. Rita married Demetrio Chavez; they had eight children, but she died young, and he took the family to California. Mi Tío Demetrio was a hundred years old when he died in 1995. Prudencia married Cornelio Anzures and moved to Winslow, Arizona, where she had four children. Onofre, the youngest, married Manuel Chavez of Seboyeta and died delivering her first child.

Don Fermín passed away in 1930, at the age of fifty-nine, and Doña Beneranda was later laid to rest by his side, at age seventy-one, in the Seboyeta cemetary. I was four years old when my grandfather died, and I vaguely remember a foggy figure in a dark suit.

Anastacio, their only son, continued the family tradition and lived in Seboyeta most of his life. He married Juanita Sandoval and had four boys and a girl. Juanita died when the children were young, and he remarried. From his second marriage, to Elisa Archunde, Leonore, a daughter, was born. All the children moved to Albuquerque except Edwina, but they return from time to time to visit the village of their birth.

Pablita was very religious and followed the tenets and commandments of the Catholic Church with fervent determination. We all bathed religiously on Saturdays, in *cajetes en la casa vieja,* and never missed Mass on Sundays. Our Franciscan priests came from Grants, and all my brothers and I served as altar boys at one time or another, as did the other boys in the village. We all got a chance to pull the rope and ring the bell and recite the responses in Latin. They called us *sacristanes.*

For many years Pablita hosted the priest for lunch. Conversation at the table was encouraged, and we all asked questions and discussed religion and other subjects of the day. A glimpse of the outside world beyond our village came to us while breaking bread with a number of priests, including Father Robert, Father Remigius, Father Cecil, Father Godfrey, and others who came from back East.

All during my childhood Pablo was building his flocks and Pablita was his helpmate. She told us, "In the middle of the Great Depression of the 1930s your father did not know how he was going to pay the taxes on the 640 acre homestead. I had quietly saved coins in a jar for a rainy day. We used them to pay the taxes . . . and kept on going!" "Prayer" she used to say, "is very important in our lives." She frequently reminded us, "Resen hijitos, Dios nos ama mucho" ("Pray my children, God loves us very much"). Our whole village was generally oriented toward prayer. Our ancestors who came to colonize New Mexico survived the tremendous hardships of the colonial days through prayer—and a lot of hard work.

Dances were an important part of our lives. Both my parents liked to dance, as did most of the people in the village. It was one of the few social outlets that gave us an opportunity to enjoy music and where our young people could meet their future spouses!

Pablita helped organize and lead the church Ladies' Sodality. She also chaired the committee that organized village festivities for the historic Coronado Cuarto Centennial in 1940, the four hundredth anniversary of the arrival of Coronado in New Mexico (see Fig. 9). When they moved to Grants, in 1962, she joined the Third Order of Saint Francis, and Pablo joined the Knights of Columbus.

In 1945 she was awarded a citation for meritorious service by

Governor Thomas J. Mabry, "In grateful recognition of your outstanding contribution for our victory in 1945. National War Fund."

Her neighbors, especially Tía Sostena Trujillo and Tía Sostia Baca, helped Pablita raise her seven children. I recall Tía Sostena telling us stories of *brujas,* but there were no children's books that I can remember. The only stories we heard were oral, and most of them scary ones about witches. She told us the story of the "mad dog" that came barking to the door of a house in San Mateo one night. The man of the house, after repeated attempts to chase the "mad dog" away, finally took his gun and shot the menacing creature. The next day came news from San Fidel, 25 miles across the mountain, that a certain lady reputed to be a bruja had died during the night of gunshot wounds!

Mother instructed us not to fight. However, in all humans there does seem to be an innate desire at times to fight, or fight back. Our village was no exception, although fights were rare. I recall being in a fistfight only once. I was being beaten up on the way back from school and I fought back. Policarpio Montaño was the constable, and he locked the three of us in a chicken coop! When word got to mother that I was in Flavio Montaño's coop for fighting, she told the messenger, "Just leave him there, it will teach him a good lesson!" It was one of the most important lessons I learned in my youth.

Eloy, our youngest brother, was a normal healthy young boy until he contracted rheumatic fever. No cure had been found for the disease at that time, but Pablita and Pablo left no stone unturned looking for medical help, as he lost more and more weight and his heart weakened. It seemed that as his body shrank, his "heart" grew, embracing the whole village. Everyone loved him and cared for him. His classmates rallied round him. The Lord took him in September 1954 at age twenty. Mother, whose own heart was broken, bravely said what all of us were thinking—"He only takes the best." His picture was on their dresser the rest of their lives. (See also pages 89–91.)

One of her happiest moments was seeing her daughter Lydia take the sacred vows of a Sister of Loretto in Nerynx, Kentucky.

She used to say, "I pray one of my children will serve God in a religious order." Her prayers were answered when Lydia left for the convent. Pablo, who had been skeptical when his vivacious daughter announced her intentions to become a nun, six years earlier, was there beaming with pride. He was her greatest champion. It made all of us happy.

Pablita and Pablo traveled to Europe, to Central and South America, to Hawaii, to Mexico—always interested in other peoples and other cultures. Mother made friends wherever she went. Many stopped to visit my parents when they came through the area.

Pablo passed away in 1986, at age eighty-seven, and was laid to rest at Grants Memorial Cemetery. Pablita ably took the reins of the family, telling us, "We must remain strong and united." And she advised us, "Do not forget to say your prayers and always remember your responsibility to each other, to our community, and to your country." Pablita passed away in 1991, also at age eighty-seven. She was the last to die of the children of Don Fermín and Doña Beneranda. Six of her children, twenty-four grandchildren, and several great grandchildren survived her. Each one of us was special to her—and she was special to each one of us.

Anastacio Márquez

Anastacio Márquez, born August 13, 1900, was not only my uncle, he was my friend. We became close friends in the 1950s, when I was managing the Peña Ranch, near San Mateo, and he was farming and ranching "El Cerro," near Seboyeta.

The 1950s were very dry years, and we purchased hay from him to get through the drought. He raised alfalfa by pumping water out of the deep arroyo that ran by his farm to irrigate his thirsty fields, and also had allotted water from the village irrigation system. The rustic water pump required a lot of attention to keep it running. He wore knee-length rubber boots and smoked his crusty pipe all day, walking between the alfalfa fields and the stubborn pump in the arroyo. From time to time, a neighbor from the village dropped by and exchanged pleasantries, talked about the drought, told stories, laughed, and went on. People liked him, and he liked people (see Fig. 10).

Anastacio was the only son of Fermín Márquez and Beneranda Márquez. He had five sisters: Perfilia, Rita, Prudencia, Pablita (my mother) and Onofre.

After grade school in Seboyeta, he attended St. Michaels in Santa Fe and later Menaul High School in Albuquerque. He was a good student and a fine baseball player. Throughout life he listened to baseball games on radio until television came along. Now he could see his favorites on the TV screen in color. He and my father were about the same age, were close friends, and had lively and loud conversations about America's favorite pastime. They argued about their teams and players. Joe DiMaggio of the Yankees was a favorite of both of them.

Mi Tío married Juanita Romero, and they had five children: Edwina, Alfredo, Rosendo, Orlando, and Anastacio, Jr. Mi Tía Juanita died relatively young, and Mi Tío married again. His new wife was Elisa Archunde, and they had one daughter, Leonore.

Tío Anastacio was very involved with the affairs of the Seboyeta Land Grant. The grant was given in 1800 by the crown of Spain to thirty petitioners from Atrisco, and Seboyeta was established as one of the first Hispanic settlements west of the Río Grande. He served as a trustee and as president for several years. The Seboyeta Land Grant is one of the few that has remained in the hands of the people, heirs of the original grantees, in New Mexico.

He also worked very hard with members of the community to procure an irrigation system and reservoir to better utilize the water from springs running off Mount Taylor down Seboyeta Canyon. He recognized the importance of water in this semiarid country of ours.

Mi Tío came from an old Republican family and remained a Republican all his life. He was a local leader in the party and believed that a strong two-party system was the best way to better government. I ran as a Republican for the New Mexico House of Representatives twice and for the Senate once in the 1960s. He was my campaign manager in the village of Seboyeta. I lost all three elections, the last one by sixty-four votes in what was then Valencia County, out of which Cíbola County was carved in 1981. Like a true friend, he never wavered in his support for me or for our party.

All his children except Edwina, who married Luis Jaramillo from nearby Moquino, moved to Albuquerque. They return from time to time to keep in touch with their roots.

Elisa was the postmaster and ran the post office as well as a small store in their house in the village. The El Cerro farm with an old comfortable house was about a mile from their home, and he spent most of the summer at El Cerro tending to his crops. Besides alfalfa, he also had a fine vegetable garden. According to Edwina, "Luis used to help him at the farm, and we remember Dad's cooking. His chile was the best, especially green chile." Seboyeta has always had a fine reputation for growing the best and most flavorful chile in Cíbola County. Apparently the southern exposure at the base of Mount Taylor combines the right conditions for producing "el sabroso chile de Seboyeta."

As youngsters we went from San Mateo to spend summers with Mi Lala, our widowed grandmother in Seboyeta. Next to the main house was a tall, two-story house that was used for storage and sleeping when guests overflowed the main house. It had a large room upstairs where the grandchildren played when we couldn't play outside. Next to the tall house was Mi Tío Demetrio's and Mi Tía Rita's house. They had a lot of children, and their ages matched our own, so we had a lot in common. That closeness has remained to this day, even though they live in California. Tío Demetrio Chávez celebrated his one hundredth birthday in May 1994 and died in March 1995. He and Tío Anastacio, besides being brothers-in-law, were good friends and had a lot of respect for each other.

As we grew older, there was less playing and more working. We learned to hitch the horses and haul alfalfa from the fields to the barn and hayloft for storage. But even in the midst of working, it was fun to lie on top of a wagon loaded with alfalfa hay as it made its swaying way to the barn or hayloft.

I also recall the sweet and succulent grapes our grandmother raised. When they ripened, she escorted us to the vineyard and encouraged us to fill our pockets, "but take only what you can eat." The peaches and apples, especially some of the colonial varieties that came with the settlers in the 1800s, had a special Seboyeta flavor.

Mi Tío Anastacio and Elisa moved to Albuquerque in the 1970s, to be closer to their family and have better access to health care. We stopped to visit them frequently. Mi Tío was a great storyteller and had a fine mind that recalled a lot of detail of things past. He liked to tell of the spring of 1946, when Pablo Peña, his brother-in-law, purchased a herd of sheep from Alfredo Mirabal of San Rafael. He asked Tío Anastacio if he would lamb the sheep at the Mirabal ranch, near Sawyer in the Zuni Mountains.

It was a relatively wet spring, and the sheep lambed very well; almost a one hundred percent lamb crop. Sheep tend to be good mothers when they have plenty of green feed. Their udders fill up with milk and require constant nursing from a healthy lamb to keep the pressure down and bearable. He had about eight men to lamb the eight hundred sheep.

As he told it, "about mid-May in the thick of the lamb drop, an electrical storm passed through. It almost killed me. I was riding my horse to check on the drop herd. As I approached a grove of tall trees, lightning struck one of them, and it splintered to pieces. A sliver whistled past me, and another struck the horse. He reared and I fell off. We both survived, but those five seconds seemed like an eternity!"

On June 4, 1987, he passed away in Albuquerque, where he had lived out his final days. He was laid to rest at Sunset Memorial Cemetery, facing west to his beloved village of Seboyeta.

PART TWO

At the Mouth of the Canyon

I have some friends in San Mateo who argue that the village was founded in the 1700s. The belief comes from the fact that two land grants were granted in the eighteenth century: la merced de Bartolomé Fernández, granted in 1767, and la merced de Santiago Durán y Chaves, granted a year later, in 1768. The latter is better known as the San Mateo Springs Grant, on which the village is situated. However, it was almost one hundred years before either grant was utilized or inhabited. There was considerable fear of the Navajos until 1862, when the first settlers came from Seboyeta, the mother village, to stay, bringing their families and starting to build homes. They had been coming for two or three summers before that, grazing their flocks and planting crops but returning to Seboyeta in the winters.

The village was built at the mouth of San Mateo Canyon, on the northwest side in the shadow of Mount Taylor, known in the colonial period as La Sierra de San Mateo, and known to the Navajos as Tsoodził, "Sacred Mountain of the South," or Dootl'izhii Dziił, "Turquoise Mountain." An abundant spring provided water to the settlers for home use, livestock, and irrigation.

The settlers chose the name San Mateo for the church, after St. Matthew, one of the apostles of Christ and the evangelist who wrote the first gospel. In the Hispanic period, villages generally adopted the name given the church. The statue of St. Matthew has permanent residence in the church and has taken part in many processions through the years, especially for La Fiesta de San Mateo, on September 21.

There's the story that one year he was taken in procession in July to the fields and gardens to show him the need for rain. The following day a hailstorm hit the fields and did a lot of damage to the crops. The villagers once again took him in procession to show him "La porquería que hizo!" ("The mess he made!")

I was born and raised in San Mateo, and the village still draws me, as it does the others who grew up there. Our roots go deep. Some of us didn't move too far away. I now live in nearby Grants, and I visit San Mateo often, especially now that my contemporaries are passing on. Many of my visits now seem to involve funerals. But in the stories that follow, you will have the opportunity to see them and our elders as they are remembered by those who knew and loved them.

I must admit that some of the individuals in the stories may sound "almost perfect," but that's the way I remember them. It is also how they were generally remembered by others whom I respected while I listened to their stories.

San Mateo Springs Grant

On February 5, 1768, Santiago Durán y Chaves petitioned Governor Don Pedro Fermín de Mendinueta for a land grant known as Los Ojos de San Mateo, on the northwest slope of the "San Mateo Peaks," today called Mount Taylor. Santiago Durán y Chaves was from Atrisco and stated in his petition that he had "80 mares, 40 mules, 1000 sheep, and some other livestock belonging to his mother" that needed grass.

The grant was made and witnessed by Mateo de Peña Redonda; it instructed Bartolomé Fernández de la Pedrera, chief alcalde, "to proceed to the place named and place said Santiago Durán y Chaves in possession of said grant . . . provided it does not displace Apache/Navajos or interfere with their cornfields." The conveyance was made by picking up rocks and throwing them to the four winds, cutting grass and pitching it in the air, and saying, "God save the King" three times, after which the land passed to the grantee. It included, "The spring and the valley of San Mateo bounded by mesas surrounding said valley and containing about 4 leagues of land more or less." Four leagues would have been approximately 17,000 acres. A year earlier, in September 1767, Governor Mendinueta had granted Bartolomé Fernández a grant north of San Mateo, "including the valley of San Miguel," amounting to about 21,176 acres. The petition read "for military services of Bartolomé, his father and grandfather in the reconquest of New Mexico."

Because of the remoteness of both grants from the more settled Río Grande Valley and out of respect and fear for the

Navajos, neither grant was utilized until almost a hundred years later. About 1834 Manuel Chaves from Seboyeta and a small group of young men went on a trading expedition into Navajo country, where they were assaulted by Navajos at Chusca. With multiple wounds, Manuel and an Indian boy raised in Seboyeta, started back to home, they were the only survivors. They reached some large oaks west of what is now the village of San Mateo, where the Floyd W. Lee ranch headquarters is currently located. While resting, he promised he would build a chapel to the Virgin Mary under the large oaks, if he recovered from his wounds. The Indian boy died. A party sent from the walled village of Seboyeta found Manuel and carried him across the mountain back home.

The village of San Mateo was finally settled in 1862 by several colonists from Seboyeta, followed shortly by Román Baca, who settled at nearby El Rito. He was a half-brother to Colonel Manuel Chaves. The Colonel, now a distinguished veteran of the Civil War, returned in 1870 to build the chapel he had promised and to build a ranch in the meadows about a mile west of the village, known as Chavesville in some of the handsketched maps of that period. The stage coach from Santa Fe to Fort Wingate passed through it. Don Román A. Baca built a home on the grant at El Rito, two miles to the south of Chavesville, and called it "La Providencia." With the blessing of his older brother, he filed a claim for the San Mateo Springs Grant as an heir to Santiago Durán y Chaves. In his claim he stated, "I am one of the present owners and reside upon same."

On April 4, 1883, after years of testimony and dispute, the claim was approved by H. M. Atkinson, Surveyor General of the United States in Santa Fe. A counterclaim was filed, however, and it was sixteen years before Chief Justice Joseph Reed of the New Mexico Supreme Court eventually ruled in favor of Don Román Baca in 1898. Don Román, a former captain in the New Mexico Volunteers, was a large rotund man and a stern taskmaster. "He expanded the ranch operations that reached more than 40,000 sheep," according to Marc Simmons, in *The Little Lion of the Southwest*, the life of Col. Manuel Chaves. In concluding his book, Simmons wrote,

In late January of 1889 a bulletin went out from Grants Station south of San Mateo. The Little Lion had finally been defeated; the light flickered out at last. Manuel's casket was a hollowed log prepared by his sons, and he was placed to rest, according to the Spanish custom of his ancestors, beneath the altar of his beloved chapel. When his devoted wife Vicenta followed him in death six years later, she was laid beside him. And as the spring winds swept off the highest crags of the San Mateo Peaks, the oak leaves whispered: He sleeps his last sleep, He has fought his last battle; No sound can waken him to glory again.

Two sons and two daughters survived them: Amado, Ireneo, Luz, and Vicenta.

In 1916 Amado Chaves wrote a letter to George R. Baucus, in which he referred to the "Fernandez Company," using the name of one of the original grantees, Bartolomé Fernández, "owned by three men, A. B. McMillen 82,000 shares; J. A. Jestro 150,000 shares and Amado Chaves 68,000 shares for a total of 300,000 shares." Later in his letters Amado mentions "a large sum of money owed to the bank." The end of the Chaves era apparently came thereafter, when he sold his shares to pay the bank.

A. B. McMillen, called "El Maxemila" by the Spanish people, assumed the operation of the ranch, and Floyd W. Lee was hired to work there. Floyd W. Lee had attained the rank of sergeant in the First World War and quickly rose to manager and eventually owner of the sheep and cattle ranch. Mr. Lee expanded the ranch. The sheep were sold off in the 1970s because of heavy losses to coyotes and a declining market for wool, and today it's one of the largest cattle ranches in New Mexico.

San Mateo

On September 21, the village of San Mateo celebrates "Las Fiestas" that date back to 1862, when the village was founded. It was named after Saint Matthew the Evangelist, and the feast revolves around the Catholic church services. There are vespers starting with a rosary and a procession on September 20, and the celebration of the Holy Mass on September 21. The padrinos, usually a young couple, make sure the church is in good repair and presentable for the occasion. The role of the sponsors was most important. The church was plastered annually, and they had the responsibility of organizing the community to mix the mud and straw, erect the scaffolds, and plaster the walls with the palm of the hand (in later years with a trowel). It kept the adobe church in good repair, gave it a fresh look, and provided the excuse for a social occasion in the close-knit community.

I recall the preparations we made in anticipation of Las Fiestas. We groomed our horses to a shine and polished our shoes as best we could. Work shoes were our Sunday best during the Great Depression and the Great Drought of the 1930s. We stacked hay and shelled corn to feed the horses of relatives and visitors who came from other villages to join us. Meanwhile the women gathered the vegetables and fruits and stored and preserved them to feed our guests, as well as provide food for the coming winter. San Mateo Spring, on the slopes of Mount Taylor ran steadily through the village and even in a drought provided water for the house, the garden crops, and hay and grain, as well as the livestock.

The pace quickened on September 19, when, El Carnaval de Don Chema arrived. A very large tent was set up. Local boys assisted with the tent, bleachers, and platforms. In return we were given a free ticket to one of the performances during the two-night stand.

Don Chema was a comic. When dressed as a clown, he used to say, "No soy chistoso porque me gusta, es la necesidad!" ("I'm not funny because I like it, it's to keep the wolf away!") As I recall there were several acts, including tumblers, jugglers, and clowns. They also set up games of chance, such as baseball throws and penny pitching. The outside world had come to us, and we laughed and enjoyed every bit of it.

Vendors also arrived and set up hamburger, fruit, and chile stands. I especially remember the first ice cream stand that kept the ice cream frozen like a rock in dry ice in an 8-inch steel cylinder. It took force to carve and scoop it, but that first ice cream was a wonderful treat. There was only one flavor, vanilla, and to this day it still is my favorite.

Sometimes there was rooster pulling, but generally that was a sport practiced earlier in the summer, for the feast of San Juan or Santa Ana. Horse races were very popular. Our horses were hardworking steeds that played as hard as they worked. They didn't look very pretty, but we thought they were handsome as they pranced down the street on the way to the starting line.

The Fiestas concluded with a big dance. The women sat on benches all around the perimeter of the dance hall, while the men stood three and four deep at the entrance. When the music started, we walked across the dance floor and invited a partner to dance. Our girls were some of the prettiest in the country. The musicians would play half a number and then stop. *El colector* then moved among the couples and collected ten cents from the men. After the collection the music resumed, and when it ended we escorted our partner with gallantry back to her bench, then returned to the entrance to wait for the next number.

Usually we danced until the lanterns ran out of gas, then went home to sleep and store the memory of another Fiesta. In my parents' day they danced till the candles burned out. ¡Viva la Fiesta!

Juan Ortega

Juan Ortega married Encarnación Perea Ortega, from Alameda on the Río Grande, north of Albuquerque. Their daughter Manuelita, one of four daughters and four sons, married my grandfather Abelicio Mariño Peña.

Juan Ortega came to San Mateo, according to my father, from the Concho country in Arizona. He came from the same corral as the Ortegas from eastern Arizona and western New Mexico, who gained prominence in the trading post and Indian jewelry business. He lived to over 100 years of age—some say 107. One time when a schoolteacher from the Río Grande Valley asked him the secret of a long life, he answered, "Hard work and a good apple." He had the largest apple orchard in the village!

I remember him as an old man with very fair skin, white hair, and a very erect posture. He probably was about 5 feet 9 inches tall, but he seemed taller. In our youth we tended to see elders and other people we admired as taller than they really were.

"Mi Paye," as his children and grandchildren called him, was a very hard worker and kept his productive orchard and farm, as well as his person, immaculately clean. He and Mi Nana Encarnación raised two grandchildren in their senior years, Efrén Ortega and Ramona Ortega Martínez. Ramona was a vivacious girl with a beautiful milky complexion, two dimples, and a Goya smile. She was always on the lookout for anyone approaching the house, so she could run and give the alarm. This included the times some of us tried to sneak in and steal an apple or two, then run for our lives! Our parents had orchards also, but the fruit was always better in our neighbor's orchard.

My brother Eddie tells of the time he overheard Mi Paye and his good friend Don Felipe Gutiérrez talking under an old apple tree. Mi Paye began, "As a young boy I was herding a small flock of sheep and goats in the San Mateo canyon when marauding Navajos approached and tried to steal the herd." He put up a fight and they ran an arrow through his arm, just below the elbow. "I was able to save some of the flock." *La Curandera* treated the wound with herbal medicines, and he recovered in short order. I remember that his arm was partly atrophied, but it didn't seem to impede his ability to use it almost normally.

He also talked about a wagon trip they took from San Mateo to the wool market at La Junta, Colorado, about 1878, with several wagonloads of wool. The most vivid images were of the problems they had crossing swollen rivers. Normally the rivers were low and easy to cross, but that year hard rains made it a grueling adventure. The task was made doubly hard because the wool, packed in 6 foot long burlap bags, weighing about 200 pounds, had to stay dry. The price was discounted by the buyers if it was wet or discolored.

His eyesight started failing when he was over a hundred. One time several of us, mostly great grandchildren, were up on one of his choice trees, helping ourselves to delicious ripe apples. We had, of course, been warned to stay off that tree. He grabbed a *barejón* (pole) and blindly struck at the tree where he could hear noises—but he couldn't see us.

In the fall during the harvest we helped husk corn, peel chile and apples and make *orejón* (dried fruit) in a large courtyard surrounded by adobe walls and storerooms. When the sun-dried fruits and vegetables were ready to store, they were put into large bins that were rodent-proof. The dried crop stored in the appropriate storehouses, coupled with what was preserved in jars, provided most of the food for winter. Mi Nana Encarnación worked as hard as he did and presided over the household in a strict manner. I remember her always in a long black dress, filling the large boxes in the store rooms with dried food. From time to time in the winter, when we were on our way to school, she'd call us and give us an apple or orejón from storage. She always had a large ring of keys attached with a safety pin to her ample black skirt.

Sometimes she was very generous, but sometimes the Perea temper flared up and there was the devil to pay. One time Junior Michael and I got upset with Ramona and called her names—"¡Ramona panzona!" Several days later she called Junior and me over to give us "orejón de manzana." When we entered the storeroom, she locked the door and pulled out a whip, giving us a few good belts and reminding us "not to call Ramona names." We both went to our nearby homes crying. I didn't tell Mother, because I figured I'd get another whipping! Mr. Michael, Junior's father, was at the store when he heard Junior sobbing and insisted in knowing what had happened. He walked to the edge of the arroyo and told her a thing or two. She was standing across the arroyo with whip in hand and her fury up, yelling, "You come over here and I'll whip you, too!"

Don Abelicio Peña of San Mateo was married to Manuelita Ortega Peña. He was a sheep and cattle rancher, as well as a farmer and a businessman. At one time or another they owned a general merchandise store in San Mateo, a saloon, a dance hall, and a smaller store north of Ambrosio Lake. Don Abelicio was my paternal grandfather; I am his namesake.

Fray Angélico Chávez, noted New Mexico historian told me that, "The name Abelicio originated in Italy from the town of Saint Abelicius. Migrations and movement throughout the Mediterranean brought the name to Spain where it changed to Abelicio. From Spain it came to Mexico then north to New Mexico." It is not a common name. I only know two other Abelicios: my Uncle Abelicio Peña, who lives in Grants, and Abelicio Barela, from the Belen area. I presume it has a biblical origin and is an extension of *Abel*, the name of Adam and Eve's younger son, brother of Cain.

C. S. Peterson dedicates his book *Representative New Mexicans*, published in 1914, "To the men of New Mexico who have fought the hard and successful fight for statehood." On page 334, under the picture of Abelicio Peña, the caption reads: "Sheep and cattle raiser, (Republican) born May 5 1874, San Mateo, Valencia Co., N. M: son of Pablo and Benita de Peña; educ. public schools, San Mateo and Albuquerque; St. Michael's College, Santa Fe; taught school, San Mateo, 1900-1; member Board of County Commissioners, Valencia Co., 1906-11., address San Mateo, N. M."

Although I never knew him, pictures of my grandfather show a vigorous and handsome man with a roundish face and a fair complexion, a prominent mustache, and light hair parted almost down the middle. He tended toward rotundness (see Fig. 11).

His father, Pablo Peña, and his mother, Benita Mariño Peña, came from Seboyeta shortly after the founding of San Mateo, in 1862. They raised two sons and four daughters: Abelicio, Rafael, Onofre, Virginia, Claudia, and Catarina. Don Pablo was a stockman with a special love for horses, especially race horses. John Barbone, a Navajo Indian from the Milpitas area near Borrego Pass, once told me, "Your grandfather Abelicio had a large herd of white horses and many of our people called him "Chief Many White Horses." We still have some horses on the reservation that trace back to your grandfather's." In the village there are still a few that remember the Big Horse Race of 1916. George Dannenbaum first told me of the race between Chino, owned by Don Pablo, and Alazán, owned by Doctor Isidoro Dávila, son-in-law of Don Román Baca. Alazán was the favorite, and most of the money was on him. Chino beat him by a nose, and Doctor Dávila, in a rage, pulled out his pistol and shot the famous Alazán on the spot!

Floyd Lee remembered Don Pablo well. He told me that when he first came to the Fernandez ranch, after World War I, he used to drive through the village. As he commented, "I was always impressed with your great grandfather. He was a dignified, neatly dressed man with snow-white hair and stood, although he was an old man, as straight as an arrow" (see Fig. 12).

Don Pablo's son Abelicio grazed sheep and cattle in the Mesa del Pino and Ambrosio Lake area west of San Mateo when it was open range. In 1916 he purchased section 9 in township 15 north, range 9 west from the Santa Fe Pacific Railroad (see Fig. 13). The same year he contracted a lease-purchase agreement with the railroad for the rest of the township.

Don Abelicio was an entrepreneur. He sold the San Mateo store and liquor license to the Lebanese merchant Merhage Michael in 1916, which started the Michael enterprises in the area. (See also the story on pages 188–91.) He was a teacher at one time and was interested in government, serving the county for two terms as county commissioner (see Fig. 14). At the state level, he served as an alternate delegate to the state constitutional convention in 1912, when New Mexico became a state.

In 1918, at age forty-three, he suffered a massive cerebral hemorrhage while milking a cow in his corrals in San Mateo and died the following day. Bells tolled at the Catholic church directly across the street from where he lived.

The family was in shock. The people of the village were in shock. A vigorous man in the prime of life had been struck down. The family mourned for a year and more, but in spite of the crushing blow, they carried on. The oldest son, Pablo, Jr., age nineteen, was attending Saint Michaels in Santa Fe and came home to help his mother manage the business. He was my father. Their daughter Eufemia, age fourteen, was at St. Vincent's Academy in Albuquerque. Antonio, age eight, and Abelicio, Jr., age six, and their younger sister Leticia, three, were all at home with their mother in San Mateo when their father passed away. An indication of their continued resourcefulness and industry during those difficult years is the 1921 warranty deed issued by the Santa Fe Pacific Railroad Company to the Estate of Abelicio Peña, deceased, receiving full payment for the Canyon Largo township.

Grandmother Manuelita (we called her Nana) remarried in 1921. She married Don Lizardo Salazar, the ranch foreman. They had one son, Lizardo Salazar, Jr., who now lives in Arizona. Abenicio Otero, a friend of the family from Peralta, says, "I remember Doña Manuelita when she was in her prime. She stood out wherever she went. She was a beautiful lady." Mi Nana lived all her life in San Mateo, where she was born; she was cared for in her old age by Eufemia Salazar Trujillo, her favorite granddaughter. She passed away in 1978, at age ninety-eight, outliving her first husband by sixty years, and seeing in those years a new world emerge that would have astounded Don Abelicio as much as it would have kept him busy.

Mi Padre

William McKinley was President of the United States when Pablo Peña, my father, was born in the village of San Mateo, Territory of New Mexico, on December 28, 1898. He died September 24, 1986, at the age of eighty-seven. He was the first-born child of Abelicio and Manuelita Ortega Peña and had two sisters, Eufemia and Leticia, and two brothers, Antonio and Abelicio, as well as a half-brother, Lalo Salazar.

His early youth was spent with his paternal grandparents, Don Pablo and Doña Benita Mariño Peña. They were among the first settlers who came from Seboyeta to settle San Mateo, in 1862. When he was in his eighties, he remembered with fondness those early years, when he "played with sticks and picked some pretty colored rocks in the arroyo." The pretty rocks were his sheep and cattle. He played alone in a *plazuela* (patio) surrounded by high walls. His brothers were about ten years younger and lived with their parents. He attended the Congregational mission school in San Mateo and recalled "playing tag, hide and seek, and other popular games" with his classmates.

After he finished the mission school, his parents sent him to boarding school at St. Michael's in Santa Fe. He adapted quickly and did well in his studies, as evidenced by a "Testimonial of Merit for Term ending June 16th 1916 . . . Special Distinction in General Excellence," signed by one Brother Edward. Although he was not very sports-minded, he did enjoy baseball and boxing. He made the baseball team at St. Michael's and later was a devoted fan of Joe DiMaggio and the world champion New York Yankees. He was also an avid fan of Joe Louis, the heavyweight boxer and champion of the world. I remember him glued to the kitchen radio listening to Joe Louis fights.

At age nineteen, while he was still at St. Michael's, his father, Abelicio, died of a massive cerebral hemorrhage at the young age of forty-three. Pablo returned home to help his mother manage their sheep and cattle ranch north of San Mateo. His father had purchased the 23,000-acre ranch from the Santa Fe Pacific Railroad two years before he died. The payments on the ranch were quite heavy, and his mother felt they should let it go, afraid they would not be able to pay for it. My father suggested that they keep it and make the next payment by selling the cattle but keeping the sheep to graze the ranch; with future lamb and wool crops they could make further payments until they paid it off. Fortunately prices of livestock went up after the First World War, and by selling most of the cattle they were able to make the payment. Good management of the sheep enabled them to pay off the ranch by 1921.

In those days there were no fences, and cattle roamed the open range from San Mateo to Ambrosio Lake to Chaco Canyon and Pueblo Pintado. Roundups took the various owners and hired hands about four weeks during calf-branding in the spring, and about two weeks to gather and deliver them to the railhead in Grants in the fall.

In 1921 his young widowed mother, Manuelita, married Don Lizardo Salazar, the ranch foreman. The following year Pablo married Pablita Márquez, the attractive daughter of Don Fermín Márquez and Doña Beneranda Chávez Márquez in Our Lady of Sorrows Catholic Church in Seboyeta. The young bride and groom struck out on their own with an inheritance of a house in San Mateo and about 225 sheep. They leased grazing land wherever they could. From Don Lizardo and Grandma Manuelita, from the Fernandez Company, from Anastacio Márquez, and others. Their sheep flock grew slowly.

They homesteaded a section of land in the Canyon Largo country and mother, who passed away in 1991 at age eighty-seven, used to say, "The hardest years were the Depression years of the 1930s. Besides the low prices for sheep and wool, the drought produced little or no grass for the livestock. . . . One year out on the homestead we made it through the winter mostly on rabbits that Pablo killed with his 22 rifle." Pablo harbored an interest in politics like his Republican father Abelicio, who had served as an alternate delegate to the State Constitutional Convention in 1910–12, as well as a Valencia County commissioner from 1907 to 1911. Pablo was elected to the Board of County Commissioners in 1928 for two terms and again in 1950 for an additional two terms. He always considered well maintained county roads a top priority. At that time most of the roads were dirt and needed frequent blading. Cars and trucks were revolutionizing transportation, and roads were essential to the progress and development of Valencia County.

His father-in-law, Don Fermín Márquez, also a Republican, had also served two terms as a county commissioner and was a model for Pablo, who idolized him. Young Pablo sought advice and received it from the older and more experienced man, a successful businessman and livestock grower.

The stately old courthouse in Los Lunas, built at the turn of the century and torn down in the 1960s, was constructed during Don Fermín's tenure as county commissioner. His name was inscribed on the bronze plaque that graced the building while it stood dominating the center of Los Lunas.

San Mateo had about 50 families when I was growing up, for a total of about 250 people. Most of the men farmed or worked as sheepherders or cowboys, both locally and away in Arizona. Other sheepowners in the village were Mariano Ortega, Román Sandoval, and Nabor Márquez. Among the cattlemen were Nazario Sandoval, Merhage Michael (Don Miguel), Reymundo Barela, and Prajeres Candelaria, all of whom had forest permits. Others with smaller herds grazed the "common lands" surrounding the village. Salaries for herding sheep or punching cattle were about thirty-five dollars per month, with groceries and a tent or house included. The largest employer was the Fernandez Company, La Compañía, about one mile west of the village.

Pablo was appointed to serve on the committee that built the first public school in San Mateo, in 1929. It was an attractive four-room adobe structure, built at the north end of the village, to house the first through eighth grades. All of us attended grade school there. Those were wonderful and growing years, where we were all raised by a caring community.

In 1942 Pablo's mother Manuelita and Don Lizardo Salazar put up the ranch for sale. My father had a lease on half of the ranch, where he was grazing his growing flock. He didn't know whether he and my mother could find the money to buy it, since the sellers wanted full payment in cash. While they had some savings, they were far from enough—but they needed the land to run their flocks. Grants had no banks at that time, but after looking far and wide, Pablo found a lender in Socorro, J. N. Mounyo, who loaned them the money in return for a mortgage on the ranch. At this point they increased their number of sheep and were able to secure a Forest Service permit for the north side of Mount Taylor for summer grazing (see Fig. 15).

Prices for wool and lambs went up during the Second World War. Wool was a strategic fiber, used in warm clothing, worn by the Allies fighting the Axis powers in Europe. With increased prices and good rains in the 1940s, Pablo and Pablita were able to repay the loan before the end of the decade. With a lot of hard work and determination, they were also able to send their children to high school, and some even went on to college.

In the early 1950s, Al Williams, from Socorro, was looking for a building to use for a "supermarket" in Grants. My father had four lots on east Santa Fe Avenue, and was approached to see if he was interested in building to suit the tenant and then leasing it. A contract was drawn up, and "Stop and Shop" became the first supermarket in Grants. A couple of years later, the aggressive chain of Barber Supermarkets from Albuquerque purchased "Stop and Shop" from Williams and continued the lease. Later on as Grants grew with the mushrooming uranium industry in the 1960s, Barber's moved to a much larger building at the Hilltop Shopping Center, built by the Gunderson family. The building on Santa Fe Avenue was then leased to Bob Daugherty and remodeled to become the Daugherty Cafeteria. It operated for about three years and a cocktail lounge was added, but then the owners got into financial trouble. The business closed and the equipment offered at a public sale. My father, in consultation with the family, decided to bid on the equipment and continue to operate the cafeteria.

At that time he was semiretired, taking care of other real estate investments while I managed the ranch. When he decided to operate the cafeteria, he and my mother moved from San Mateo to Grants. Mother, always the devoted wife, left her beloved San Mateo with a heavy heart, to join her husband in a new venture twenty-three miles down the road. But in time she also became an enthusiastic supporter of Grants.

Pablo hired Escolástico "Esqui" Mazón, an experienced restaurant man and founder of the Monte Carlo Cafe, to manage the business. Dad liked the name "Starlite," and that's the name he gave it. After a year Esqui left to start another restaurant, and Dad decided to manage the cafeteria and lounge himself. The "Starlite" became a landmark in Grants and a well-known stop on historic Route 66.

He was again working full-time and enjoying it. He and mother made many friends from near and far who repeatedly stopped to eat and say "hello." The Starlite became a gathering place for businessmen on their coffee break, as well as for "snow-birds" on their way to southern Arizona from frigid northern climes in the fall, and back again when it thawed out in the spring. Californians stopped in droves when the schools let out in June. In midsummer it was not unusual to see the large parking lot filled with California license plates. In the evenings the softly lit and thickly carpeted cocktail lounge offered a respite for travelers as well as for a fine local clientele. Dad had made the Starlite a successful business that helped the local economy with jobs, sales, and services. With the bypass of Grants by Interstate Highway 40 and the demise of the famous Route 66 in the 1970s, the Starlite closed and the building rented, first as an auction center and later to a church group. In the 1980s the building that had served for so many functions over the years burned down. Larry and Angela Baca purchased the four lots in 1991 and built the attractive and popular "El Cafecito" restaurant on the site of the old Starlite.

Dad and mother traveled to Europe to visit their daughter Sister Lydia, who was doing graduate study in Spain, and together they traveled through France and Italy. Later they traveled to Central America to visit my own family in Honduras, later in Costa Rica, and after that in Paraguay, in South America, when I was in the foreign service. They enjoyed their travels and wisely paced themselves to come back home rested rather than exhausted—and that is an art.

Among other activities in his full life, he served as president and founder of the Paisano Senior Citizens. He was a member of the Knights of Columbus, a member of the Rural Electrification Administration (REA) board, a director of the First National Bank of Grants, a member of the board of the Good Samaritan

Center, a member of the Grants Chamber of Commerce, and a member of the New Mexico Wool Growers Association. He and mother were honored one year as grand marshals in the Grants Fourth of July Parade. In San Mateo they helped obtain electricity, running water, and telephones for the village.

An era was coming to an end. Pablo Peña, a dedicated, successful, and most gracious man, held in high regard by the community, passed away on September 24, 1986. He died of pneumonia after a short illness, at age eighty-seven. His wife, Pablita, joined him in death on June 24, 1991, also at the age of eighty-seven.

In an editorial the *Grants Daily Beacon* said, "Pablo Peña never stopped working for his community . . . until Wednesday, when he died at the age of 87. Pablo Peña contributed to his community and kept right on contributing until the end. He was also a gallant gentleman of the old school of etiquette and ethics. With his presence the community was a better place. With his passing, the community suffers a great loss."

Figure 1
Our Lady
of Sorrows
Church in
Seboyeta

Figure 2
Part of
the early
nineteenth-
century wall
in Seboyeta

Figure 3
Fermín Márquez surrounded
by grandchildren

Figure 4
Automobile trip
in 1921

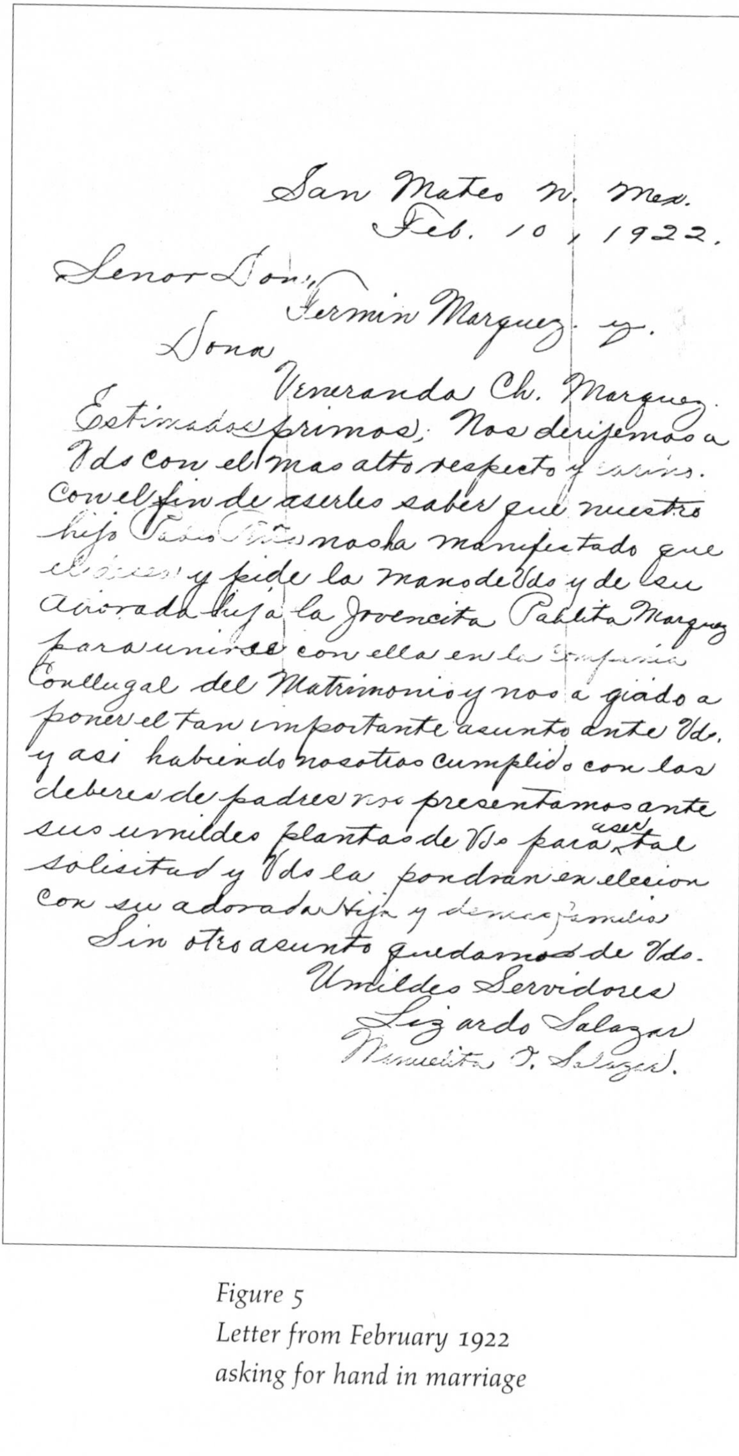

San Mateo N. Mex.
Feb. 10, 1922.

Señor Don.
    Fermin Marquez. y.
Doña
    Veneranda Ch. Marquez.
Estimados primos, Nos derijemos a
Uds con el mas alto respeto y cariño.
Con el fin de aserles saber que nuestro
hijo Pedro Frias nos ha manifestado que
el ... y pide la mano de Uds y de su
adorada hija la Jovencita Pablita Marquez
para unirse con ella en la compañia
Conlugal del Matrimonio y nos a giado a
poner el tan importante asunto ante Ud.
y asi habiendo nosotros cumplido con los
deberes de padres nos presentamos ante
sus umildes plantas de Uds para tal
solisitud y Uds la pondran en eleccion
con su adorada Hija y demas familia
    Sin otro asunto quedamos de Uds.
        Umildes Servidores
            Lizardo Salazar
        Nunuita T. Salazar.

Figure 5
Letter from February 1922
asking for hand in marriage

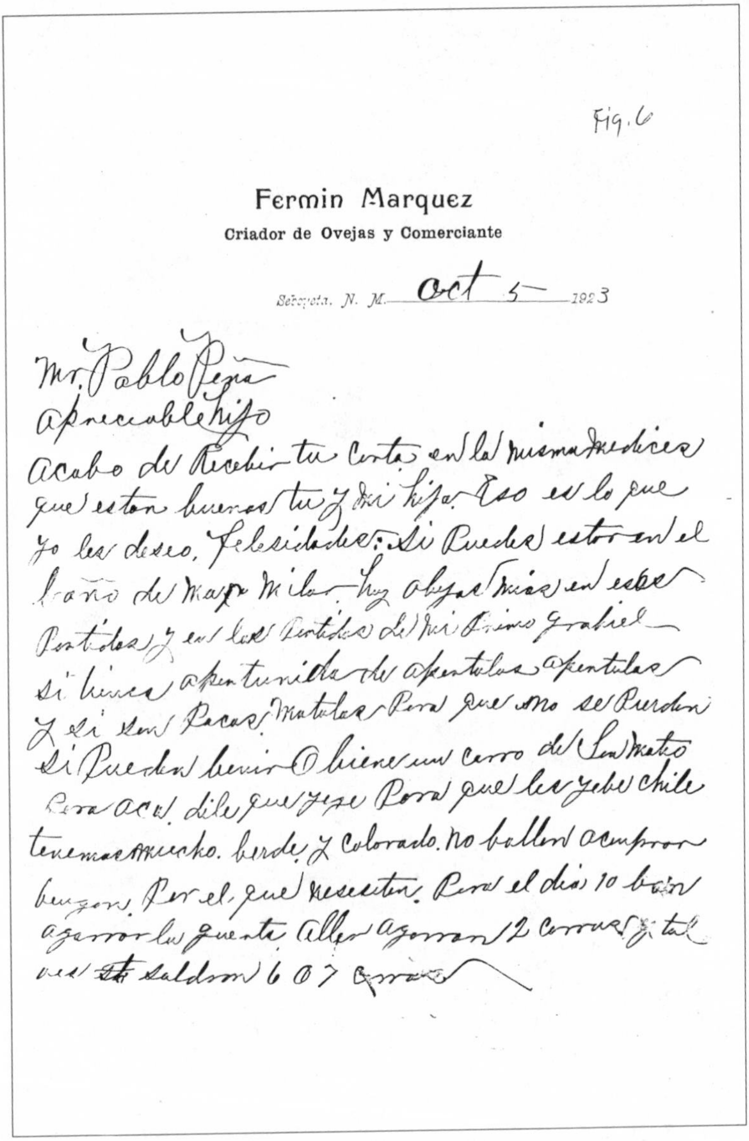
Fig. 6

Fermin Marquez

Criador de Ovejas y Comerciante

Seboyeta, N. M. Oct 5 1923

Mr. Pablo Peña

apreciable hijo

acabo de Recebir tu Carta en la misma me dices que estan buenos tu y mi hija. Eso es lo que yo les deseo, felicidades. Si Puedes estar en el baño de Mayo Milar hay obejas mias en esas Partidas y en las Partidas de mi Primo Grabiel si hines apurtunidad de apartalas apartalas y si son Pocas matalas Para que no se Puedan Si Puedes benir O biene un carro de San Mateo Para aca dile que pase Para que les yebe chile tenemos mucho. berde y colorado. no ballen a comprar bueyes. Por el que necesitan. Para el dia 10 ban agarrar la guenta. aller agarran 12 carros y tal vez ~~ste~~ saldran 6 O 7 carros

Figure 6

Father-in-law's business letter to his son-in-law, 1923

Figure 7
The wedding of Pablo and
Pablita Peña, February 1922.

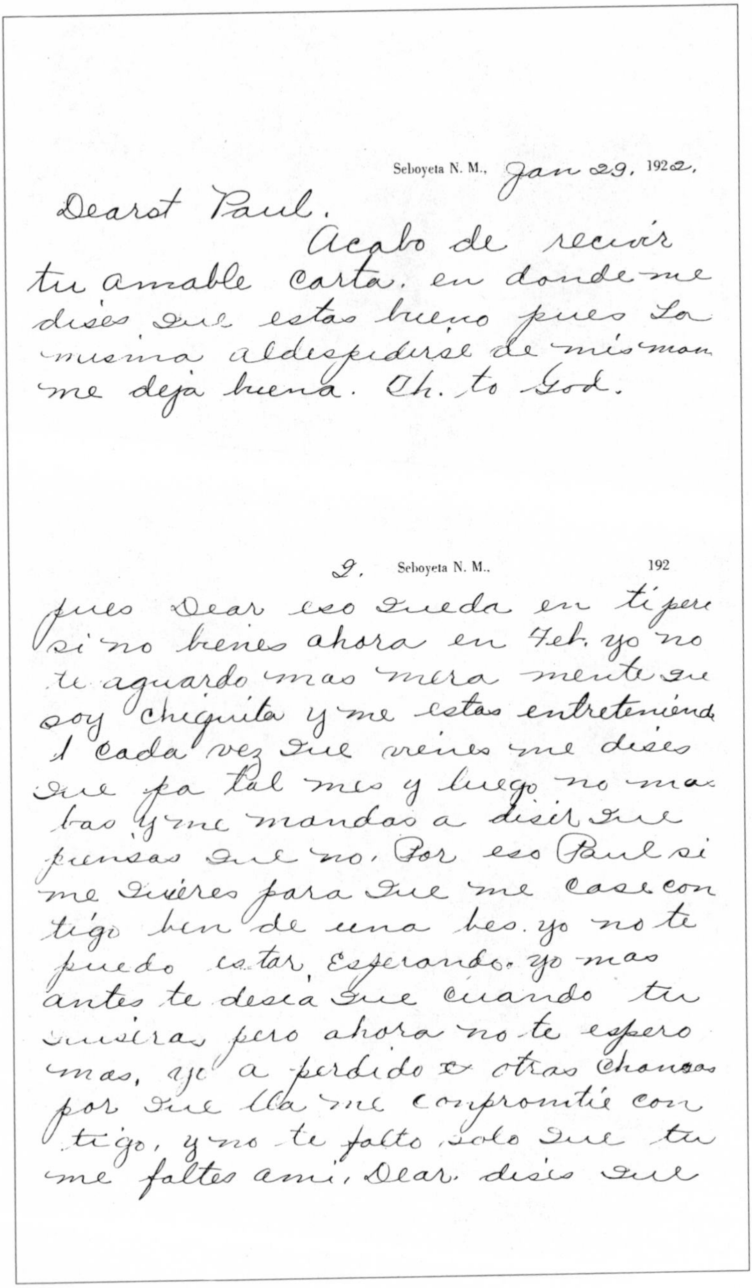

Dearst Paul.

Acabo de recivir
tu amable carta. en donde me
dises que estas bueno pues la
misma aldespedirse de mis mano
me deja buena. Ch. to God.

pues Dear eso queda en ti pero
si no bienes ahora en Feb. yo no
te aguardo mas mera mente que
soy chiquita y me estas enteteniendo
1 cada vez que veines me dises
que pa tal mes y luego no mas
bas y me mandas a disir que
piensas que no. Por eso Paul si
me quieres para que me case con
tigo ben de una bes. yo no te
puedo estar Esperando. yo mas
antes te desia que cuando tu
quisieras pero ahora no te espero
mas, ye a perdido x otras chansas
por que lla me compromtie con
tigo, y no te falto solo que tu
me faltes a mi, Dear. dises que

Figure 8
Pablita's letter of January 1922
setting a marriage deadline

Figure 9
Coronado Quarto Centennial
celebration in San Mateo, 1940.
Pablita (left) and Lydia Peña
with hat.

Figure 10
Anastacio Marquez (right)
and nephews, Reyes and
Benjamin Chavez,
c. 1920

Figure 11
Abelicio Peña and his son
Pablo, c. 1916

Figure 12
Pablo and Benita Peña,
c. 1900

Doña Virginia, *la curandera*, delivered hundreds of babies and treated the sick in San Mateo and other neighboring villages in Cíbola County. When she died in 1966, at age eighty-five, this remarkable lady had brought two generations of her "children" to life, including me. To this day I think of Doña Virginia Perea Sánchez as my surrogate mother, someone who was there when I breathed life and gave that first cry. How fortunate we were to be raised in a village where all the elders, whether related or not, were our guardians and teachers. Doña Virginia saw us grow to adulthood, and along the way she tousled our hair and reminded us "to behave and listen to your elders." How blessed we were to share the love this singular woman brought to our world.

Doña Virginia was a devoted wife and mother. Her husband, Don Protacio Perea, died when their six children were young, so she raised them by herself. They are all dead now except for Leonardo, who lives in Albuquerque. Later she married Don Rafael Sánchez, a quiet-mannered man who shared her care and compassion for the sick and for others. In her older years she was usually dressed in black and used to say, "I'm always in mourning for one of my children." She felt the loss of any infant and others as her own personal loss.

The first doctor came to San Mateo with the Civilian Conservation Corps (CCC) camps in the 1930s, but only in emergencies were they permitted to treat the sick in our village. But Doña Virginia was always there, and in many ways she was more than a doctor to us. In her curandera bag were such herbs as *yerba buena, poleo, yerba del manso, ochá,* and other home remedies. She also carried some patent medicines, such as "Aceite Mexicano" and "Aceite Volcánico," and most important of all, love and compassion.

She gave us a sense of hope and security. Her bedside manner was legendary. According to Mi Tío Antonio Peña, she learned the skills of nursing and midwifery from Doña Martita Salazar and Doña Regalada Chávez. They in turn learned the skills from a schoolteacher from back East, who taught at the Congregational Mission School in San Mateo, shortly after the turn of the century.

The life expectancy in those days was around fifty-five years; today it's seventy-five. The lack of prenatal care caused high infant mortality—many died before reaching the age of five. However, there are cases of some who lived beyond 100 years. My great grandfather Juan Ortega lived to be 107, as near as we can determine, and his daughter Manuelita, my grandmother, lived to the age of ninety-eight. And there were others in the village who lived as long or longer.

Doña Virginia was a devoted member of the Hermandad de Nuestro Padre Jesús Nazareno, also known as Los Penitentes. She, along with Doña Beneranda Romero, Doña Sostena Trujillo, and a few other women, in addition to many men, did special penance for Lent. I recall this pious lady carrying a large crucifix in her outstretched arms while on her knees on the way to Mt. Calvary, a quarter-mile from the *morada*. It was a sobering sight to see this good woman alone with her God, suffering as He did on the Via Dolorosa. Dressed in a long black dress, a black shawl over her head, her feet bare, and perspiration running down her face, she was unquestionably on another plane. The gravel would tear through her knees, and blood marked her trail as she painfully made her way back to the chapel. She was helped to her feet, but was unable to stand. Then she was carried to the interior of the morada, where her knees were treated. But that same evening, she was back on her knees during the Rosary, singing the *alabados* and prayers in a strong voice!

Celito Jaramillo, now deceased, remembered their trips to the woods to pick *piñones*. "She advised everyone not to pick all the piñones under a tree, but to leave some for the little animals. They too are creatures of God." Eleito Anzures, her son-in-law, recalls her carefully asking them not to poison the ants— "They're beneficial to the environment." She was a natural-born conservationist. All forms of life, whether plant or animal, were dear to her. But no doubt "her children" were the dearest.

The search for lodging by Joseph and Mary in Bethlehem on the night Christ was born started the Christian tradition of Las Posadas ("The Inns"). The reenactment of Las Posadas spread throughout the Christian world over the centuries, as Christianity grew. It reached Spain early in the Christian era, and from Spain it came to Mexico, then north to New Mexico, in the sixteenth century. The colonists who came with Don Juan de Oñate in 1598 started Las Posadas in San Gabriel, the first capital of New Mexico, near Española, then brought the celebration to Santa Fe in 1610. The custom kept spreading throughout the colony. It arrived in the country to the west of the Río Grande in 1800, with the settling of Seboyeta, then spread to other villages as they were founded.

In San Mateo, as in other Hispanic villages, Las Posadas still begin on December 16, nine days before Christmas. As the custom spread, changes were made in the text and prayers and procedures, but the main theme, denial of shelter and finally a stable where the Christ Child is born, has never changed. We would gather at the church at dusk to pray a decade of the Rosary then proceed in prayer up the *luminaria*-lit street. Each house on the route lit one luminaria (bonfire) to illuminate the path of Mary and Joseph. At a predetermined house, representing an inn, Joseph would ask for shelter in song, "In the name of Heaven may we have shelter for the night? We come from Nazareth and my adored wife is cold and tired. Only a corner for the night." The response from inside: "Keep on going and leave us alone, we will not open for you. Who knows, you may be thieves. Just keep on going." Generally a second home was visited the same night.

The procedure was repeated on the seventeenth of December at different houses, and the street would be lit with two luminarias at each house along the way. The luminarias were built of crisscrossed piñon or juniper from our woodpiles. On the eighteenth three luminarias were lit, and so forth, until the twenty-fourth, when we built nine luminarias at each house, and the street was literally ablaze with light from one end of the village to the other. On Christmas Eve Joseph is very tired but perseveres, as Mary is fast approaching her hour of delivery. "My wife is Mary, she's the queen of heaven. She will be the Mother of God." The response is, "You are Joseph and your wife is Mary. Come in pilgrims, sorry we didn't recognize you." The pilgrims are greeted and offered shelter in a protected stable. At this point the pageant of Los Pastores usually followed. Los Pastores are shepherds who have heard the angels announcing the birth of Christ and follow the star to Bethlehem to adore the Christ Child—the newborn King!

Mrs. Jane Madrid Valencia of Grants, born and raised in Villa Nueva, near Pecos, New Mexico, says, "In our village Mary rode a donkey led by Joseph and we followed. I have some wonderful memories of Las Posadas and the traditions they represent. My mother and father were very devoted and we participated in all religious activities in our village." She came to Grants during the uranium boom and helped organize a group that reenacted Las Posadas in Grants. There were other and earlier groups that kept the tradition alive, especially when Grants was a small village. Jane laments the fact that the tradition is disappearing. Those of us who were raised in rural villages and participated in Las Posadas lament with her. However, urban settings, where cars have to be used to transport the pilgrims from the church to a subdivision, do not lend themselves to pilgrims walking or lighting luminarias along the way. To their credit some groups are still braving the cars.

To Jane Valencia, and to all of you who remember Las Posadas with its pure and simple message of love and devotion to the Holy Family, let me suggest you get involved and keep the message alive. Many churches have inspiring Christmas services, and although they cannot replace them, maybe they can substitute for the traditions of our small villages, and all of us can be a part of those services. Keep in mind that there are many ways to serve our Lord.

"Los Pastores," "The Shepherds," is the beautiful and ageless story of the birth of Christ. The pageant has been performed in all the Hispanic villages in Cíbola County since the arrival of the first Spanish settlers in the early nineteenth century. Seboyeta, founded in 1800 by thirty individuals who requested and were given a land grant by Spanish Governor Don Fernando Chacón, was one of the first settlements west of the Río Grande. "Los Pastores" spread from Seboyeta with the settlers to San Mateo in 1862 and to San Rafael in 1865.

When I was a young man in San Mateo, auditions and rehearsals for the pageant begin about December 1 and ended on Christmas Eve in a colorful and touching story of the shepherds' initial confusion, eventual understanding, and finally adoration of the Christ Child in the stable. The cast of about twenty, led by a director or directors, met nightly for rehearsals. In between school and chores, we worked on costumes and regalia, assisted by our parents and friends who in most cases had been a part of an earlier pageant. I can remember that the pastoral scenes we were recreating were familiar to all the cast. We all were shepherds or at least knew about their life. We all farmed and tended or herded sheep, and we were largely self-sufficient.

I recall the sincerity and the intensity of our feelings as we stepped up to adore the Christ Child. Today I try to recapture that feeling, a feeling that I believe only country people growing close to nature can feel. There was nothing sophisticated in our recreation of the greatest story ever told—only a simple radiance that touched us all.

While rehearsals were going on, Las Posadas started. On December 16 practically every house on the route Mary and Joseph took was lit up with a luminaria, a bonfire made of firewood crisscrossed about two feet high. Generally two houses were visited and shelter was denied. On the seventeenth two luminarias were lit at each house, and by December 24 there were nine luminarias illuminating the entire route, which culminated at the stable where Los Pastores awaited to reenact the ageless story

of Christmas. The most touching and memorable part of the
play was when Bártolo, an old and lazy shepherd who had spent
his life lying on a sheep pelt, refused all our efforts to get him
up. Finally when the angels announced the momentous birth,
Jila, a shepherdess, would get him up on his wobbly legs and
with help from Bato, another shepherd, he would approach the
child and behold! Bártolo would stand there awestruck. He would
hold on tightly to Jila, his legs barely holding his weight. Focusing on the child, he would do a little spontaneous dance. Then he
would let go of Jila and break into a full dance and song, wanting
to share his happiness with the whole world. His lethargy would
be gone. He has seen his Savior and rejoiced—and we all rejoiced with him!

Los Comanches

As a youngster in the village of San Mateo, I recall excitedly
painting my face red with *almagre*, putting on a feathered head-
dress, and dancing Los Comanches for Christmas. According to
this custom the image of the Christ Child would be kidnapped at
a velorio from his crib and taken by Comanche Indians to their
distant lands. Preparations and rehearsals started about the second week in December. The producers were older and generally
very talented singers and composers. The best known in my day
were Evaristo Gonzales and Delfinio Salazar. They had a special
talent for drama and deep devotion to the Christ Child. About
fifteen Comanches, both boys and girls and some older villagers,
learned the steps, verses, and chants.

At the rehearsals, which took place at night, we also got guid-
ance in making our costumes from Delfinio's wife, Senaida. She
was the director and inspired us all with her enthusiasm and
good cheer. On Christmas Eve there was a velorio at someone's
home. The living room was arranged with an altar, generally a
small table covered with a finely embroidered white linen cloth,
with the image of the Christ Child in a crib resting in the center

and a candle on each side. The padrinos were generally a married couple and sat at each end of the altar, representing Mary and Joseph keeping watch over the Child. People sat in chairs around the room and prayers were constantly recited as they kept their vigil over Christ the King.

Around 8:00 P.M. a band of Comanches arrived silently at the door. After some clearing of throats, our chief gave a sign and lead us a cappella into the first song:

> En el marco de esta puerta,
> El pie derecho pondré,
> A los dueños del velorio,
> La venia les pediré.
> ("At the threshold of this door,
> My right foot I'll place,
> Of the sponsors of this vigil,
> Permission to enter I will ask.")

After about a dozen or more verses telling about the long and arduous journey from the plains, the door opened and we'd glide into the room, singing at the top of our lungs. At this point the padrinos would double their hold on the crib, as the spirited Comanches danced past the altar singing and chanting with their eyes glued on the Child:

> Qué bonita la cunita,
> Qué bonito está el altar,
> Más bonito está el niñito,
> Si yo lo pudiera robar.
> ("How beautiful the little crib,
> How beautiful is the altar,
> But more beautiful is the Child,
> Could I but steal him.")

We sang to his beauty, we sang to his sanctity. We told him we would take care of him if he came with us across the miles to our far away lands. After lulling the padrinos to relax their hold on the crib, a darting Comanche grabbed the Child in a flash and held him up in the air as we withdrew in triumph, singing:

Se retiran los Comanches,
Ya cumplen su devoción,
Con tu mano poderosa,
Échanos tu bendición."

("The Comanches are withdrawing,
With satisfied devotion,
With your all-powerful hand,
Give us your benediction.")

In those days I never thought to ask how and where this custom originated, but in recent years I've started asking the old-timers, and the answer usually has been, "I don't know—it was always done." Curiosity and good fortune finally led me to one of the most outstanding researchers and writers of Hispanic history in the Southwest, Fray Angélico Chávez, author of more than twenty books who died in March 1996, confirmed my suspicion that it originated in the Río Grande villages during the colonization period, between 1600 and 1850.

The Comanche Indians, coming out of the Great Plains of Kansas, Oklahoma, Texas, and eastern New Mexico, raided the Hispanic villages, kidnapping our children, both boys and girls, and taking them to serve as warriors or as servants to augment their declining tribal numbers. They also stole Spanish-introduced horses, sheep, and cattle, giving a start to the livestock industry among Indian tribes. To the credit of the Indians, they became excellent horsemen and very good sheep and cattle raisers.

Hispanic villages began the custom of Los Comanches to keep alive the memory of their captured Christlike children, kidnapped by Comanches in war paint and feathers and taken to the distant plains. In 1800 the custom was brought by colonists from the Albuquerque area to Seboyeta. From there settlers took it to San Mateo in 1862, where the custom is still a part of the Christmas tradition. In most of the other villages in Cíbola County, the custom has disappeared, but in San Mateo it has remained a part of our rich and colorful heritage.

Tía Sostia

In her senior years Tía Sostia was losing her eyesight and was virtually night-blind. Rosalio, the grandson whom she had raised from infancy, would light *el farol*, the lantern, and escort her on her night visits to neighbors and the sick throughout the village. Rosalio says, "I enjoyed escorting Mi Nana," adding with emotion, "I loved my grandmother dearly, but during her night visits I kept wondering what you guys were up to!" We were boyhood friends and lived across the community *acequia* from each other. Across the arroyo in the other direction lived Junior Michael and Sifredo Sandoval. We were all about the same age and spent a lot of our free time together.

Mi Tía Sostia Márquez Baca was related to my mother through the Márquez family in Seboyeta. When she was a young girl, about 1895, she was ordered to marry Anastacio Baca, a farmhand of Don Román Baca, the largest sheepowner in the area, with headquarters at El Rito, near San Mateo. I remember her telling the sad story of her wedding day. "I did not want to marry Anastacio. They put the bridal veil on my head and I grabbed it and threw it on the floor and stomped and stomped on it!" Rosalio says, "My grandmother, a most reluctant bride, finally stood but never took the vows. Don Román Baca had arranged the wedding to marry off his illegitimate son Anastacio, the offspring of an affair with a Zuni girl who was a servant at his ranch." Nevertheless Tía Sostia had two children, Santiago and Manuelita. According to Rosalio, "My father Santiago was called 'Zunie' by some in the village because his grandmother was from Zuni Pueblo." From time to time I go to Zuni to visit the Gaspers, our relations from the distant past.

Santiago married Rafelita and they had three boys and a girl: Anastacio, Rosalio, Elfego, and the pretty Deluvina. He was a veteran of the First World War and had fought the Germans in France. He received a disability pension from the War Department. Rafelita died relatively young, and Santiago married Elviria Mirabal; they had a son, Jimmy. Manuelita married Andrés García, and they had two boys, Dimas and Tránsito. Rosalio is

the only one still living in San Mateo. He married Ruma
Romero, the granddaughter of Doña Beneranda of "Comanche dance" fame, and they have six children: five boys and a girl. Ruma died in the early 1990s. Tía Sostia, like Tía Sostena, helped Mother when we were growing up. Sometimes she stayed with us when our parents went on trips. At night she told us stories of witches, brujas.

I recall the story of "La Brasa Colorada," "The Red Ember." It seems there was a woman in a distant village who turned into a red ember and traveled the roads and byways by night, spooking people. The ember, glowing a fiery red, made a whizzing sound at times, but it never spoke. Years later when I was about fourteen, I was riding El Vallo to San Mateo from the ranch at Canyon Largo, some 15 miles away. It got dark on the trail. I knew the trail well, and so did the horse. There was no reason for fright that dark night. About half a mile from the village, I suddenly heard a loud whizz and saw a glowing red ember approach. I furiously spurred the horse to a run, but the ember kept pace with us, a little ahead and about twenty yards to our right.

At full speed, with hair standing on end, I was racing toward the village with the ember keeping pace. When we slowed down, it slowed down—when we ran, it ran. When we reached the first houses at the north end of the village, the glowing ember made a louder whizzing sound and mercifully disappeared into the dark night. Looking back there's no doubt it was my vivid imagination seeing and hearing things that had remained dormant in my mind from stories told by a kindhearted woman. I keep thinking it was also an indirect way of keeping us home at night, through fear of witches in the dark!

In our minds Tía Sostia, with her concern for her neighbors and for the sick, still walks the streets of our village, with a *tápalo* over her head escorted by her grandson Rosalio, holding a lantern and lighting the way.

The men sang:

En el marco de esta puerta,
El pie derecho pondré,
A los señores casados,
Los buenos días les daré.

("At the threshold of this door,
My right foot I'll place,
To the married couple,
I come to bid good day.")

A version of this song was also sung by "Los Comanches." When the door opened, the guitars and the singing stopped and the men shouted, "Mis días, Mis días!" and were invited in. Later, as Christmas was commercialized, they added, "Mis Crismes, Mis Crismes." The custom of Los Días came to San Mateo and other Hispanic villages in Cíbola County from Seboyeta. To Seboyeta it came with the grantees from Atrisco, and to New Mexico with the Spanish colonists through Mexico, from Spain.

A busy Christmas Eve started at dusk, with Las Posadas—Mary and Joseph searching for shelter—followed by El Velorio and Los Comanches. Then followed the pageant of Los Pastores, The Shepherds, and finally Midnight Mass, at the Catholic church. At dawn on Christmas Day came the men celebrating the birth of Christ by singing and walking from house to house to wish the villagers "los buenos días," "good morning." At the various homes in the village they were usually offered a glass of wine or whiskey, sometimes two glasses. When there was little money, such as during the Depression, a cup of coffee was in order, along with tamales, frijoles, chile, and tortillas, followed by pastelitos and biscochitos. Delfinio Salazar used to say, "During Prohibition many homes kept a bottle of *mula*, moonshine, for medicinal purposes. And sometimes, in the spirit of Christmas, they shared it with their neighbors!"

The numbers in the party kept growing, as men joined the group when Los Días passed by their house. Only men joined in, and as the hours passed, the gaiety as well as the numbers grew. The women and children had celebrated in religious activities, but this was the men's turn.

Some years the snow was several inches deep. In San Mateo, which sits on the north side of Mount Taylor, there usually was more snow than in other villages with a southern exposure, and in the snow, the slipping and sliding by cheerful greeters was amusing. They held onto each other for dear life. Sometimes two or three went down at the same time. Getting up in the slipping and sliding was hilarious! I don't recall any arguments or fights—the men enjoyed each other's company. The most important thing was to keep the guitarists on their feet. Music was important to the celebration, and guitars were precious and expensive. After rolling in the snow, it sure felt good to get to the next home and stand by the fire to warm up and dry out. The ones that didn't have overshoes got their feet pretty cold, but they hardly complained.

By ten or eleven in the morning, some of the men would begin to drop off and go or be taken home. It didn't take too many turns at the spirits to weaken the legs of most of the men, who usually indulged only on feast days. By noon only the very hardy were left in the group. They had managed to take greetings to most of the homes in the village before going home to join their families.

Larraniaga

Up the canyon in a rustic two-room adobe house lived Rafael and Cruz, his wife. He was an artist in our village of San Mateo. He made art objects out of discarded tin cans and aluminum pots; both metals were scarce and hard to find in our isolated village. He pounded designs into the cold metal and produced work of art: picture frames, mirror frames, sun faces, bracelets, conchos, buttons, birds and many other designs in beautiful patterns. He was an unappreciated tinsmith, generally ignored by his neighbors as *poco raro* (a little strange). Rafael was a self-made artist, and his nontraditional skills and manners were suspect in our traditional agrarian isolation. He came to San Mateo from elsewhere—Alfredo Barela thinks he came from the Santa Fe area to herd sheep for the Fernandez Company. In San Mateo he met and married Doña Cruz, who had a daughter, Adelaida. Doña Cruz was a cousin of Doña Beneranda Saavedra Romero, the wife of Don Gabriel Romero, a fine gentleman. Doña Cruz was a large and very tall woman. She had a crippled left foot and partly dragged it when she walked. I remember her always dressed in black, with a large tápalo over her shoulders and a large black purse hanging on her arm. The mail came to our village on Mondays, Wednesdays, and Fridays. She walked about 3 miles round-trip for the mail, three times a week, with the aid of her cane.

Rafael herded sheep for a living and created art for the soul and for its beauty. I was a boy when this man was in his creative stage, during the Great Depression of the 1930s. I occasionally sat and watched him create magnificent picture frames out of a ragged piece of tin! He also herded sheep for my father, Don Pablo Peña. One time while at a lambing camp, the men talked Rafael into getting in an empty cylindrical water tank, convincing him that he had a good voice and that if he sang real loud, Don Pablo could listen to him on his truck radio. He got into the tank and sang for all he was worth. When Don Pablo returned, they asked him if he had heard Rafael singing in the radio, and he played along saying, "Yes I did, and he sounded real good!" Looking back sometimes, I'm certain Rafael played along with the men for his own amusement.

I'm pretty certain there was no market for Rafael's art. To my knowledge little or nothing survived him. I have tried to find some of his work, with no luck. There may be a piece of his work at La Morada (the Penitente chapel). I have not seen any there, but they may have one or two pieces in the storeroom in the back. Some of the walls of Rafael and Cruz's house are still stand-

ing. I believe whoever emptied the house after their death simply threw everything away. It just might be that some arroyo or
trash dump near the village holds Larraniaga's creations and
works of art. ¡Dios nos salve!

Severo Gutiérrez

"¿Cómo están los frijolitos?" Severo asked Pablo, while eating
breakfast around the sheep camp fire at daybreak. Don Pablo
Peña, without answering, continued to eat the tasty beans that
had been buried in the coals during the night and were as delicious as only camp fire beans can be. Don Severo asked again,
"¿Cómo están los frijolitos, compadre?" Then again for the third
time, and finally Don Pablo answered in mock agitation, "¡Están
buenos! ¡Están muy buenos los frijolitos!"

These two men had a lot of respect for each other, but they
were very different personalities. Severo Gutiérrez liked to talk,
and Don Pablo liked to think. Severo was outgoing, and Don
Pablo was at times retiring. When Don Pablo stopped thinking,
he was a good listener and a good conversationalist, and Severo
enjoyed the moments and visited with his compadre to his
heart's content.

Severo Gutiérrez was married to Doña María, and they had
one daughter, Herminia. Doña María had been widowed young
and had two sons and three daughters from her previous marriage to Don Manuel Mirabal: Moisés, Lionel, Tonia, Lita, and
Inez. When Herminia was born, they asked Don Pablo and Doña
Pablita, my father and mother, to serve as padrinos, godparents
for the baptism of their daughter.

Mom and Dad served many times as padrinos for children of
relatives, friends, and neighbors. Mother especially remembered
the baptism of Herminia and talked about it all the time.
"Herminia was a very pretty child, and we dressed her in white
chiffon to receive the important sacrament of baptism at the San
Mateo Catholic Church." The ceremony was followed by a lun-

cheon at the Peña home. "Pablo butchered a sheep and our guests savored *morcillas, burriñates, menudo, sopaipillas*, and all the fine trimmings prepared by Mi Tía Sostena. Mi Compadre Severo, a dedicated mutton man, still talked about the fine meal years later."

Don Severo was one of the best sheepherders of his time. He was always interested in the welfare of the sheep. Every waking moment of his day he was wondering where to graze his herd to keep the sheep fat, healthy and productive. In the summer of 1941, at age fourteen, I was the camptender to Don Severo, herding about a thousand sheep and lambs at Los Bancos, on the San Mateo mesa above Ambrosio Lake, on the Peña ranch. One day after a big rain in early July, he said, "Hijito," (he called every boy "hijito") "you take care of the herd. I'm going to see if the tank at Canyon de Los Alamos caught water to move the sheep and camp there." He returned late in the day, announcing that the tank was full of water and "tomorrow we move the sheep and camp to Los Alamos—I'll leave at daybreak with the herd, and you load the camp and follow me."

I didn't sleep much that night, thinking this would be my first time packing and loading the four burros by myself. At daybreak I went looking for the hobbled burros, and by the time I got back to camp Don Severo had gone with the herd. Each burro had its individual packsaddle. El Pardo was very gentle and stood still while being packed, so I packed him first. I loaded the two 5-gallon barrels on him, then Don Severo's *mochila* (bedroll) on top. Then I took the long pack rope and tightened it as tight as I could, made a crisscrossed figure 8, and went on to the next burro. It took me about an hour to pack all four of them, and then I started on the trail, praying that they were cinched and packed well enough to go all the way without dropping their packs.

About half a mile on the trail, we started down into El Cañon Chamizoso, and the packs started slipping. I stopped the burros and tried to center their packs by pushing and shoving, but I could tell the packs were not tight enough, and trouble would be looming ahead once they started up the other side of the canyon. Sure enough, when they started up the trail out of the canyon, one of the packs slipped to the underside and the burro stopped—he couldn't walk! I had to unpack him and start all over again. In the meantime the others kept going up the rough trail, and another pack slid and started dropping pots and pans. When I finally caught up with them, I was carrying half the camp pots in my arms! I felt like crying but, "I was too old to cry and it hurt too much to laugh." In all honesty I shed more than a tear or two in El Cañon Chamizoso that long day in August!

Don Severo was patiently waiting when I finally reached him, sometime after noon. He was smoking away on his ever-present pipe, and his only comment was, "Ya las grandes se comen a las chiquitas, hijito" ("The large intestines are about to eat up the small ones, son!"). He was a hearty eater and liked his lunch on time.

Don Severo was raised on a homestead north of San Mateo, near the present Lee Ranch coal mine. He was a rugged outdoorsman and liked to tell of the summer of 1945, when we were herding sheep on the north side of Mount Taylor. "I remember we were drinking a cup of coffee at daybreak. It was a cloudless morning and we were facing south, when the southern horizon lit up momentarily. It seemed like the good Lord had lit a giant flame and quickly blew it out. We had never seen anything like it." Some time later we learned that it was an atom bomb, detonated near Alamogordo, New Mexico. That was the first time we'd heard of an "atom" bomb.

Don Severo suffered from diabetes, and the ravages of the disease took him in the 1950s; diabetes affects a disproportionate number of Hispanics. Doña María lived a long life by herself and spent the final years close to her daughter, in Grants. She passed away in the 1980s. Herminia has two sons and a daughter. The boys live in Houston and the daughter in Grants. There are three grandchildren. Both Don Severo and Doña María are gone now, but they left their mark on the community. She was a reserved lady with a Mona Lisa smile and a placid personality. The world was a better place because of Doña María.

Yes, Don Severo, we saw that summer morning in 1945 the dawn of the atomic age. The tranquil life of the shepherd, known to us since biblical times, was ending.

Eufelia

We didn't call her just Tía Eufelia, we called her Mi Tía Eufelia, My Aunt Eufelia.

Mi Tía Eufelia, who lived from 1880 to 1964, was married to Leandro Sandoval. Leandro's brother Abel was married to my Great Aunt Claudia Peña Sandoval, which is why we called Eufelia "tía." She was a Chávez and had come as a young bride to San Mateo from the Cubero area, about 1899. Reynaldo Mirabal, now deceased, a grandson who lived in Grants, told me she used to talk of relatives in Cubero. They had five attractive and talented daughters and two sons: Josefita, Perfetita, Dolores, Feliz, Trinnie, José, and Bernardo. They have all passed away now.

Eufelia and Leandro homesteaded at Tinaja, north of San Mateo. She also filed her own 320-acre homestead near Canyon Largo, a little farther north. It's the only homestead filed by a woman that I am aware of in that area. She was a pioneer in every sense of the word. Don Lizardo Salazar used to tell the story of how he and my father, Pablo Peña, had ridden their horses about 1916 to the Canyon Largo Ranch and stopped to visit the Sandovals. They were served coffee at the ample kitchen table, where generally country people visited. The rustic but comfortable kitchen occupied one end of the two-room rock house. Mi Tía Eufelia poured the coffee and put out *galletas* for her guests, but no sugar. My father kept stirring his spoon in the tin cup—stirring and stirring and stirring. They simply didn't have sugar. America was in World War I, and sugar was rationed and unavailable most of the time, especially out in the country. Dad always liked sugar with his coffee, and Don Lizardo, with tongue in cheek, said, "He kept stirring and stirring as if by stirring he could sweeten the coffee! Young Pablo's mind was elsewhere, and didn't realize my comadre Eufelia was embarrassed as he stirred and stirred, and she without sugar!"

There was a school at Tinaja at that time. Reynaldo Mirabal says, "My mother Perfetita used to talk about going to school there. She remembered with fondness her teacher, Miss May. They kept in touch through the mail for years." Mi Tío Rafael Peña also taught school in the two-room schoolhouse. His daughter Nora Peña Sandoval says she remembers when they lived "in the house close to the brick school building."

Water came from a tinaja and from a well dug by hand by Don Epifanio Leyba, according to his son Amado Leyba, who married Trinnie, the youngest daughter of Mi Tía Eufelia. I remember stopping there with my father in the late 1930s, and the buildings were gone. We did find some broken bricks, which were a bit unusual, since all the homesteaders built with sandstone or adobe. But the school was in McKinley County and had been built with bricks from the Gallup kilns. My good friend Reyes Romero says, "There was a cemetery near the school and there was talk of a still or two during Prohibition." Other homesteaders were Alfejo Montaño, Salvador Apodaca, Vicente Mártinez, Eduardo Montaño, Perfeto Chávez, Pedro Chávez, Sebastián Mirabal, Severo Gutiérrez, Felipe Gutiérrez, Epifanio Leyba, Isidro Chávez, and others.

When I first knew Mi Tía Eufelia, she was living in San Mateo. She was a tall, attractive gray-haired lady. I remember her neatly dressed in light gray dresses that matched her gray hair, beautifully groomed in a chignon. She had widowed relatively young and after selling the homestead, moved to San Mateo. In the 1920s M. B. McMillen, "El Maxemila," bought most of the homesteads north of San Mateo, including Tío Leandro's, and consolidated most of the lands known as the Fernandez Company, known today as the Floyd Lee Ranch. Mi Tía Eufelia sold her homestead to Don Lizardo Salazar, who sold it to Pablo Peña, and today it's part of the Peña Ranch.

Mi Tía and her daughters were very active in the choir and led the singing at the Catholic church in San Mateo. Josefita and

Perfetita had high voices, while Dolores and the younger sisters had lower voices, giving their alabados a special quality. Today when I go to church in San Mateo, I tend to close my eyes and try to recall the days when we were altar boys listening to their singing while serving Father Robert at the classic white altar of our church. The Mass was prayed in Latin, and I still recall some of the Latin responses. "Ad Deum qui litificat juventutum meum." For funerals the voices took on a sorrowful and painful tone, appropriate for the occasion. Nearly every one was dressed in black or gray. As the funeral procession left the church and headed toward the cemetery up town, bells tolled, mourners cried, and the singing led by Mi Tía and her daughters followed the shoulder-carried bier and casket to its entombment. Usually after the priest had said the last prayers, a person was asked to speak and bid farewell to the deceased.

Funerals ended with almost everyone crying and dropping a handful of dirt onto the loudly echoing pine casket. In 1964 Mi Tía Eufelia, a beloved homestead pioneer, passed away. She was eighty-four years old.

Don Eduardo

Don Eduardo was a builder. He built homes, he built cabinets, and from time to time he built coffins. At one time in our youth my older brother and I were assigned to be his helpers. He was building a pitched roof over an old adobe warehouse on our farm in San Mateo. Somehow he missed the upper step on the ladder and fell to the ground with a hard "thump." He shook his head and shoulders, kept wringing his hands to deal with the pain while we were making a fuss over him. In a little while he stood up, dusted himself off, climbed back up, and continued building the roof!

Don Eduardo Montaño was of medium height, with strong arms and body. He was fair-skinned with blue-green eyes and

gray hair, and he spoke with a bit of a lisp. His hearing was also
somewhat impaired, and we made it a point to face him when we
spoke to him. He was married to Doña Idela Castillo Montaño,
and they had four daughters and three sons: Refugio, Demetria,
Lala, and Mary Esther, Cándido, Willie, and Eugenio. Their home
faced the main village street, and their orchard and garden were
in the back, paralleling other garden strips. The land was irrigated from a ditch that ran between the house and the orchard.
The Montaños had a very fine orchard, with a diversified mix of
fruits. Among them was one of the best improved pear trees in
the village. We kept an eye on that tree to slip in and "help ourselves" to a pear or two when they ripened.

Doña Idela also watched and guarded her tree jealously, knowing that her fine pears attracted boys. One night several of us
slipped into the orchard and climbed the pear tree. Sifredo
Sandoval did not climb up, however, and when the rest of us
were in the tree, he yelled at the top of his voice, "Doña Idela,
Doña Idela, the boys are stealing your pears!" We heard the
back door open, and she ran to her pear tree with a kettle of hot
water to throw at us. We were too high for her to reach us, but it
scared the devil out of us, and we never returned. Sifredo had a
lot of fun and enjoyed playing jokes and pranks on us. We were
cousins and good friends. He raised his family in San Mateo and
became a successful businessman and cattle rancher in the foot-
steps of his father, who was a prominent sheep rancher in an
earlier era. He passed away in March 1993, at the age of sixty-
seven.

Another time Don Eduardo was building a retaining wall with
rock and mortar. Again Bennie and I were his helpers, mixing
the mortar and carrying it to him as he laid the rock wall. One
side of the wall was to be filled in with dirt, and would not be
seen, so Bennie suggested he not groove the mortar and save
time, saying, "Nobody will know you didn't groove it." Don
Eduardo thought about it for a moment and quietly responded,
"I will know," and continued grooving the mortar very carefully. He was a true craftsman, with a remarkable sense of pride
in his work.

In those days there were no mortuaries nor embalming in the area and we buried our dead as soon as possible, generally the next day. I recall the hammer blows at night when Don Eduardo was building a casket. He would plane the one-inch boards and carefully round them off. His care and skills gave the finished coffin a professional quality. When he was through, the ladies took either white, gray, or black cloth and lined the casket. White was for children ,whom we called *angelitos*, while either black or gray was for adults. The mortality rate of children under age five was very high.

Their two older daughters, Refugio and Demetria, married two Gonzales brothers that came from Albuquerque to work for the Fernandez Company. Alcario Gonzales married Refugio, and his brother Telesfor married Demetria. Alcario rose to be *el caporal mayor* (head foreman) of one of the largest sheep and cattle ranches in New Mexico. They both raised fine families, and many of their children and grandchildren are living in the Grants area, as well as in California and elsewhere. Lala married Herminio Jaramillo, and they had a daughter. Mary Esther moved to Albuquerque. She inherited Don Eduardo's blue-green eyes, with a special radiance to them. The three brothers moved to the Los Lunas area, but they still come back to San Mateo from time to time to visit their past.

Don Eduardo was a builder. He not only built houses and walls, he also helped build character in those whose lives he touched.

Román Sandoval

Román Sandoval, who lived from 1906 to 1975, was the son of Don Procopio Sandoval and Doña Luz Ortega Sandoval. His mother and my grandmother Manuelita were sisters. My father, Pablo Peña, and Román were first cousins. Both boys had a similar upbringing in the village of San Mateo, where they were born and raised. Both of their fathers homesteaded grazing land,

and their flocks grew. Their mothers were widowed relatively young. The sons started in the sheep business with small flocks of about two hundred sheep and built them into commercial-sized flocks over the years. Román attended the mission elementary school in San Mateo, then went on to Menaul High School in Albuquerque. After returning from school and starting in the sheep business, he married Francisca Jaramillo Sandoval, from Cubero. She is a quiet, soft-spoken lady, now living in Grants. God has given her good health, and she is still able to take care of herself. Their home in San Mateo was up the canyon, near the old flour mill. I never saw the mill in operation, but old-timers remember when it ground all the grain for the village. The coming of the railroad through Grants in 1882 brought wheat flour at a lower cost and put almost all the flour mills in Cíbola County out of business. Their daughter Maggie, their only child, married Tomás Márquez, of Bibo. They were blessed with six children, and Maggie calls on her mother daily. Pablita, her sister-in-law, lives in the same apartment complex. They have been close friends over the years and still look after each other.

During World War II tires and tubes had gone to war and were hard to get. All of us had to patch and limp along as best we could. One time on the way to Grants, Dad arrived while Román was trying to fix a tire. After exchanging greetings, Dad said, "Looks like you had some bad luck, Román." Román, aggravated with the tire, his hat on the ground and sweat running down his brow, responded, "Qué mala suerte ni mala suerte— ¡malas llantas!" ("It's got nothing to do with bad luck—just bad tires!")

Both Román and the other sheep and cattle growers in the area patriotically responded to President Franklin D. Roosevelt's call to produce more wool and meat to win the war. Flocks and herds increased beyond normal grazing capacity, in order to help save the world from Hitler and the Axis powers. Increased livestock numbers, coupled with a severe drought, eroded the range, and environmentalists took us to task after the war for overstocking our ranges. We asked them to pause and reflect—we reminded them that freedom was preserved. The alternative was ugly.

Mi Primo Román, like his wife Francisca, was a quiet, soft-spoken man. I remember hearing about a problem he and José María García had on their way to San Mateo from Grants one night years ago. While in Grants they tipped the bottle once or twice, and on the way home they missed the bridge at Puertecito! The ton-and-a-half bobtail truck landed on its nose, down in the twenty-foot-deep box arroyo!

My father and my brother Eddie were the first ones to get there the next morning. Román was sitting by the road, a little dusty and a little bloody, but alright. When Dad asked him what happened, José María, Román's companion, friend, and employee, spoke up and said, "The darned steering wheel on that truck is loose, and in the dark we missed the bridge and fell in the arroyo." Román sheepishly added, "Yes, the steering wheel on the truck was loose, but our steering wheel was loose also!"

The Sandoval family was a large one. Manuel was the oldest, followed by Román, Procopio, Carlos, Flora, Aurelio, Fela, Benjamín, Pablita, Sifredo, and Lucy. Román, Procopio, Aurelio, and Sifredo are now deceased. The boys, as was the custom, were kept busy helping on the farm in San Mateo and at the ranch, which was about seven miles west of the village, near what we know today as Ragland Village, at the turn-off to Ambrosio Lake. The original homestead is still standing, and the old windmill until recently squeaked and groaned. Some of the grandchildren run cattle on the ranch. The sheep are gone, though, victims of predators and changing economic times.

Nabor Márquez used to tell the story of Manuel Sandoval, Román's older brother, stopping at their ranch on the way to San Mateo. "Manuel stopped to have coffee with my father and me, and asked if we were going to the wedding and the big dance in San Mateo? We told him we couldn't, we had to take care of the sheep." They had a flock of about a thousand sheep. Manuel continued his ride to San Mateo, and two days later, on the way back, he stopped again. "My father Eugenio asked him, 'How did the wedding go, Manuel?' Manuel looked at him, looked at Nabor, and said with a perfectly straight face, 'You know what? A poor man can make a devil of a lot more noise with a chile string than you can with a thousand sheep!'" Grinning, Nabor turned to his dad and asked, "Any other questions, Papa?" Nabor married Isabel Ortega Márquez, the daughter of Mariano Ortega, an uncle to Román and to my dad. Mi Tío Mariano, Isabel's father, was also in the sheep business.

Let us always remember that San Mateo, like other villages in Cíbola County in the early 1940s, not only sent young men to war, but also produced the wool and the meat to clothe and feed our soldiers and sailors—and win a war.

Marcelino Jaramillo

Another interesting villager was Marcelino Jaramillo. Both his and Doña Flora's hair turned gray, literally white, early in life, and they made a most handsome couple. They had twelve children, seven strapping sons and five beautiful daughters: Leonor, Herminio, Marcelino, Jr. (Celito), Refugio, Trinidad, Víctor, Albino, Conce, Tita, Teresa, Tonia, and Benina. The oldest of their sons, Leonor, made the supreme sacrifice in World War II. After he had chased the German General Rommel and his Afrika Korps in the African Campaign, a letter came stating that Pfc Leonor Jaramillo was killed storming the beaches at Anzio, in Italy. They were attempting to establish a foothold on the continent of Europe. The village mourned. War touched us all.

Don Marcelino was a lean and robust man, with a deep voice and a fine sense of humor. He worked as a cowboy for the Fernandez Company, La Compañía, and sometimes herded sheep in Arizona. Later he became a fence contractor and built hundreds of miles of netwire fence for La Compañía and other ranchers. He and his sons were noted for the speed at which they could build a mile of quality fence. They were hard workers and tough as nails.

His storytelling was legendary. He was gifted with an exceptional memory and remembered every tale, every joke, and every ghost story he ever heard—and recited them with pleasure! I recall as a boy sitting at a respectable distance from him and other villagers, hearing their stories *en la resolana*. Popular gathering places were the front porch of the Michael store or la sala de Mi Tía Onofre.

In an unassuming way those men were philosophers who interpreted their times by observing nature and the world around them. Don Marcelino was a good friend of Mr. Merhage Michael and they often teased each other. Both had strong opinions, which sometimes led to heated arguments. Don Marcelino once called the store, "la tienda de la averiguata," "the store of arguments"! Mr. Michael would argue the point till he ran out of Spanish, then continue in Lebanese!

Sometime in the 1960s the Jaramillos moved to Grants. However, Doña Flora once told me, "I miss San Mateo—it's alright here, but . . ." My mother, who moved to Grants from San Mateo about the same time, felt the same way for a long time. It's hard to let go of our roots—even when they're only twenty-three miles away.

Doña Beneranda

It was Christmas Eve and Doña Beneranda lost her voice in the middle of the song. Whispering, she said, "Se me fué, se me fué" ("It is gone"). The rest of us carried on, while she rested her voice, keeping step with the "Comanche" drummers. The celebration of Los Comanches was part of Christmas folklore in our village of San Mateo, as well as in some of the other villages in Cíbola County. It was a memorable tradition, because it kept alive the memory of the captive children taken by Comanche Indians from our Hispanic villages along the Río Grande to Indian country, to the east, where the sun rises.

Doña Beneranda Saavedra Romero was our Comanche leader. Her thin, short gray hair was tied at the back and she wore a red band around her forehead. Her aging face showed the calm of a life of hard work lived in a state of grace. She lost her hearing in her old age, but never her enthusiasm for life.

Over her shoulders she draped a soft Navajo blanket, and her skirt stretched to a little below the calf. She wore low heel shoes, sometimes tennis shoes for comfort, and in her right hand she carried a tambourine. She was a very pretty and petite lady and light as a feather on her feet. She was also an accomplished composer of verses and songs. She truly was a troubadour. Sometimes while she was singing her memory would fail her, but she would just compose and improvise as she went along!

Don Evaristo Gonzales, Doña Beneranda's son-in-law, was her assistant and took special interest in training us to sing and dance the stories of Los Comanches. He also had a flair for dancing and dressed the part of a colorful Comanche. On his head he wore a feathered warbonnet that trailed almost to the floor. With almagre (ocher) war paint on his cheeks and wearing a frilled leather vest and pants, he cut a dashing Indian figure. He carried a bow and several arrows in his hands and small bells tinkled around his ankles. He walked with the confident authority of an Indian chief.

The rest of us also dressed like little Comanches and imitated Don Evaristo, dancing and preparing to capture the Christ Child from the crib on the altar and take him to the distant plains. The image of the Christ Child, protected by los padrinos, representing Mary and Joseph, represented the children taken by the Comanches.

Doña Beneranda was married to Don Gabriel Romero. Don Gabriel was over six feet tall and towered over almost everyone in the village. No one knows where he came from, but Celito Jaramillo says, "He used to say he came, el año de los tres ochos, 1888" ("the year of the three eights"). People believe he came with the railroad crews and met Beneranda in Cubero, where she was raised. They had a son and a daughter, Santiago and Sofía. Santiago married Lauteria Montaño and had two children, Reyes Romero and Ruma Romero Baca. Santiago died in a tragic car accident, hurrying to the hospital in Winslow, Arizona, where Lauteria was delivering Ruma. Lauteria herself died on the delivery table, but the child survived. The children were raised by their grandparents, Don Gabriel and Doña Beneranda, in San Mateo. They also raised Zacarías, one of Sofía's sons. Sofía married Don Evaristo Gonzales, and they had three children.

Doña Beneranda was probably the best *enjarradora* (plasterer) in the village. Every summer, or at least every other summer, almost every house in the village would be replastered. She used her bare hands as a trowel for the finishing touches. It took a special skill to apply the clay mud and make it stick to old adobe walls.

The village took on a very clean appearance as homes were replastered and windows and doors painted. By late September our village sparkled. Our homes were modest but immaculately clean. Even homes with earthen floors had a fresh smell to them—the floors were sprayed daily with water and swept with a grass broom.

The San Mateo fiestas took place on September 21, and the Catholic church, like our homes, also took on a fresh coat of adobe in early September. It was a major community project. September 21 was the last day of summer and an appropriate time to thank God for giving us a bountiful harvest. The Penitente chapel up the canyon also took on a fresh coat of plaster at that time. Doña Beneranda was a member of La Hermandad de Nuestro Jesús Nazareno, one of three or four women who were members of the Brotherhood, also known as Penitentes. Her singing gave the alabados a special reverence when we attended and prayed the Rosary or recited other prayers at the morada during Lent and Holy Week.

Don Gabriel was a fine sheepherder. He worked for Don Lizardo Salazar in the sheep camps for many years and later for my father and Román Sandoval. Rosalio Baca, a boyhood friend of mine who married Ruma, told me, "Don Gabriel fell and hurt himself and caught pneumonia and died." And he added, "Remember how he called us all 'chiquitos'?" His right index finger had been bitten by a rattlesnake in the sheep camps, and it remained stiff all his life.

Doña Beneranda died of old age respected and venerated by the whole village. She who kept the story of our people alive through verse and song will live in our hearts and minds forever.

Los Hermanos Penitentes

In our youth the Lenten prayer services at the morada of the Penitentes were part of our religious life in San Mateo and other villages in Cíbola County. Today there is some confusion regarding the origin and history of the Penitentes, La Hermandad de Nuestro Padre Jesús Nazareno, in New Mexico and southern Colorado.

Charles Lummis in *The Land of Poco Tiempo* says they were introduced into New Mexico by Franciscan in the sixteenth, seventeenth, and eighteenth centuries.

On the other hand, Fray Angélico Chávez, one of the most notable historians and writers on the colonial period and author of *My Penitente Land*, says, "Charles Lummis was a well meaning but impetuous author, who resolved that Penitentes had come with the very first Spanish settlers and Franciscan missionaries who accompanied them. . . . Subsequent writers kept on parroting Lummis's mistaken assumptions. . . . As it turned out, New Mexico's particular society of penitentes had not come with the original colonists more than three centuries and a half ago, but only appeared at the beginning of the nineteenth century."

My research confirms that of Fray Angélico. In 1821, when it won its independence from Spain, Mexico claimed all the territories to the north, including New Mexico. Mexico did not trust the loyalty of the Spanish priests, and deported them back to Spain. The concern was that they would be loyal to Spain and influence their parishioners to be disloyal to Mexico. Only a few native-born New Mexico priests, who had trained in Durango, Mexico, remained. New Mexico did not have any seminaries to train priests at that time. The handful of Mexico-trained priests could not minister to all the far-flung parishes. Distant and isolated parishes were closed, and our people were left without priests, the only people who can celebrate Mass in Catholic churches. When the churches closed, the people built moradas to continue their communal prayers and Rosaries as best they could.

They organized as La Hermandad de Nuestro Padre Jesús Nazareno. An *hermano mayor* was selected from among themselves to serve as leader. The Brotherhood had a very loose connection to other brotherhoods in other villages. There was some contact, especially during Holy Week, when visiting Penitentes arrived, usually on foot, from other moradas on the eastern and southern sides of Mount Taylor. Most of the Brothers were men, but some women were also members. Many of the *cantos* and alabados blended the self-taught voices of men and women to give a moving, primitive quality to our prayers. During Lent, starting on Ash Wednesday, there was a Rosary prayed at La Morada every Friday. The chapel was usually full of people. In my youth there were about 250 people in San Mateo, and between 30 and 35 were members of the Hermandad.

In 1846, when the United States claimed New Mexico and the rest of the Southwest after the Mexican War, priests returned, but this time they came from the See of Baltimore and spoke English. Our ancestors spoke Spanish, and naturally there were misunderstandings. Especially misunderstood were Los Hermanos Penitentes, who had grown in numbers and had become a part of our religious culture and tradition. Archbishops, starting with Jean Baptiste Lamy in 1850, never recognized the Brotherhood, until the Most Reverend Archbishop Edwin D. Byrne accepted them in 1947. In a statement issued at that time, he wrote, "The Brotherhood constitutes a society of men, united in charity to commemorate the passion and death of the Redeemer, and the society is a part of the Catholic church and deserves its protection as long as it observes and practices the teachings of the church." He concluded the lengthy statement, "In a way we owe these groups of Penitential Brothers, although certain excesses entered their practices, the preservation of the faith during those sad and harsh days, and they have my blessing and help."

There are still some Penitentes in some of our villages, observing the Lenten days of prayer and penance. San Mateo and San Rafael hold well-attended Friday Rosaries. I recall the long service, prayed on our knees. After the five mysteries of the

Rosary, plus other assorted prayers and songs, our knees had gone numb and our legs felt like jelly! It was an effort to stand and walk.

During Holy Week the Stations of the Cross were prayed along with a nightly Rosary starting on Wednesday, when all the Hermanos, *se encerraban* (locked themselves up), and they didn't go to their homes until Good Saturday. All of the Holy Week services were sad reminders of the mocking, the accusations, the trial, the scourgings, the carrying of the cross, and the death of our Lord Jesus Christ on that cross. Holy Saturday services were for children to celebrate La Gloria, parading and singing around the altar at La Morada, carrying flowers and happily awaiting the Resurrection.

On Easter Sunday, with scrubbed faces and polished shoes, we joined our Franciscan priest in his most colorful vestments at the church to celebrate the Holy Eucaristic Mass of the Resurrection. The transformation of bread and wine into the body and blood of our Lord Jesus Christ has given Christianity meaning here and around the world for nearly two thousand years.

The Postmaster

Rafael Mariño Peña was a schoolteacher, a farmer and rancher, a notary public, and the postmaster in San Mateo. He and wife, Rosita Montoya Peña, were a handsome and hardworking couple. She also assisted with the post office and had been a schoolteacher in the village of Márquez. The post office occupied one of the front rooms of their home, so that it was convenient for them to take care of the post office and also of their family. There were about fifty post office boxes and a service window in the neat and efficient office that served the village for many years.

Don Nazario Sandoval, the mailman, brought the mail from Grants three times a week, on Mondays, Wednesdays and Fridays, weather permitting. The twenty-three-mile dirt county road from Grants was troublesome in both rain and snow.

Rafael and Rosita had three sons and five daughters: José, Alfredo, Rafael, Jr., Nora, Minnie, Margaret, Frieda, and Rosa. Before they ran the post office, it had been run by Joaquín Sandoval, and before him by Dubijinia Montoya Chávez, Rosita's older sister. Dubijinia was married to Abrán Chávez, brother to my grandmother Beneranda Chávez Márquez.

Tía Rosita was born in Cuba, New Mexico, and was very young when the family moved to Seboyeta. Nora, the oldest daughter, told me, "Mother and two of her sisters went to school at Sherman Institute, an Indian school in Riverside California through some arrangement with the school." Tío Rafael was the son of Pablo and Benita Mariño Peña. His older brother Abelicio was my grandfather.

Margaret Peña García, one of Tía Rosita's daughters, told me recently, "Mother came to San Mateo to visit her sister who was the postmistress and met my father! . . . It was love at first sight!" They were married in 1915 and started a long and productive life together. They were members of the Congregational Church. Near their home the Church had built a two-story mission school, which served the village until 1929, when the public school was built (see Fig. 16).

Nora told me, "Mom and Dad used to say there were some wonderful teachers at the mission school. They talked about Miss Dorothy Blotter, who had taught in a mission school in Turkey. Also, about Miss Gertrude Marsh, Miss Flossie Nichols, and Miss Anna Swanson. Miss Swanson had some nurse's training and she brought the news of Don Procopio Sandoval's death in the middle of the night in 1926." Nora later married Don Procopio's son, also named Procopio, in the 1930s. Miss Swanson had been at the school for many years and apparently trained Doña Martita Salazar and Doña Regalada Chávez, curanderas, who in turn trained Doña Virginia, who assisted in the delivery of many San Mateños through the years, including me.

After the Mission School closed, Tío Rafael and Tía Rosita purchased the building, which had been built around 1905. The first floor was built of adobe and the second floor of lumber. Quarters for the teachers were in the same building. By the front door it had a fine improved pear tree that attracted youngsters when the pears ripened! And there was a hand-dug well on the side, with a hand pump on it—the first pump handle in the village. Years later some of the teachers traveled to the village to visit my aunt and uncle and other villagers.

In 1943 the family moved to Albuquerque. They purchased a farm in Pajarito, where coincidentally a great, great, great grandfather of Tío Rafael, José Mariano de la Peña, had been a merchant in Spanish colonial times. His grandson moved to Seboyeta, and his great grandson to San Mateo, from whence the Peñas descended. Their oldest son, José, married Ramoncita Sandoval. They moved to Gallup in 1940, a year after the birth of their first son, John. The rest of the family lives in Albuquerque, where they have raised their families. Minnie is the only one in the family who has passed away, and the only one who has remained in San Mateo is Nora, who married Procopio Sandoval. They were childhood sweethearts and married shortly after they graduated from Grants Union High School, in the 1930s.

In early 1953, shortly after I was discharged from the army, I took pilot lessons at Cutter-Carr Flying Service in Albuquerque. I went to visit my aunt and uncle, who by then were retired and living alone. When I told them I was driving from San Mateo twice a week to take flying lessons, they asked if I'd like to stay with them. I happily accepted and stayed with them from time to time.

They both aged gracefully. Tío Rafael stood perfectly erect, with a full head of wavy white hair, an ever-present smile, and his pipe with its fine aroma. Tía Rosita was still interested in civic and Presbyterian Church affairs and devoted a lot of her time to community service. She was also a fine cook and a great conversationalist. She had gray hair and was most attractive in her golden years.

When I asked Sister Lydia what she remembered most of Tío Rafael (born in 1890, died in 1984) and Tía Rosita (born in 1894, died in 1976), she answered without hesitation, "They were great hosts. They made you feel welcome. They had the grace to go with their hospitality—they were very special." Their daughter Frieda Peña Salazar says, "They both lived long lives and we enjoyed every moment with them. They were truly great parents, grandparents, and great grandparents. We miss them." According to their grandson John Peña in Gallup, "They were both hard workers and expected the same from their family. I feel very fortunate and proud to be their grandson." And when I asked my wife, Viola, what she remembered most, she answered, "They were the perfect couple. Besides, Tío Rafael was the handsomest man I ever met!"

Blas Trujillo

Colorful and interesting best describes some of the people from San Mateo I knew during the 1930s and 1940s. Times were tough, especially during the Great Depression of the thirties, but hard times did not defeat the character, determination, and humor of the people.

There was Blas Trujillo. He was a big man with a round, expressive face and a round, portly body, who always wore bib overalls. He walked with short quick steps and a lot of determination and held sway with a commanding voice wherever he was. It was the sort of voice worthy of an operatic tenor. I can't remember hearing him sing, but he looked like a handsome Pavarotti. He had many friends and made a living for himself and his wife, Ventura, two sons, Vivián and Eduardo, and daughter, Veronica, operating a pool hall and driving a school bus. In 1940 when I started riding the bus to high school in Grants, he owned and drove it. He bought the ton and a half truck chassis, then built a relatively comfortable cabin with seats running lengthwise; it carried up to fourteen students. The exhaust pipe was turned and extended into the cabin, to serve both for heat and as a footrest down the center isle.

One Christmas Blas was codirector of Los Pastores, with his sister-in-law Geneveva Trujillo. There were about a eighteen

shepherds, Jila (a shepherdess and cook), three devils, and a
couple of angels in the cast. We rehearsed every night for two
weeks in preparation for presentation of the pageant on Christmas Eve.

I was thirteen years old and played the shepherd Aparrado,
Lolita Castillo Mandagarán played Jila, Reyes Romero was Bato,
Merhage Michael, Jr., was Cucharon, my older brother Bennie
was the angel St. Michael, Don Santiago Baca was the devil Lu-
cifer, David Salazar was *el diablito*, Leandro Márquez was Bártolo, Andrés Salas was Melicio, Sifredo Sandoval was Bras,
Vivián Trujillo (Blas's son) was Tulio, and to the rest of the cast,
please forgive my memory. The codirectors and our parents
helped us prepare our shepherd costumes.

The ageless story of the birth of Christ played to a full house.
The most touching moment in the play was the finale, when
Bártolo, a lazy sheepherder who spent his days lying on a sheepskin, was picked up by Bato and Jila and carried to adore the
baby Jesus. When he saw the Christ Child, he was simply
stunned—he held his breath, carefully tried his wobbly legs, did
a little twirl, then broke into a spirited dance! He had seen his
Savior and rejoiced . . . and we rejoiced with him!

Don Blas was also a very good pool player. The only one who
could compete with him was his son Vivián, who was a carbon
copy of his father, but not quite as tall. On Sunday December 7,
1941, we were playing pool when the squeaky radio flashed the
news of the Japanese attack on Pearl Harbor. We were stunned
into silence after hearing the news, until Don Blas broke the
silence in anger, "Wait till we go after them. We'll beat the tar
out of those SOBs." It may have sounded like bravado at the
time, but it gave us hope—and how right he was. It took four
years, but many bold and courageous men, many from our village, including two who died, brought the Axis powers to their
knees and freedom was preserved.

"Go invite Don Desiderio to *la matanza*," said my mother. Pig killing was not only an important source of villagers' food supply, it was much more—a social event, a working feast, and a ritual in San Mateo and other villages in Cíbola County. Don Desiderio García, an old widower, was considered an expert in bleeding the swine to produce tender and flavorful pork and properly rendered lard.

Almost all the villagers had pigs, fed the leftovers from our tables, but most importantly, corn. Generally the pigpen, built of pine logs or heavy lumber, was adjacent to the corral where the milk cow and other livestock were penned. The chicken coup was nearby also. The animals were kept about 200 feet from the house, far enough away for hygiene but conveniently close for doing chores. The average sow gave birth to about eight pigs in the spring. Pigs were butchered at various times during the year for meat, but la matanza, for lard, was the big one in the late fall or early winter, in preparation for Christmas. It yielded as much as 150 pounds of lard, enough to serve the cooking needs of a family for several months.

Pigs selected to be fattened were generally two years old or older. The heavy corn feeding started with the corn harvest in September. A couple of pounds in the morning and a couple in the evening was increased gradually to as much as the animal could eat. By November or December, they were sometimes so heavy they couldn't rear up on their hind legs. It was time for la matanza. The day before we would hand carry water in 2-gallon buckets from la acequia and fill two 50-gallon drums, which rested either on a stand or on large rocks. Then we would arrange firewood under the barrels. Even before daybreak the firewood would be lit and the water heated to a boil, before Don Desiderio and the other invitees arrived. At sunrise the pig would be walked or hauled in a wheelbarrow to the butchering platform constructed nearby of planking elevated about a foot off the ground.

With the blunt heel of an axe, the pig would be struck hard

between the eyes and knocked out. Then Don Desiderio would take his special sharp, long-bladed kitchen knife, saying, "Jesus y Cruz," and pierce through the breast to the heart. A bucket or large pan would be held to catch the gushing blood, which would be made into morcilla, a fine food rich in proteins and minerals. The pig would then be rolled onto the platform and after boiling water was poured over the animal, it would be covered with gunny sacks. In a few minutes the hair would loosen and could be pulled off easily with razor-sharp knives. The naked pig shone like a freshly shaved face.

The animal would then be carefully cut open and the internal organs removed one at a time. In a very fat pig this would be quite a task, because the fat layers would keep covering the organs. It was especially important to remove the gall bladder intact without spilling the gall, or the meat would take on a repugnant bad flavor. When the liver came out, it would be cut into large slices and roasted over the hot coals, turned with a sharp-pointed stick or long forks. The smell of the roasting liver would start the gastric juices flowing, and all the killing crew, usually six or eight, plus the children, would have their first taste of the well-fattened pig.

The blood and some meat would be sent to the kitchen crew, and the cooking of red chile with the fresh meat, the central activity of the matanza feast, would begin. The killing crew sometimes helped the kitchen crew cook the chile in large Dutch ovens over the coals, while the kitchen crew made piles of blue corn tortillas on the wooden stove in the kitchen.

When all the innards had been carefully removed and sent to the kitchen, the *lonjas* would be removed and hung on a clothesline. Lonjas are 2-inch strips of skin with about a 3-inch thick layer of fat, cut lengthwise; the pig butchers would literally skin the pig in strips. While the lonjas hardened, the crews feasted, joked, and visited. Most of the talk would be about the fine pig, and the guessing game would be on. How much lard would it render? Stories of legendary pigs that rendered up to 200 pounds and the men who raised them were told and retold. Some would even boast of having heard of one that rendered 300 pounds!

In about an hour the lonjas would harden and the stripping of the fat from the skins would begin. The crew would sit around the planking and dice the fat into about one inch cubes. Large cast-iron or brass *ollas* would be filled with diced fat and stirred and stirred for about two hours over the fire, to render the precious lard.

Then the distribution of the food would start. Children would be sent in all directions throughout the village to deliver food in *botes de cinco*—some chile, two or three tortillas, and a handful of *chicharrones*, and sometimes a small strip of meat. We would deliver food to different houses according to the instructions of the kitchen crew. Some trips would take longer than others, as we crisscrossed the village delivering the bounty. By the end of the day most of the pig would be distributed and shared by the village, except for the lard. It would be stored in *botes de diez o de viente*, 10- or 20-pound tins, and carefully put away in a storeroom.

Others in the village would also have matanzas, so there would be a constant sharing with each other in the fall and winter. In this way the meaningful custom of sharing was not only carried out at Christmastime but all year long. Hardly a day passed when we would not be sent somewhere in the village with a container of food to someone who was sick, or had visitors, or had a baby, or who simply liked our mother's *sopa* or *panocha*.

Today there are still some matanzas in our villages. However, there are fewer and fewer, as the lifestyle of the village is changing. In most of the households, both husband and wife are employed; the supermarket is not far away, and it's a lot more convenient in today's busy and hurried world, where sharing with others has been almost forgotten.

Songs of My Village

In the village of San Mateo, most of us sang or whistled, or both. I remember Ricardo Salazar, our neighbor and an early riser, whistling on the way to milk the cow before sunrise. On the way

back from the corral, he generally changed to another song.
Ricardo was a happy man. My father's favorite song, as he drove
out to the ranch with one of us at his side, was "Un Ramillete de
Flores":

En una mesa te puse,
Un ramillete de flores.
María, no seas ingrata,
Regálame tus amores.
("I placed for you on a table,
A bouquet of flowers.
Maria, don't be ungrateful,
Give me your love.")

He was a gentle man and sang very softly, with a lot of feeling; but you would never hear him singing in public. Singing
was a very personal matter for him. However, he enjoyed listening to others sing. In our living room there was a beautifully
polished Victrola, with a crank, and he enjoyed listening to
records of Lydia Mendoza, one of the most popular singers of
the 1930s. She made such an impression on him and on Mother
that they named their first daughter Lydia. She is now a Sister
of Loretto, teaching at Regis University.

Mother was a whistler, but not in the usual way. When she
was concentrating hard on a task, she pursed her lips and whistled
and blew air at the same time. In those moments we didn't dare
interrupt!

Doña Beneranda Romero, our leader in "Los Comanches,"
had an extensive repertoire of songs. The one I recall best was
the religious "Bendito":

Bendito, bendito,
Bendito sea Dios.
Los ángeles cantan
Y alaban a Dios,
Los ángeles cantan
Y alaban a Dios.
Yo creo, Dios mío,

Que estás en el altar,
Oculto en la hostia,
Te vengo adorar,
Oculto en la hostia,
Te vengo adorar.
("Blessed, blessed,
Blessed be God.
The angels are singing
And praising God,
The angels are singing
And praising God.
I believe, my God,
That you are in the altar,
Hidden in the host,
I come to worship you,
Hidden in the host,
I come to worship you.")

And then there was Salvador Chávez, a composer of note, who spent a large part of his life on the range punching cattle. His most famous composition was "El Rincón de Marcos":

Mi casa es de rama,
No tiene zotea,
Cuando no cae agua,
Pues no se gotea.
Tengo en un sabino
Mi puela colgada,
Porque los ratones
La usan de guitarra.
Las víboras pasan,
Casi galopeando,
En mi cabecera,
Bailan sus fandangos.
("My home is made of brush,
It has no roof,
As long as it doesn't rain,
Well, it doesn't leak.

I have a juniper tree,
Where my frying pan hangs,
Because the mice
Use it for a guitar.
Poisonous snakes come by,
Almost galloping,
At the head of my bed
They dance their fandangos.")

Mi Tío Ismael Salazar, known to many as Smiley, liked to sing and play the guitar. One of the songs he liked best was "Adelita":

Adelita se llama la joven,
La que yo quiero y no puedo olvidar,
En el campo yo tengo una rosa,
Y con el tiempo la voy a cortar.
Si Adelita se fuera con otro,
Le seguiría la fuella sin cesar,
Por vapores o buques de guerra,
O por tierra en un tren militar.
("Adelita is the name of the young woman,
The one I love and cannot forget,
In the field I have a rose,
And in time I will pick it.
If Adelita should go off with another,
I would follow her trail without pause,
By steamboat or warship,
Or on land in a military train.")

Don Francisco Baca, probably the best dancer in the village, liked to sing "Las Gaviotas":

¿Qué andan haciendo esas gaviotas?
¿Qué andan haciendo a orillas del mar?
Andan buscando nidos de amores,
Nidos de amores encontrarán.
("What are those swallows doing?
What are they doing on the shores of the sea?

They are searching for love nests,
Love nests are what they'll find.")

Possibly the best singers of all were Delfinio Salazar and his wife, Senaida. They directed pageants of "Los Pastores" and "Los Comanches" and trained many of us to sing. One of their favorites was "Venid Pastorcillos":

Venid pastorcillos, venid adorar,
Al rey de los cielos, que en el cielo está.
("Come little shepherds, come to worship,
The King of the heavens, who is in heaven.")

Another of their favorites was "Belen":

Vamos todos a Belen con amor y gozo,
Adoremos al Señor, nuestro redentor.
("We will all go to Bethlehem with love and pleasure,
To worship the Lord, our Redeemer.")

Mi Tía Josefita Márquez Price sang with her sisters in church, but she also sang the popular songs. She had a high-pitched voice and could belt out in fine fashion her rendition of "Cuatro Milpas":

Cuatro milpas tan solo han quedado,
De aquel rancho que era mío,
De aquella casita tan blanca
Y bonita, lo triste que está.
Los potreros están sin ganado,
Toditito se acabó,
De aquella casita tan blanca
Y bonita, lo triste que está.
("Only four cornfields remain
Of that ranch that was mine,
Oh, that little home so white
And beautiful, how sad it is.
The pastures are without livestock,
Every little thing is finished,
Oh, that little home so white

And beautiful, how sad it is.")

Possibly the most famous and most sung of the old songs was
"El Rancho Grande." It was the favorite song of Mrs. Frances
Lee, from the Fernandez Ranch nearby. She always requested
the promenading musicians at the annual wool growers' con-
ventions in Albuquerque to sing it. Her husband, Floyd, headed
the Wool Growers' Association for years:

Allá en el Rancho Grande,
Allá donde vivía,
Había una rancherita,
Qué alegre me decía,
Qué alegre me decía.
Pues ¡Qué te decía!
Te voy hacer tus calzones,
Como los que usa el vaquero,
Te los comienzo de lana
Y te los acabo de cuero.
("Over there at the Big Ranch,
Over there where I used to live,
There was a little house,
How happily I used to say to myself,
How happily I used to say to myself.
Well, what was I telling you!
I'm going to make you some pants,
Like the ones a cowboy uses,
I'll start them with wool for you
And finish them off with leather.")
Most of the songs came from Mexico. Many were campesino
songs, composed during the Revolution, such as "Adelita,"
"Cuatro Milpas," and "Borrachita":

Borrachita, me voy,
Hasta la capital,
Para ver al patrón,
Que me mandó llamar anteayer.
("A little drunk I go,

To the capital,
To see the boss,
Who summoned me the day before yesterday.")

Don José Gutiérrez, a good sheepherder, used to sing "Puro Mexicano":

Yo soy puro Mexicano,
Y me he echado el compromiso
En la tierra en que nací,
De ser macho entre los machos,
Y por eso muy urfano
Yo le canto a mi país.
("I'm pure Mexican,
And I made myself a promise
In the land where I was born,
To be a man among men,
And for that with pride
I sing to my country.")

Another favorite was:

Una noche con la luna,
Yo me la voy a llevar,
El que no me tenga miedo,
Que me la venga a quitar.
(One night with a full moon,
I'm going to carry her off,
Let him who isn't afraid of me
Just try to take her from me.")

There were many others, such as "Cielito Lindo," "La Vecina de Aquí en Frente," "Ya Tú no Soplas," "El Zapatero," "La Cucaracha," "Alta y Delgadita," and a number of ballads also. My wife, Viola, who studied voice, sang to my father "Paloma Blanca" ("White Dove"), his favorite in his golden years. At age eighty-seven, in his final hours, as Viola sang softly, he responded with a smile, associating my mother, his bride of sixty-four years, with the song:

Buenos días, Paloma Blanca,
Hoy te vengo a saludar,
Saludando tu belleza
En el reino celestial.
Eres madre del criador,
Y a mi corazón encantas,
Gracias te doy con amor,
Buenos días, Paloma Blanca.
("Good morning White Dove,
Today I come to salute you,
Saluting your beauty
In the kingdom of heaven.
You're the mother of the Creator,
And my heart you've enchanted,
Thanks I give to you with love,
Good morning, White Dove.")

Eloy

In 1954 at the age of twenty, our youngest brother, Eloy, passed away. Rheumatic fever weakened a strong heart and eventually led to his untimely death. Eloy was born October 6, 1933, and sometime in his early years he contracted the disease, for which there was then no cure. Mother and Dad took him to doctors everywhere, with no success. He was the youngest of five boys—Bennie, Abe, Fermín, Eddie, and Eloy—and older than his two sisters—Lydia and Dorothy. Sandwiched between siblings was a good place to be. We gave him love and tried to comfort him as much as possible. We knew he was hurting, but if we asked him if he was in pain, he answered no, or shook his head. And yet we could see pain etched on his face. I believe all of us learned a lesson: take pain in stride, do not let it consume you. Eloy was very intelligent, and his philosophy was, "death may take me, but pain never will"—a committed stoic. He had black hair, brown smiling eyes, a fair complexion, and stood lean and straight. He was a neat dresser, and even toward the end he maintained his poise (see Fig. 17).

I recall some episodes from his youth. One day when he was about eight years old, before he got ill, we were docking lambs at the ranch. Wrestling with a lamb, he grabbed him by the tail while the lamb was on the run, but he could not keep pace with the frisky lamb. His legs gave way, and he fell to the ground, coming to a stop headfirst in the middle of the dusty corral. Everyone laughed. He was embarrassed and left the corral to go sit in the truck. While in the pickup he evidently put a matchstick in the ignition switch, and it broke inside. When Dad later went to put the key in the switch, he couldn't insert it. He tried, we tried, but the switch wouldn't yield the broken matchstick. After several hours of trying, Dad sent one of the men to San Mateo, about eighteen miles away, to get Lizardito Salazar, a mechanic, to work on the switch. If nothing else he knew how to bypass the switch and get the truck started. Eloy was very contrite, and no one in the family ever mentioned the incident again.

Another time I was driving the pickup and Eloy, then fifteen, was with me. I parked the truck downhill at El Rincón. While I was gone from the truck, Eloy took it out of gear, and the truck started rolling down the road. I heard the yells, ran back, and saw the truck headed into a shallow arroyo, where it stopped. When I reached the undamaged truck, Eloy was speechless and white as a sheet. On the way home I gave him his first driving lesson. He became a very good driver, even though he was ill. Mother trusted him more as a driver than she did the rest of us.

I recall early in 1954, while traveling in Spain on my way home from Australia, where I had studied for a year, climbing the bell tower of a church in Valencia. In letters I had received from home, I could read between the lines that he was getting weaker. There were several bells in the tower, and one of them was named "Eloy." When I asked the caretaker if I could ring it, he obligingly handed me two stones. Ringing that bell was like sending a prayer across the seas to a brave young man whose heart was failing in distant New Mexico. The bell had a beautiful tone. To this day I can still hear the sound of that bell when I think of my brother.

His heart finally stopped on September 8, 1954. The pallbearers were his classmates and friends—Jimmy Gonzales, Eddie Gonzales, Ernest Michael, Silvano Sandoval, and Eddie Trujillo from San Mateo; Fred Mirabal from Bluewater; and Buddy McBride from Grants.

Mother carried the memory of her son engraved in her heart to the day she died in 1991. On her dresser in my parents' bedroom was the ever-present picture of Eloy. Father, a quiet man, spoke with emotion whenever he mentioned his youngest son. Eloy had touched everyone. Several hundred people came to San Mateo to his funeral. Listening to the church bell toll, I kept hearing the tolling of the bell in far away Valencia.

The following poem, anonymous as far as I know, summarizes his life and death far better than I can.

God saw you were getting tired,
And a cure was not to be,
So He put His arms around you,
And whispered, "Come with Me."
With tearful eyes we watched you suffer,

And saw you fade away,
Although we loved you dearly,
We could not make you stay.
A golden heart stopped beating,
Hardworking hands to rest.
God broke our hearts to prove to us,
He only takes the best!

Sister Lydia

Lydia was born shortly before midnight on December 4, 1934, in San Mateo, to Pablita and Pablo Peña, who were anxiously praying for a daughter after five sons. Pablo, our father, took his pearl-handled .45 Colt revolver and joyfully fired several piercing shots into the starlit night, breaking the silence of the sleeping village—announcing to the world that a daughter had been born!

We five brothers, awakened by the shots, celebrated and danced for joy in our long john underwear! She brought joy to all of us, especially Dad. "Six men thereafter," Mother used to say with a smile, "spoiled my daughter!" She was a charming baby, with jet black hair, olive skin, and sparkling dark eyes. Doña Virginia, who delivered her, said, "She is a very special child." The midwife had delivered hundreds of babies, but found this one very special. How prophetic she was. This "very special" child has certainly made a difference for the benefit of humankind.

I recall that when she was about six, I was saddling a horse and she kept pestering me for a ride. I couldn't resist her, standing there tomboyish in bib overalls like a boy, so I finally picked her up and sat her in the saddle. El Vallo, usually a very gentle horse, spooked and took off like a bullet across the freshly irrigated vegetable garden. Lydia fell off in the chile patch! I ran wildly after the horse and found her in a mud puddle. All I could see were smiling dark eyes peeking through a muddy face. I took her to the nearby irrigation ditch and washed the mud off. While I washed her down, she kept insisting, "I want to ride again, I want to ride again!"

That year another daughter was born, and she is very special too. If the truth be known, we probably spoiled Dorothy even more than her older sister! She was the opposite of Lydia. She was all girl in dresses and curls, fair-skinned with brown hair and pretty brown eyes.

Lydia finished grade school in San Mateo and attended high school at St. Vincent's Academy, in Albuquerque. She was an outstanding student and charmed both her schoolmates and her teachers. The brother closest to her in age and temperament was Eloy, who was one year older. He never let her out of his sight if he could help it. When he died, Lydia was nineteen and a junior at Loretto Heights College in Denver. In 1955 she got her BS degree in dietetics. That same year she was maid of honor at Viola's and my wedding, at St. Francis Cathedral in Santa Fe.

And then the week after the wedding, she surprised everyone
by announcing that she was going to a convent in Kentucky to become a Loretto nun!

This lovely, energetic, and resourceful girl made Mother very, very happy, but Father was dubious and confused. In a short time he accepted her choice, however, and became her champion. His daughter could do no wrong! We all applauded.

At the convent they recognized her talent for art. At that point she wore the habit of the Order of Loretto nuns. All white as a novice and black and white when she received her vows of poverty, chastity and obedience as a full-fledged nun. She cut a striking figure. The sparkling dark eyes were still perpetually smiling and radiated a special contented glow from behind the nun's hooded veil (see Fig. 18). A happy girl was now a happy religious sister of the teaching Order of Loretto, and she became a happy teacher. She taught at St. Mary's High School in Denver for several years, and from there she went on to get her master's degree and her doctorate in art history from Webster College, in St. Louis. She wrote and published a book on the life of the artist Agnes Tait, of Santa Fe.

Later she went on to study art history at the University of Madrid, in Spain, the land of her ancestors. While studying in Spain, she traveled extensively through Western Europe and Greece. Mom and Dad traveled to Spain to visit her, and together they traveled through some of Europe in the 1960s, including Italy, where they were in a group that had an audience with the pope. It was a highlight in their Catholic lives, especially for Mother.

On her return she joined the faculty at Loretto Heights College, in Denver, teaching art and art history. She was a leader in the movement for "relevancy" in the order. After Vatican II, Pope John XXIII said, "Let's open the windows of our church and let the fresh air come in." Change did indeed come to the church. She and others changed from their religious habits to street clothes. "Conservative clothes," she said, "that gave us relevance in our service to people, rather than simply the 'awe of the habit.'" They left the convents and rented houses in the poorer sections, always ministering to the needs of people, especially the most vulnerable. "They need us more." She joined some of the marches for civil rights, marching with Corky Gonzales in Denver. She championed the liberal causes of the day. She was appointed to a church commission to travel to Nicaragua in the early 1980s, to observe and report the effects of the Daniel Ortega regime in that country. She had visited Costa Rica earlier and had a good understanding and appreciation for Central America's traditions and culture.

Later Loretto Heights appointed her coordinator of the "University without Walls" program. She traveled the state of Colorado in her duties. When Loretto Heights merged with Regis University, a Jesuit institution, she continued with the "University without Walls" and teaching some classes. In addition she was selected as an advisor to Teikyo University, which purchased the Loretto Heights campus, and she went to Japan to consult with the university administration in that country. Regis University has since appointed her director of special gifts in the Department of Development, and she loves raising money for the university. She is very skillful at fund-raising and still teaches a few classes, teaching being her first love.

Mayor Federico Peña (no relation) appointed her to the Advisory Commission of the new Denver Airport, which opened in 1995. In between all her duties and assignments, however, she always finds time to remain close to her family in New Mexico.

Doña Meme

In my opinion and the opinion of many of her neighbors, Doña Meme was an angel. She was born in Lebanon, christened Tameme, and married Merhage Michael in that distant country. In 1909 they immigrated to the United States with their young son, Mike.

Mr. Michael had been in America working for a couple of years, then returned to Lebanon to finish his education and marry his boyhood girlfriend, Tameme, before returning. They came through Ellis Island in New York, where millions of immigrants from the Old World were processed at the turn of the century. Mr. Michael used to tell of the hardships they suffered on the boat that brought them to our shores. It was a miserable experience, bunched up for weeks in close quarters, having to cope with overcrowding, sickness, filth, and insults.

They came west from New York and temporarily settled in Lemitar, on the Río Grande in central New Mexico. From there he peddled merchandise from the back of a wagon west to Seboyeta, Cubero, and San Mateo. In San Mateo he saw his opportunity and purchased a store and bar from Abelicio Peña, my grandfather, and went into business. The wagon vending days were over. The Michaels raised a large family and prospered. Their eleven children—Mike, Azize, Selfa, Lorraine, Albert, Merhage, Jr., Lillian, Kate, Ernest, Betty, and Florence—were primarily Spanish speakers, but they learned some Lebanese at home and learned English when they started school. In the small village of San Mateo, they mingled and were completely integrated into Hispanic village life. I've heard Merhage, Jr., one of my closest boyhood friends, say, "Yo soy mexicano, casi" ("I'm Hispanic, almost").

Doña Meme's life revolved around her family, her vegetable garden, and the store. She was always cooking or washing, both clothes and dishes. In the spring, summer, and fall she could be found in her vegetable garden. She had one of the best in the village. In between those activities, she answered the call of customers to the store, who yelled down the alley between the store and the residence, "Vengo pa' la tienda" ("I've come to the store"). I recall as a youngster standing at her kitchen door, savoring the pleasant smells of her cooking, which mixed New Mexican cooking with Lebanese dishes such as kibbe and huge *tortillas árabes* ("Arabic tortillas"). As the family sat down to eat, she'd give me a piece of tortilla, and I'd run home across the street and arroyo, sit on a bench, and eat the delicacy. I learned later to call it pita bread.

Merhage, Jr., and I were approximately the same age and were close friends. We shared everything and were inseparable. We learned to smoke and were altar boys together. We slipped into the store and took a sack of Bull Durham tobacco from time to time rearranging the rest in the carton to make it appear that nothing was missing. We would take the tobacco to the corral and hide the sack in dry manure, near the stables. After lunch we'd meet at the corral, roll a cigarette, and smoke away. Sometimes we took the sack to mock dances in the arroyo, where we cut willows and pretended they were girls. We danced to the music of our older brothers, Albert Michael the drummer, who banged away on an old tin tub, and Bennie Peña, who blew away like a trumpeter on a curled old pipe.

Doña Meme personified patience. She was patient with her family, with her neighbors, and with the world at large. On the other hand, Mr. Michael, known as Don Miguel, tended to be on the nervous side. If he lost to Doña Meme at cards, he flung the deck and stormed out of the kitchen, raving mad and talking Arabic to himself. My mother, a good friend of the Michaels, used to tell the story of Don Miguel deciding one day in a fury to go back to Lebanon. He started walking down the road toward Grants, speaking Arabic to himself. Doña Meme went to our house and asked Dad, a good friend of Don Miguel's, if he would follow him and bring him back. Dad took the truck and followed him. "When I caught up with him, he was looking back, apparently wondering whether anyone would follow him and take him back. When I asked him why he was going to Lebanon, he answered, 'Because in the old country the women don't try to run everything. Here they want to run everything!'"

Doña Meme passed away in the 1960s, as did Don Miguel. They were buried in Albuquerque, where other Lebanese related to them are buried.

Ernest Michael, the youngest of the boys, married Mary Martínez and lives in the old Michael home, where they raised their family. Ernest inherited the patience and green thumb of his mother and brings in some of the finest produce to the farmers' market in Grants during the summer. The memory of Doña Meme's garden lives on through her son.

PART THREE

The Village at Ojo del Gallo

Ojo del Gallo, "Spring of the Rooster," is a rich watering hole, used by Indians long before the Spanish came to Cíbola. In 1862 the army decided to build a fort at Ojo del Gallo, to keep an eye on the Navajos. The fort was named Fort Wingate, after Capt. Benjamin Wingate, killed in the Civil War battle at Valverde, in Socorro County.

In 1863 the army arranged with Kit Carson to round up the Navajos and move them to Bosque Redondo, on the Pecos River, some 225 miles to the east. The purpose ostensibly was to improve the lot of the Navajos by making them farmers. But the noble Navajos were nomads and could not stay long in one place. They needed space to move and to roam—they were hunters and did not take to farming. Unfortunately thousands died in the "Long Walk," before the misguided orders were rescinded and the Navajos at Bosque Redondo returned home.

In 1868 the army decided to move the fort to Ojo del Oso, "Spring of the Bear," near Gallup, to be closer to the larger concentrations of Navajos farther west. Some of the Hispanics that had come from Seboyeta to provide materials for building Ft. Wingate at San Rafael petitioned the president of the United States, Grover Cleveland, to grant them the site to build a village. A patent was granted to them, which protected their land and water rights, and San Rafael was settled and started growing. It developed into a prosperous community that claimed several large sheepmen, with tens of thousands of sheep, a number of cantinas to wet the sheepherders' and cowboys' thirst, and a number of stores selling groceries and hardware. Some of those buildings are still standing, and many of the attractive houses of the ricos are still in use.

The village was named after Father José Rafael Chávez, a Franciscan priest, brother to Esquipula Chávez, one of the founders of San Rafael. The good friar was suspended from his priestly duties by Bishop Lamy and became a very successful businessman.

San Rafael, three miles south from Grants on Highway 53, is considered the gateway to the west side of El Malpais National Monument, the Ice Caves, Inscription Rock at El Morro, Zuni Pueblo, and to the most direct route from Albuquerque to Phoenix.

Capt. Rafael Chacón arrived in October 1862 with a military troop to build a fort at Ojo del Gallo, today San Rafael, by orders of Lt. Col. José Francisco Chaves, assigned as post commander, and by General James Carleton, commander of forces in New Mexico. In his memoirs Capt. Chacón wrote, "Upon receiving orders I used my wits to take my wife Juanita and my little daughter Gumecinda to the new fort. . . . When we arrived we made an acequia from the spring, about two miles southward, and there established Fort Wingate. The soldiers and officers were in their respective tents. Four sentinels constantly walked around to safeguard the provisions and barrels in the open."

Although the good captain does not mention the grim conditions they encountered, winter was fast approaching, and conditions must surely have been harsh and primitive, especially for young families.

In *Legacy of Honor: The Life of Rafael Chacón*, edited by Jacqueline Maketa, he says, "Timber had to be cut, roads and a water supply system built, and buildings erected. Soldiers were employed as carpenters, millwrights, masons, timber cutters, road constructors and adobe makers—all in addition to their myriad military duties. Some civilians were also hired and a contract for 350,000 adobe bricks was awarded." General Carleton estimated the fort would cost $45,000 and that it would provide for two companies, one mounted.

Several individuals from Seboyeta, all veterans of the Civil War who had fought at Valverde and some at Glorieta, came to work and help build the fort, according to Josephine Barela in her book *Ojo del Gallo*. "Among them were Mónico Mirabal, José León Téllez and José Fermín Gallegos. They cut timber, harvested grass, made adobes and sold them to the fort."

Vidal Mirabal of Grants, now in his eighties, says that "They dug a 4 foot by 4 foot by 4 foot hole in the ground and cut meadow grass and packed and stamped it into bales and sold the hay to the fort to feed the horses." A blessed and happy event happened in June 1863, when a boy, Luis Antonio, was born to

Doña Juanita and Capt. Rafael Chacón, the first child born at Ft. Wingate. He was baptized by Father Rafael Chávez. A stage-coach line came from Santa Fe to Fort Wingate, passing through Peña Blanca, San Isidro, Cabezón, and San Mateo. It served the area until about 1882, when the railroad came through Grants.

According to Chacón, the fort was to be "a permanent one surrounded by a stockade with walls 8 and 13 feet high, containing in addition to the officer and company quarters, a quartermaster storehouse, a magazine, corrals and stables, and a hospital." Progress on the fort was slow, however, as the soldiers fought skirmishes with the Navajos. Then came the infamous order from General Carleton in 1863 to round up all the Navajos and move them to Ft. Sumner (Bosque Redondo), on the Pecos River. Col. Kit Carson was put in charge of the move. The misguided order was intended "to give them a better livelihood as farmers." Approximately twenty-five hundred were rounded up in the San Rafael area and another thirty-five hundred in San Isidro and taken on the "Long Walk" to Ft. Sumner. Many died on the way. Orders were given to burn the Navajos' cornfields and destroy their hogans, to force the reluctant ones to move. Delgadito and Barboncito, Navajo leaders, fought desperately, but finally gave up.

Conditions at Fort Sumner were miserable, and the Navajos could not adapt to a farming life. Many more died, and some escaped and came back to their beloved sandstone country. By 1868 it was evident the order to move had failed, and the surviving Navajos were permitted to return to their homes in the piñon and juniper country of northwestern New Mexico and eastern Arizona. That same year the military decided to move Fort Wingate to Ojo del Oso, near Gallup, to be nearer the center of Navajo country and began the shutdown of Fort Wingate at San Rafael. By 1869 most of the soldiers were gone, and the government invited the settlers around the fort to stay and occupy the land. The settlers decided to name their village San Rafael, after former priest Rafael Chávez. A proclamation signed by 115 villagers was sent to President Grover Cleveland in 1884, stating, "we have broken the ground, dug ditches, built homes and fences, establishing a town called San Rafael." A patent was then granted to them, and their land rights were protected from that time on.

And so ends the story of Fort Wingate at San Rafael.

San Rafael

Three miles south of Grants, on Highway 53, sits the historic and tumultuous village of San Rafael. At one time it was called Ft. Wingate, and before that Ojo Del Gallo. San Rafael was named after Father José Rafael Chávez, a Franciscan priest who came to Ojo del Gallo with the original Hispanic settlers from Seboyeta, in 1863. Among those settlers were Mónico Mirabal, José León Téllez, José Fermín Gallegos, Esquipula Chávez, brother of Father Chávez, and others, veterans of the New Mexico Volunteers in the Civil War. Father Chávez was suspended from his priestly duties by Bishop Lamy, but he went on to be a very successful businessman.

The settlers came to supply the new cavalry fort then under construction with hay and grass for the horses and adobes and lumber for the buildings. The new fort was named Fort Wingate, in honor of Lt. Benjamin Wingate, who was killed by Confederate forces in the Battle of Valverde, on the Río Grande south of Socorro. The fort's purpose was to keep an eye on the Navajos and Apaches and provide security to settlers moving west into this new country. The first Fort Wingate had been quartered for a year or two in Seboyeta, but then it was relocated at Ojo del Gallo.

Mónico Mirabal applied for a veteran's land patent to the rich meadow at the spring, which covered several hundred acres. The meadow is irrigated naturally from the overflow of the Ojo del Gallo spring, which still produces about 500 gallons per minute. Vidal Mirabal told me he heard the old-timers say that "To bale hay, Don Mónico dug a hole in the ground approximately 4 feet by 4 feet by 4 feet, then tramped the grass into large bales and sold them to the fort to feed their horses and milk cows." The fort under construction was commanded by Col. José Francisco Chávez. He was gone most of the time on other duties, however, and the provisional commander was Capt. Rafael Chacón. According to Chacón's autobiography, *Legacy of Honor*, written some forty years later, "The soldiers lived in tents while building with adobe, terrones and lumber."

Capt. Chacón and some of the other officers brought their young wives to live with them in the harsh and primitive conditions, especially severe during the first winter, in 1862. He writes, "In the month of October 1862, we went to El Gallo. . . . All went well on the trip except for two mishaps. Across from Isleta Pueblo was a narrow passage, and when we passed by there the soldiers saw that the wheels of the wagon, on the river side, were off the road and in the air. It was a miracle that it did not overturn. In it were my wife Juanita and Gumecinda, my little daughter, and Doña Simona, the wife of Lieutenant Martin Quintana."

The Seboyetanos decided to bring their families to Ft. Wingate in 1865. Among the children came one-year-old Silvestre, the son of Mónico and Juana María Mirabal, who grew up to attain prominence in ranching, banking, and the political arena after the turn of the century.

In 1868 the army decided to move Fort Wingate, after six short years at Ojo del Gallo, to Ojo del Oso, near Gallup, to be closer to the Navajos. During World War I, it was converted to an ordinance depot. In World War II it handled millions of tons of munitions and employed hundreds of people; it was finally phased out in 1993.

San Rafael adopted its new name in 1868 and prospered as an important economic center in west-central New Mexico. When the Atlantic and Pacific Railroad came through Los Alamitos, now Grants, in 1882, it pretty well signaled the decline of commerce in San Rafael, 3 miles south of the railway line. The thriving community had several general merchandise stores and some large and luxurious homes, many of which are still in use today. There were a few bars, also. Josephine Barela, in her book *Ojo del Gallo*, says that Don Leopoldo Mazón, a prominent sheepman from the

Tinaja country, rode his buggy into San Rafael, and although he generally did not patronize bars, he stopped at Don Eliseo's cantina. "After a few drinks, he looked up and saw himself in the mirror. Not liking what he saw he whipped out his pistol and shot the mirror to splinters! Knowing he was drunk, my father did not say anything." The following day he sheepishly sought out Don Eliseo, to apologize and tell him to order the best and most expensive mirror he could find. The mirror graced the Barela bar and later their home, for years.

Ms. Barela also writes, "In the elections of 1888 the Militia assigned Captain Dumas Provencher, called Don Damacio, to supervise the election. Two Indians attempted to vote, and knowing they were not citizens, he refused to let them vote. . . . That night as he watched the tallying of the votes, it was said some chairs had been pulled back by the other election officials and a shot rang through the window and he was killed. His assailant was never found and the case remained open for years."

The U.S. census of 1880 shows San Rafael with a population of more than eight hundred inhabitants. Today San Rafael is home to about fifteen hundred people. The Guadalupe Plaza, across from the attractive Guadalupe Catholic Church, is well-kept, and in a corner of the fenced plaza is the gravestone of its first priest, Padre José Rafael Chávez, who gave the historic village its name, San Rafael.

Don Silvestre

On May 10, 1864, a son was born to Doña Juana María and Don Mónico Mirabal, in the village of Seboyeta, in western New Mexico. They baptized him Silvestre, and at age two his mother moved to San Rafael, to join her husband where Silvestre grew to manhood and became a legend in his own time. When he died on October 9, 1939, at the age of seventy-five, he had built a land and livestock empire stretching from the Acoma Reservation on the east to the Navajo Reservation on the west. He did it by dint of hard work, resourcefulness, and the instinctive ability, given to a few, to glimpse the future and act on it.

There were eight children in the family, six boys and two girls. Silvestre was the oldest and attended St. Michael's, in Santa Fe. His sisters, Premia and Reyes, attended Loretto High School, also in Santa Fe. His younger brothers Federico, Nabor, Telesfor, Remigio, and Gilberto also attended St. Michael's as they grew up. Don Mónico and Doña Juana María were believers in education, although they had little formal education themselves. As a young boy I recall seeing Don Silvestre, whom people pointed to, at the Fernandez Ranch, near San Mateo. We were the guests of Mr. and Mrs. Floyd W. Lee for the inauguration of a new "Big Red Barn" at the ranch headquarters, about 1936. A barbecue and barn dance were held, and the people of San Mateo were invited to break bread and share the day with friends of the Lees, who came from all over the state. Some of them flew in, touching down on the dirt strip in a cloud of dust. The airplanes came to a stop near the new barn, which dominated the landscape; it still stands today. It was very exciting watching those planes touch down and take off. Some had the open cockpits of barnstorming fame, and the pilots were dashing, with their goggles and their scarves flying in the wind.

Don Silvestre, as I recall, was dressed in a black suit with a black bow tie, a white embroidered shirt, and a black bowler hat. I remember him as a tall man, but I'm certain his reputation made this uncommon man taller than life. Neither the embroidered shirt, nor hat, nor the black suit were his ordinary dress. Although he wore formal dress for the occasion, and that with aplomb, his usual dress was bib overalls (*de pechera*), a cotton shirt, and ankle-high work shoes. People who remember him well say that it was hard to distinguish him from those who worked for him. In fact he prided himself on confusing people by becoming one of the many and pretending to be someone else.

They tell the story of the time when he was president of the Bank of Commerce in Albuquerque, which he helped found, and a nervous client from back East needed the approval of the president to secure a rather large loan. He was told that Don Silvestre would be in Albuquerque on a certain day. The client arrived at the bank smartly dressed and in a hurry and was told that Don Silvestre had just walked out of the bank and was on his way to his Albuquerque home on Twelfth Street. The gentleman rushed out and saw a man sitting on the stairs in his work clothes and asked him if the buggy was his and would he take him to Don Silvestre's home. They got in the buggy and trotted to Twelfth Street. He tipped the driver generously, and the buggy went on to the back of the house, while the passenger went to the front door and knocked. After a bit of a wait, the door opened and the gentleman asked, "is Don Silvestre in?" Suddenly he realized that the man who answered the door was the same one who had driven him there. "I am Silvestre," the president said, and with tongue in cheek added, "and I wonder whether a man as generous with his tips as you are needs more money?" The fellow got the loan, but he also received a big lesson in humility.

There's also the story of a trip he and his oldest son, Mónico, made to Gallup in one of the first trucks to come into the area, about 1916. The first road followed wagon tracks to Gallup, paralleling the railroad tracks and up on the railroad bed from time to time, to cross arroyos. An entrepreneur at Thoreau with barrels of gasoline for those first vehicles, saw the Mirabals going toward Gallup. The following day on the way back, the truck quit running near the Continental Divide, and Don Silvestre, or "Pantaleo," as many of his friends called him, decided to walk home, while young Mónico tried to get the truck started. The fellow with the gas barrels saw him walking and asked, "Did your truck break down?" Don Silvestre, without breaking stride, answered, "No, Mónico's truck broke down back there, mine's still going strong!" And on he walked, with the familiar wool shawl over his shoulders, still some thirty miles from home.

He served as a delegate to the New Mexico Constitutional Convention in 1889, as chairman of the County Commission from 1889 to 1891, as a member of the New Mexico Territorial House of Representatives from 1891 to 1905, as a member of the National Rivers and Streams Commission, as chairman of the board of the Bank of Commerce, and was inducted into the National Cowboy Hall of Fame in Oklahoma posthumously, in the 1960s.

He also had a general merchandise store in San Rafael, and during the Great Depression of the 1930s, he provided food to many people whether they could pay or not. He also helped many homesteaders by providing sheep and cattle on shares to get them started. He was a generous man, but did not tolerate idleness and had little patience for laziness. If someone was standing around, he handed him a shovel and sent him to clean out the corrals or pigpens.

His wife, Lorencita, was also from Seboyeta, and they raised six children: Mónico, Alfredo, Josefita, Prudencia, Vitalina, and Beneranda. Beneranda married Salvador Milán, the founder of the village of Milan, and the three older sisters married three Candelaria brothers from the Concho area, in Arizona. Beneranda was named after one of her aunts and also after my maternal grandmother, Beneranda, who was related and a good friend of Doña Lorencita. My grandmother remembered "many happy hours spent at la Casa Grande in San Rafael, quilting with mi prima Lorencita." When Don Silvestre died, in 1939, the large herds and landholdings were divided among six heirs. Most of the properties are still in the family and grazed by livestock, while some have been commercially developed, such as the village of Milan. Part of this vast empire embraced the land and shearing shed near the golf course in Milan, the Ice Caves, Tinaja and Campo Nueve, El Muerto and Tampico, La Jara and El Morro, and the large meadow and big three-story mansion in San Rafael. Also included in the holdings were the plot across from the church in San Rafael, where the Guadalupe Plaza is located, the property where the Cíbola General Hospital stands in Grants— the litany goes on and on.

Beneranda Mirabal Milán, known as Bennie by her friends, is the only one of the children now living. She has a home in Milan and an apartment in Albuquerque.

Isidoro had very little money, but from time to time he purchased a small can of paint and painted the weather-beaten crosses at the San Rafael cemetery. The artist Leona Nellis, of Grants, painted an oil portrait of Isidoro Solís. She told me, "Isidoro sat for me and other painters in the 1960s." Leona has many fine paintings, but in my opinion Isidoro's is one of her best (see Fig. 19). He is adorned by a magnificent white beard and a large dark hat, and soft light illuminates his handsome face, showing a contented individual reminiscent of the subject of an El Greco painting. Leona said that when she was painting him, Sue Cook of Cook's Hardware, in Grants, told her about Isidoro buying paint to refurbish the cemetery crosses. She would throw in an extra can to help him go further in the beautification of the cemetery, his own adopted project.

Frank Barela told me Isidoro also cut the weeds around graves when they weren't cut by the families, and that he reprimanded him, "You haven't cut the weeds around your mother's grave!" Frank smiles and says, "To this day, for Memorial Day, I clean mother's grave, afraid that Isidoro, even though he is gone, will scold me if I don't!" Frank also remembers as a youngster going to a small farm near San Rafael, where Isidoro was taking care of pigs, and seeing books in Spanish, French, and English on the table. "To my knowledge he did not have a formal education, yet he could read in several languages!"

I met Isidoro in San Rafael in the 1950s, when we were building a pipeline to distribute water for livestock on Oso Ridge in the Zuni Mountains. I stopped at Elias Saavedra's gas station to gas up, and Isidoro was there. After visiting with him briefly, I asked if he wanted to go work in the high country. He said, "Sure. What do I need to take?" I told him all he needed was a mochila (bedroll), and the job would last about a week. There was something very profound and graceful about Isidoro. I sensed a free spirit in him that reminded me of an intellectual unafraid to let his mind go where it will. The other men on the job greeted him cordially, but tended to leave him alone. I kept him with me, and learned that he had been born in Zacatecas, Mexico. His family came to the United States to work in mining and later settled in San Rafael. Mrs. Belinda Mirabal told me, "His father had a crippled leg, his brother Vicente and his mother lived here also. She apparently came from French heritage . . . her maiden name was Bavian."

The job was over in a week, and I brought him home. Money did not interest him much; he told me when I needed help to call on him, which I did from time to time. I especially appreciated his company. I never saw him angry or quarrel with anyone. He minded his own business, a refreshing quality in an age when so many of us want to manage and reform everyone else's life.

For the Fourth of July parade in 1962, Viola and I rode matching palominos we had raised on the Peña Ranch. They were born a week apart, and we called them Amos and Andy. We were loaned matching silver-trimmed black saddles and bridles by our friends Dan and Flora García Powell, owners of a tack and feed store near Bluewater. We put on black boots, black pants, black shirts, and black hats, and I must add we cut quite a figure as we paraded down Santa Fe Avenue in Grants in style! When the parade was over, a light Fourth of July shower caught us on the way back to our horse trailer. We stopped at La Tiendita, owned by Don Melecio Calzada, to shelter and have a soft drink. Isidoro was standing by the door of the store, and I asked him if he'd hold the horses and share a pop with us. When the shower passed, we were mounting our horses when Isidoro said, "Oye Abelicio, you better get out of politics!" I asked, "Why, Isidoro?" He looked at Viola and back at me. "You have a very beautiful wife, and if you stay in politics, you're going to lose her!" It took me a moment to recover, but I had a pretty good idea where he was coming from.

I was the Republican candidate for the state legislature that year, and he had seen some men in San Rafael get into politics and fall for the temptations of flattery, flesh, and late nights away from home. Some lost their wives and families in the process. Although he usually minded his own business, in this case he gave me a barrelful of timely advice. I've never forgotten his admonition! For the record, I lost the election, and the election after that, and the election after that, but Viola and I are still going strong, after forty-one years of caring and sharing.

In the late 1970s we periodically received the *Grants Beacon* in Bolivia, where I was directing the U.S. foreign aid program (USAID), and read that our friend Isidoro Solís had been found dead in the malpais, between San Rafael and Grants. Frank Barela told me recently, "He usually walked on the old road to San Rafael, but we found him near an old trail that's hardly ever used." With emotion for a lost friend, he added, " I don't know what the devil he was doing over there!"

I do: Isidoro preferred the uncharted way. That's the way he lived, and that's the way he died.

Casimiro the Goldsmith

Casimiro Lucero was a goldsmith, an accomplished goldsmith. His gold rings, necklaces, bracelets, pins, brooches, and earrings are priceless. Some are still being worn today, but many have gone into safekeeping as heirlooms. He learned his skills from a master goldsmith, Anastacio Burgos. Josephine Barela, in her book *Ojo del Gallo*, writes, "My uncle, Anastacio Burgos, a goldsmith, came from Burgos, Spain, to settle and practice his trade in San Rafael." Burgos came in the 1880s. His business thrived, and it appears that sometime later he took the young Casimiro Lucero under his wing and turned out a gifted craftsman. Mrs. Belinda Mirabal of San Rafael, the widow of Mónico Mirabal, told me they melted 18-carat gold coins that were in limited circulation as legal tender to make their jewelry. The intricate art of filigree is most evident in the necklaces, bracelets, and pins with grapes and grape leaves in clusters. I wear a gold ring made by Casimiro about 1915 for my grandfather Fermín Márquez, of Seboyeta. The ring passed down at his death to his only son, my uncle Anastacio, who passed it on to his son Anastacio, Jr. Then Junior gave it to me, several years ago. He told me, "I'm passing this ring to you because you have taken an interest and are preserving our family history." I wear it with pride in deference to my grandfather, whom I never knew but have always admired. The ring had a part of the shank cut off, where they filed it to take it off his finger when he died. I had it reshanked and originally stored it in the safety deposit box. Recently I asked Junior if it was alright if I wore it, and he said, "I gave it to you. You do what you want with it. If you want to wear it, wear it. I think our grandfather would want you to."

My mother had a Casimiro necklace with a large ruby and other gems beautifully set off by filigree. It was a beauty. It was given to her by her mother-in-law, Manuelita, when she was married, and mother treasured the necklace. Unfortunately it was stolen with some other jewelry in a break-in of her home in San Mateo, one of the few break-ins I remember occurring in our village up to that time. Most of the other jewelry was recovered, but the Casimiro necklace was never found. Even when the jewelry is no longer physically present, Casimiro's memory lives on through the magnificent masterpieces he created.

Nicolás

Nicolás Maestas hailed from La Plaza Vieja in Albuquerque; he was a fine sheepherder. He took a lot of pride in what he did and was one of the best in the country. In the 1920s and 1930s, Nicolás worked in the sheep camps of Don Silvestre Mirabal, of San Rafael. Nicolás sometimes considered himself a San Rafael-eño. In the late 1940s, when he came to work at the Peña Ranch, he frequently spoke of his friend and former boss as Don Pantaleo. It was an affectionate nickname the herders gave Don Silvestre, one of the most successful businessmen in western New Mexico.

Not only was Nicolás a good shepherd, but he was also a good man. He did have one blinding weakness—alcohol, but I should add that many herders liked their spirits when they came to town after months of herding sheep. Nicolás was very generous with his friends, and others, while his money lasted. Usually he stayed for four to six months in the sheep camps (see Fig. 20). The average salary in those depression years of the 1930s and early 1940s was $30 per month, with room and board provided. He generally had about $125, and his philosophy was that money was to spend—not to save—so he spent it!

He was about 5 feet 11 inches tall, taller than most of his friends. He weighed about 170 pounds and had a relatively flat belly in his fifties. He was dark-complexioned and had a parrot nose and jet black hair and smoked a sack of Bull Durham a day. His camptenders liked him. He had a placid personality, was good-natured, and liked to cook. He baked excellent *breles* (bread) in the Dutch oven, over the coals of an open fire. He had a *buena mano* (a gourmet) cooking red chile to go with the hot breles coming out of the trusty Dutch oven. The camp was moved every five to six days by pack burros, to provide fresh grass for the flock of about one thousand sheep. One time he was herding sheep on Oso Ridge in the Zuni Mountains, straddling the Continental Divide. The herd was resting during the noon hours near the camp, when suddenly the sheep spooked, running wildly and terrified. Nicolás and his camptender saw a black bear chasing them. He pulled out the .44 Remington rifle and leveled it at the beast. The bear went down, and after some anxious moments, both the men and the sheep settled down. They skinned the large bear and planned to turn the skin in to the game warden, in accordance with standing instructions. However, one of his friends from nearby Tinaja stopped to visit, and Nicolás, in a generous mood, gave him the skin. The friend told his friends, and his friends told their friends, and the word quickly got back to the warden. He arrested Nicolás and brought him to the "pokey" in Grants.

The warden notified us of the incident, and hurriedly we found the judge. After a brief trial, he fined Nicolás fifty dollars plus twelve dollars in court costs and released him to us. He returned to his herd on the mountain a considerably wiser man. The judge hit him in the pocket, where it hurt the most.

Later he would say, "I made an error in judgment. . . . If I have to kill another bear to save the sheep, I'll do it. But the warden will be the first to know."

Nicolás died in 1971 in his beloved Plaza Vieja de Albuquerque, at the age of seventy-one. His friends still remember him.

Remijio (Ray) Chávez

Remijio's grave is in front of La Morada in his native village of San Rafael. This exceptional man was totally blind, yet he was one of the most talented musicians in Cíbola County and certainly one of the kindest individuals in west-central New Mexico.

He was born in San Rafael on January 17, 1926. His parents were Patricio and María Baca Chávez. He had two brothers and three sisters. Joe married Josie Padilla and lives in Gallup, Rafael lives in Houston, Delfida (Fefi) married Ray Baca and lives in Albuquerque, Esther lives in New York, and Alfídez, the oldest, died in her teens.

As Joe told me, "Our parents were living and working in the Zuni Mountains, either at Paxton Springs or Sawyer, around 1932, when the lumber camps were in full swing. Remijio, who we called Ray, was about six years old and was having trouble with his eyes, and they took him to a doctor in Gallup or the doctor came by the camp, I can't remember, and he put eye drops in his eyes and his eyes dried up." Juan Padilla has said, "I heard he fell face first into loose dirt from a carrito while playing and his eyes started bothering him and a doctor treated him." And Paul Milán told me, "It seems the doctor accidentally put acid in his eyes and Ray went blind."

His parents took him to the School for the Blind in Alamogordo; Ray was a very good student, and among other things, he learned to read in braille. He also learned to play the piano, the accordion, the guitar, the violin, and various other instruments. He had a natural gift for music. Ben Chávez says, "He could take

an instrument, feel it, mess around with it, and start playing. I
saw him do that with the clarinet."

He was provided with a seeing eye dog. According to his brother Joe, "He had two dogs and both were killed by automobiles." Ray developed a keen sense of hearing and could identify a person by voice, even in a noisy room. Frank Barela, who has a missing hand, says, "I was gone for several years. When I returned, I greeted him and he asked, 'Where have you been, mocho!' He also had a great sense of humor!"

His mother, Doña María, became his eyes and his constant companion. Ray was very neat and liked white shirts. Sometimes he wore bow ties. They lived on San Jose Drive in Grants and walked everywhere hand in hand. He was always in demand to play his music at weddings, at receptions, at dances. At a piano bar he could take requests all evening and never repeat himself.

At one time he played with a band in Albuquerque and met and married Celia, a blind girl. The marriage dissolved, but they had a charming daughter, Patricia, known to her family and friends as Patty, now living in Albuquerque.

Through the years he played with several bands, including one led by Wilford Murrieta and Rosario "Challo" Rodríguez, who played guitars, while Ray played the accordion or the piano or the guitar, or whatever the situation demanded. He was a member of La Morada, Los Hermanos Penitentes, and played the *pito*. "We play the flute to call and gather los Hermanos," says Frank Barela, the hermano mayor of Los Hermanos in San Rafael. "He also knew when the candles on the altar were burning out, even though he was in another room; and when things were very quiet, he could identify a person by their walk—incredible!"

When Doña María died, Ray lost not only his mother but his companion and his eyes. In his loneliness he became a chain smoker and started drinking. His many friends gave him drinks while he was playing—we felt it was a way to repay him for his music. In reality we were hurting him. ¡Dios nos salve! When he got ill he lived with members of his family until he needed nursing care and went to the Good Samaritan nursing home in Grants. Many friends and family stopped by to visit him frequently. He died at St. Joseph Hospital on July 7, 1994. On his gravestone are inscribed the following words:

He gave so much through his music
and asked for so little in return.
REMIJIO CHAVEZ
"RAY"
Jan 17, 1926–July 7, 1994

PART FOUR

Los Alamitos

Before the town was known as Grants, it was called Los Alamitos. There were only three or four Hispanic families living in Los Alamitos when the railroad came through, in 1882. Some of the families had come from Seboyeta, looking for grass for their livestock and fertile soil for crops; one of these families was that of Antonio Chávez. The family of Jesús Blea came from Santa Rosa, on the Pecos River. Many of the descendants of those original families still live in the area.

The coming of the railroad led to the rapid development of Grants and the land of Cíbola. The tent city on the west side of town sheltered thousands of workers who came to build the Atlantic and Pacific Railroad, work that was subcontracted to the three Grant brothers, from Canada. Among the workers was a large contingent of Filipinos, who helped to cut the railway heading west.

The entrepreneur Simon Bibo purchased 160 acres from Jesús Blea and started a store and hotel, as well as selling land to others. Several other businesses also sprang up along the railroad. Grants was a water and fuel stop for trains, both passenger and freight. The railroad drilled a water well on the south side of the tracks and built a tower to elevate the water tank. I can remember in the 1930s a tall, black elevator chute near the depot that loaded coal on trains to produce the steam that powered the trains going east, and across the Continental Divide going west. The Santa Fe Super Chief was one of the most popular passenger trains that stopped in Grants. Many recruits who went off to the world wars boarded trains in Grants on their way to forts, camps, and bases around the country. I used to ride the train to Las Cruces, when I was at New Mexico A & M in the late 1940s. I still remember how the collar of my shirt would get black after a twelve-hour ride, but there was something special about a steam engine puffing away.

Sheep were followed by cattle and cattle were followed by timber, in the evolution that moved Pueblo Indians, Hispanics, and Anglos into the cash economy. Carrots followed the timber industry, bringing the Navajos into the cash economy. The rich volcanic soil of the Bluewater Valley, west of town, produced pre-

mium carrots that brought high prices in the eastern markets. In 1950 when the price for carrots started slipping, the uranium boom began. Grants grew from twelve hundred people to nearly twelve thousand, and Milan grew from two hundred to three thousand. By the time the boom ended, in 1985, Grants was on its way to diversifying its economy, which has brought stability and prosperity to the land of Cíbola.

Grants, where ancient trails meet modern highways, is now the county seat of Cíbola County and the commercial and banking center for the area whose people and customs you'll discover in the following pages.

Grants

Long before the first Europeans came through Grants, the Anasazi Indians, and later their descendants, the Zunis, the Acomas, and the Lagunas, hunted and traveled extensively through the area. The nomadic Navajos and Apaches later settled in "rancherías," and sometimes there were conflicts between them and the Pueblos.

The Spanish explorer Hernando de Alvarado and some twenty men were the first Europeans to pass through the area, in August 1540. He was sent by the conquistador Francisco Vásquez de Coronado from near Zuni Pueblo on an exploring expedition to the east. Coronado and a larger party passed through what was to become Grants later in the year, to winter near present-day Bernalillo. Some fifty years later, Juan de Oñate, the first Spanish governor of New Mexico, passed through in 1598. On a later expedition he carved his name on Inscription Rock at El Morro, "Pasó por aquí el adelantado don Juan de Oñate del descubrimiento del mar del sur . . . abril 16 1605." ("There passed through here the Adelantado Don Juan de Oñate from the discovery of the sea of the south . . . April 16, 1605.")

In 1862, some 257 years after Oñate, came Antonio Chávez and his family from Seboyeta, to build the first home in Grants, according to the Grants *Daily Beacon* centennial edition. In 1872 Jesús Blea, veteran of the Civil War Battle of Valverde, came from Santa Rosa with his family and added to the home. They called the settlement "Los Alamitos" ("The Cottonwoods"); the trees were thriving on the edge of the malpaís, near a spring that provided permanent water for the settlers. The original adobe and lava house is still standing, but in disrepair, on Valencia Street, off San Jose Drive, in South Grants. George Dannenbaum had it listed in the New Mexico State Register of Cultural Properties in 1976.

With the coming of the Atlantic and Pacific Railroad, in 1882, came three Canadian brothers, Angus, John, and Lewis Grant. They won the contract to build the railroad through "Los Alamitos" and established a camp there. Over four thousand men and more than two thousand mules worked the line as it inched its way toward California. People begin to call the greatly expanded settlement "Grants' Camp." Later when a station was built, it was known as Grants' Station. Eventually the name of the whole settlement became simply "Grants." The year of 1882 is recognized as the founding of Grant's. The U.S. Postal Service removed the apostrophe in 1937, and it's been "Grants" ever since.

Next came the enterprising merchant Simon Bibo. He and several members of a Jewish family came to the United States from Prussia, in 1866. He purchased most of the 160 acres of the original townsite from Jesús Blea and built a store facing the railroad tracks, where Falcomata Motors on Santa Fe Avenue is now. The railroad built livestock loading pens nearby, and thousands of sheep and cattle were shipped to markets around the country. The livestock industry gave Grants a shot in the arm. A hotel and general merchandise store were opened, and Grants began to develop as the commercial center of the area.

In the 1920s came the Breece Lumber Company, which built a railroad to the heart of the Zuni Mountains, in order to haul the timber to Grants, then on to Albuquerque, on the main line of the Atchison, Topeka and Santa Fe, successor to the Atlantic and Pacific Railroad and now known simply as the Santa Fe. The timber industry became the largest provider of jobs, bringing the local Hispanic people into the cash economy. To that time we had been mostly a self-sufficient and barter society. Grants grew slowly but surely.

The year 1929 was one to remember. The first electricity lit up a few homes and businesses. The first telephones came in. The first street was paved. The first high school in Spanish colonial architecture was built, which is now the attractive Cíbola County courthouse. The first Fourth of July rodeo was started. Bluewater Dam was built. And the stock market crashed and started the Great Depression of the 1930s.

By 1940 the timber in the Zuni Mountains was harvested, and the rails were taken up and sold, in large part as scrap iron to the Japanese. Some of those rails probably came back at us, in the form of bombs and bullets at Pearl Harbor.

The vegetable industry, from Milan west to Bluewater, was started by some enterprising Bluewater farmers after Bluewater Dam was built. In time it attracted large planters from the Phoenix area, who planted some 4,000 acres of carrots and lesser acreages of other vegetables for America's tables. Several packing sheds were built, hundreds of people were employed, and thousands of railroad cars were shipped to eastern markets. Large numbers of Navajos came from the reservation to work the fields and help harvest the carrots (see Fig. 21). It was truly a spectacular sight to see hundreds of Navajos, including the women in their colorful velveteen blouses, working together. Carrots brought our Navajo friends into the cash economy.

World War II saw the development of the cellophane plastic bag, and after the war American homemakers wanted their carrots packaged in them. The attractive Grants deep green carrot top was generally cut off and disappeared from produce counters, and Grants carrots lost their advantage in the markets. Rising freight and pumping costs for water from irrigation wells meant that Grants could not compete successfully with areas closer to consumers, with less expensive irrigation water. The commercial vegetable industry in the area went out of business by the 1950s.

But as the fates would have it (some call it "Grants luck"), our good friend Paddy Martinez brought in the rock that changed the complexion of our area for all time—uranium! The fever that ran through the area was catching. Many of us invested in Geiger counters and took to the hills. It was not uncommon to see landowners posting their land "No Trespassing. Trespassers Will Be Prosecuted Or Shot." In many cases the landowner owned the surface but not the mineral rights, and this situation created problems, especially if there was Bureau of Land Management acreage on the same ranch that was eligible to "claim." Lawyers had a field day, but when the dust settled, the Grants uranium industry developed about six thousand jobs and produced about 63 percent of all the uranium mined in the United States. The town grew from twelve hundred people to twelve thousand. The village of Milan was born and grew to three thousand. Trailer parks dotted the landscape, where hundreds of mobile homes provided housing for a mushrooming population.

In 1979, after the meltdown scare at the nuclear power plant at Three Mile Island in Pennsylvania, the price of uranium began dropping, and layoffs followed by more layoffs on the part of the mining companies were necessary, but devastating. The price per pound of uranium dropped from an average of thirty-two dollars to less than eight dollars. The last mines to close operated at a loss, hoping for times to improve. By 1991 all the mines were shut down, and the number of jobs fell to less than one hundred. Today land reclamation is going on at the huge tailings ponds left by the mills. The giant A-frames, sentinels of Ambrosio lake, are disappearing from the landscape.

Grants and Cíbola County by their grit have survived the dismantling of an industry and are turning the tide. Interstate 40, our monuments, our museum and riverwalk, our nearby pueblos, our Hispanic villages, our championship golf course, our small industries, our service industries, our coal mine and generation plant, our cardboard factory, our government facilities, our retailers, and residuals from sheep, cattle, timber, and vegetables are all contributing to a strong recovering economy.

Carroll Gunderson

Carroll Gunderson, generally known as C. G. Gunderson, came with his family from Laguna to Grants in 1928. He came to manage the Bond-Sergeant General Merchandise store, which became the Bond-Gunderson store in 1940, and later, the Furniture Mart. The Furniture Mart closed its doors in recent years, bringing an end to an era.

From the day they arrived, he and his wife Frieda got involved in their community. He was appointed to the School Board of Grants Union High and served several terms as chairman of the board. Their two sons, Charles (Bud) and Ray (deceased), attended school in Grants, then went on to the University of New Mexico and returned to help with the expanding businesses. Like their father and mother, both were tall fellows, showing their Scandinavian heritage; both were active in sports, especially basketball.

Bud says that Jackie Harrison got the first bicycle when Santa Fe Avenue was first paved, in 1931. Bud got the second one, and Wilbur Thigpen got the third! Jackie was the son of Will Harrison, the editor of the *Grants Review*, the predecessor of the *Beacon*. He went on to fame and many awards as the political columnist who wrote "Inside the Capitol" from Santa Fe, which was carried by most newspapers in the state for many years.

Grants had no electricity when the Gundersons came from Laguna. He purchased a Fairbanks-Morse generator and generated electricity for the store and warehouses, as well as for nearby neighbors. In 1930 the Fairbanks-Morse Company purchased the generator and expanded into the Inland Utilities Company, subsequently purchased by Continental Divide Electric Cooperative (under the Rural Electrification Administration) in 1947 and still going strong.

Beside his interest in business and commerce, G. C. Gunderson was interested in government and was elected the first mayor of Grants when it was incorporated. He was a founding member of most clubs and organizations formed in Grants prior to World

War II. He also served as a "banker" to many of his customers, carrying them on credit until their wool or crops or livestock were sold. He was one of the principals who chartered the Grants State Bank in 1947, the first bank in Grants. The Republican Party of New Mexico nominated him as candidate for the office of governor in 1944. I was too young to vote, but we campaigned hard for a man who we believed would be a dynamic and progressive governor for our great but poor state of New Mexico. He lost by only a narrow margin, in spite of the dominance of the Democratic majority, a majority that established itself during the "New Deal" days of Franklin D. Roosevelt.

In 1952 he was a delegate to the Republican National Convention, in Chicago. At that time I was in the U.S. Army, serving in the veterinary service in Chicago during the Korean War. As I recall it was the first fully televised political convention ever, and Mr. Gunderson, a commanding figure in any crowd, was followed by the cameras throughout the proceedings. I recall sitting in the visitors' gallery, watching. He supported former General Dwight D. Eisenhower to be the standard bearer for the party. Ike's principal opponent at the convention was Senator Robert O. Taft, of Ohio. Floyd W. Lee of San Mateo, also a delegate to the convention, supported Senator Taft. In a close race for the nomination, Eisenhower won and went on to become president.

After the discovery that was to change the course of Grants history, Paddy Martinez, a good friend of the Gundersons, brought a yellow rock into the store in 1950. It was sent off to be assayed and turned out to be high-grade uranium! A prospecting stampede followed that brought people and money and jobs to the area. George Dannenbaum, a former mayor of Grants, has written a book of the uranium days entitled *Boom to Bust*. The book adds to the history of our area and is a good source of information for people who shared those days in a booming mining community. George Dannenbaum, a Democrat and Mr. Gunderson, a Republican, were fierce opponents in the political arena.

Mr. C. G. Gunderson will long be remembered as a friend. Those Hispanic people who knew him well called him "El Gunso." Every time I drive past the Saint Teresa Community

Center on High Street, I recall another example of generosity from this uncommon man; he and his wife, Frieda, donated the land on which this landmark was built. There are dozens, and probably hundreds, of individuals in Grants and the surrounding area who worked summers or part-time at the store. Some of them were students, home for the summer, who needed to earn money to continue their education. Somehow he always employed them and encouraged them to continue. Among these aspiring scholars were a sister and a brother of mine. Mr. Gunderson was a leader in the best sense of the word.

Salvador Milán

Salvador Milán was the founder of the village of Milan, next door to Grants in Cíbola County, on historic Route 66 (now I-40 west). He was born on the Hacienda San Carlos in Coahuila, Mexico, on September 9, 1910. His parents, Don Bartolomé Milán and Doña María de los Frutos Milán, came from Alicante, Spain, to Mexico to manage an hacienda owned by Francisco Madero, president of Mexico. Mary Milán Gunn, Salvador's sister, told me that the four older children were born in Spain and the four younger ones in Mexico, adding with a smile, "While we were growing up, it was a constant war between the Spaniards and the Mexicans!"

When Madero fell from power, there was an antiforeign wave in Mexico, and the Miláns, including their eight children, were put in refugee camps. While in one of these camps, word reached them that Gallup, in far-off New Mexico, needed coal miners and others to provide services to the growing industry in the area. The family then came to Gallup, and according to Paul Milán, son of Salvador, "They started managing a couple of boarding houses. It made sense, because they had six daughters to help take care of the place. In a short time they bought the houses and branched into other businesses. Pedro, Salvador's older brother, had a strong business sense and started some meat markets and a store in Gallup. At age 28 he was assaulted and killed by robbers." Salvador stepped in, and while managing the various businesses, met and married Beneranda (Bennie) Mirabal, the youngest daughter of Don Silvestre Mirabal and Doña Lorencita, of San Rafael.

When Don Silvestre passed away in 1939, their large land-holdings were distributed among their heirs—four daughters and two sons. Each one got approximately a township and a half (about 34,000 acres). Don Silvestre's ranch was one of the largest in western New Mexico. Mónico Mirabal, Salvador's brother-in-law, told my father that at the distribution table, all the heirs wanted land as far away as possible from populated areas, to graze their sheep and cattle without disturbance. Salvador and Bennie, with more of an urban orientation, asked for and got some land west of Grants, which was crossed by Route 66 and fronted the Atchison, Topeka and Santa Fe Railway. The location had great potential for commercial development and rich volcanic soil for agricultural production.

In the early 1940s Salvador and Bennie built a home and a motel in which later would be called Milan. They drilled several irrigation wells and planted hundreds of acres of carrots. The Miláns, as well as Carter and Eden, John Church, Stanley and Card, Fred Freas, and other farmers, produced flavorful, high-quality carrots. The 6,400-foot elevation gave the carrots a unique flavor and tops a deep green that brought premium prices in markets across America. But plastic bags developed during World War II became popular for packaging produce, and after the war, America's housewives wanted their carrots bagged in the transparent bags, for a more hygienic product. The supermarkets began to cut the tops off carrots and bag them in plastic. When the flavorful Bluewater carrot lost its deep green top, it became just another carrot at the produce counter. It lost its premium price and could not compete with California or Arizona carrots, since their growers enjoyed lower irrigation and freight costs. The carrot industry began to disappear from the area and was gone by the end of the 1950s.

When uranium was discovered by Paddy Martinez in the early 1950s, however, Milan began to mushroom into a village, with house trailers everywhere. Salvador subdivided land along Route 66, and businesses and individuals came to develop and mine the new bonanza. According to Salvador's son Paul, "Dad tried to get Grants to annex Milan. Senator Joe Fidel, at that time a member of the Grants City Council, made the motion to annex Milan, but it died for lack of a second." Grants city fathers were barely coping with growing pains of their own and showed little interest in a proposition that would cost them money to provide paved streets and water and sewer lines.

Salvador was not deterred and proceeded to incorporate the village as Milan, having first secured a contract post office, which was a requirement for incorporation. Salvador was elected the first village mayor and was later reelected several times, serving the village until he died, on October 5, 1979. Today what began as an unpromising grazing area on Don Silvestre's huge ranch is a thriving village of over fifteen hundred people.

Salvador and Beneranda had three children—Peter, Paul, and Kathy—and they too have made lasting contributions to the community. Peter lives in Milan and is retired from the real estate business. Paul was a banker, then went to work for the federal government, in Dallas. Kathy married Bill Hocker, a partner in the Grants Mortuary and a former president of the National Funeral Directors of America.

The Fourth of July

The Fourth of July was celebrated with firecrackers, when we could afford them. In the Depression years of the 1930s, firecrackers had an honest-to-goodness bang, but it was a dangerous bang. We set them off at dusk on July 3. The following morning we came in from San Mateo and joined other villagers in the patriotic activities in Grants. We came in cars or trucks that could barely negotiate the dirt roads into town. The ladies and young girls wore colorful gingham dresses and skirts, and the men wore the original no-nonsense Levis, together with a vividly colored silk shirt and a ten-gallon hat. We boys wore our newest bib overalls over a white shirt and our ankle-high laced work shoes. Around our necks we wore a red or blue bandanna and on our heads an old dusty felt hat with a lot of character. Straw hats had not come into vogue yet.

The kick-off was the big parade to celebrate our national day of independence. It formed on the west end of Grants, at the Bernalillo Mercantile store, and went east on Route 66, Santa Fe Avenue, to Bond-Gunderson's store, on First Street. The always stirring VFW color guard, carrying the American and New Mexico flags, led the parade, followed by the high-stepping Grants Union High School band, in their flaming red and black pirate colors. The bristling flags coming down the street made for a colorful spectacle. I would get goose bumps and stand a little taller as the Stars and Stripes passed by. Tourists on Route 66 were detoured through back streets, and many stopped to watch and take in some of our local color. The parade had very few floats but a lot of horses, buggies, and riders.

The parade was followed by a barbecue, sponsored by the fledgling Grants Rodeo Association, founded in 1929 by ranchers Mark Elkins, Hamp Eaves, and I. K. Westbrook. Working cowboys and their wives took the beef from the pit and served it steaming hot, along with beans and hot coffee, at the rodeo grounds on Mountain Road, now the parking lot of Grants High School. Probably over five hundred people attended, representing at least a third of the population in the area. The barbecue was a social event that gave us the opportunity to visit with friends and relatives from other villages. And as our friend Paddy Martinez from the Navajo country used to say, "panza llena, corazón contento!" ("Full belly, happy heart!")

The crowd moved into the grandstands at twenty-five cents each to see the rodeo, now the oldest continuous rodeo in New Mexico and still going strong. Our cowboys were local working cowboys. They competed in wild-cow milking, team tying, bull-dogging, calf roping, bronco and wild-cow riding, and the at-

tempt to ride an occasional bull. All the livestock came from
nearby ranches, and most them were range Herefords. I recall
riding a wild cow and winning a dollar for crossing the white
chalk line! The dollar paid for several dances that night.

The purses, according to Mrs. Mark Elkins, a fine lady who
passed away recently, were twenty-five dollars per event, which
represented about 10 percent of the entry money. Sometimes a
cowboy from as far away as Quemado or Magdalena showed up,
and interest would heighten even more. Our cowboys were
tough as rawhide, and they gave us our twenty-five cents worth!
Side bets were also made on the calf roping, and enthusiasm
escalated until the contest was decided by the cowboy who averaged the best time after roping five calves. Another popular challenge was "my horse against yours," in races after the rodeo and
before the dance started. My brother Eddie had a mule that ran
well, and he usually won a few dollars—if the doggone mule
didn't get stubborn!

Sometime in the early 1940s, girls begin to ride the barrels
and compete. They are always a joy to watch, as they turn around
those barrels and add so much beauty and color to our present-
day rodeos. They were the first girls to wear jeans, which have
become the dress of the modern girl.

The rodeo dance was held in a wooden hall next to the grand-
stand. There were a few electric bulbs, burning with power supplied by Inland Utilities, a subsidiary of Fairbanks-Morse, who
purchased the original plant from Carrol Gunderson in 1928.

Guitars and violins were the most popular instruments used
to provide the music, and schottisches, polkas, and squares were
the most popular dances. We had some of the prettiest girls in
the country and danced till midnight and sometimes until 1:00
A.M., with special permission from the town marshall.

It was a cold and windy day, with snow blowing furiously across the Ambrosio Lake plain. Approaching a cattle guard, I saw a blurry human figure leaning into the wind by the side gate. It was late October, and the Moleres sheep were on their way back to winter country at Navajo. The man at the gate was the owner, J. B Moleres, counting the herd as they made their way north. I stopped the pickup and turned up the heater.

When he finished counting the more than thirteen hundred sheep, I saw him nod to the herders that the count was okay and to keep on going. He was covered with a mantle of snow, but he heard the horn of my truck. I signaled him to get in. In the corner of his mouth he had a hand-rolled cigarette butt, still lit. He kept sucking away, as if his life depended on it, saying, "Está poquito frio!" ("It's a little cold!") Things were never extreme for this gentle man with the biblical patience of Job and the proverbial goodness of Abel. When I got to town, I saw my brother Eddie and told him, "I ran into your father-in-law counting sheep at Ambrosio Lake, and I swear if his cigarette had gone out he would have frozen to death!" Eddie was married to J. B.'s daughter Marie.

J. B., also known as "Bautista," was one of the best sheepmen in the area. He knew his sheep and his sheep knew him. I am convinced, after working sheep in the early years of my life, that sheep, like house plants, respond to love and to care. We all recall stories of the shepherds of old playing the flute, and the sheep following to the soft strains of the music. But sheep are very delicate. Frank Hubbell, a sheepman I worked for in the Quemado country, told me as we looked over a hospital pen full of sick sheep, "You know Abe, I'm convinced sheep were born looking for a way to die!"

Jean Baptiste Moleres came to the United States from the Basque country of France in 1916. He worked for La Compañía, a sheep company in the Vaughn area, for two years, then came to Grants as a partner with Jean Carrica. Mr. Carrica also came from the French Pyrenees. The two of them bought a ranch in the Hospah country, north of Ambrosio Lake. The ranch was next to the Navajo Reservation, and they called it Navajo. They also owned and leased lands south of the Ice Caves from the Arizona–New Mexico Land Company, where they summered their sheep. For many years they trailed the sheep about 100 miles, from their summer pastures south of the Ice Caves to their winter pastures north of Ambrosio Lake in the fall, reversing the trail in the spring.

From time to time Bautista's heart would go back to the old country, to Marianne Arrosa, a young lady he had known in the Pyrenees. After twelve years of hard work getting started in the sheep business, he finally felt able to support a wife, and sent for Marianne. They were married in Albuquerque in 1928, at the Immaculate Heart of Mary Catholic Church. When Marianne came, she spoke only French Basque. In a short time she became trilingual, however, adding Spanish and English to her repertoire. She immersed herself in raising a family of three boys and a girl, and in helping the priests of St. Teresa Parish.

As their children grew up, Carrica and Moleres decided, after forty years, to split their partnership. Each got half of the sheep and half of the land, in an amicable agreement. They successfully continued to manage their respective sheep ranches, independently.

In 1964 the Moleres family traded the sheep for cattle to Gordon Bond, who represented a prominent livestock-trading family in New Mexico. According to Marie, "they traded 8 sheep for one cow and started their cattle herd with 165 mother cows." Sheep herders were hard to find, the coyote population had gotten out of control and was killing too many sheep, and the price of wool dropped when polyester fibers came onto the market. All these factors were significant in the demise of the sheep industry in western New Mexico. But J. B., the sheepman, missed his sheep. He'd say, "Cattle are alright, but . . . " Other Basques followed this pioneer into the area, playing a prominent role in the development of the commercial sheep industry. Among them were Juan Iriart, Filiberto Arretche, Ramón Amistoy, Martín Borthagaray, Pedro Mandagarán, León Iriart, Juanito and Pascual

Iriart, Pierre and Johnny Arrosa (brothers of Marianne Moleres), Luis Sena (brother of Mrs. Carrica), and Jean Ithurria. Most of these men married local girls, and their families are playing an important role in the continued development of Cíbola County. Only Pierre Arrosa and Jean Ithurria still live in the area. Most of the others have passed away, and one or two returned to the old country and their homes in the Pyrenees.

Marie says, "They were all single when they came from France. The only two women that came from the old country were my mother and Mrs. Marie Carrica . . . they were like surrogate mothers to the men who gathered at our homes during the Christmas Holidays, when they came from the sheep camps for a couple of weeks. In our youth we considered them all like members of our family." All of them in time also became trilingual—in Basque, Spanish, and English. Marie says, "They played cards till one or two in the morning. Mother fed them and sometimes joined them in some noisy Basque card games!"

When Mr. Moleres died, in 1988 at the age of ninety-two, I was asked to say a few words at his funeral mass. I quoted the 23d Psalm, "The Lord is my shepherd, I shall not want," then said that he had been my friend as well as my model. There was thirty years difference in our ages. He was more my father's age, and they were good friends and compadres, but I always felt completely at ease with this uncommon man. Mr. Moleres was very special to me.

Two years later Mrs. Moleres passed away, at the age of eighty-nine. Father Godfrey in his eulogy called her "Mother of Priests," a beautiful title and very appropriate. She had devoted her life to her family and to her church, St. Teresa of Avila. She cleaned the altar, she washed the linen, she arranged the nativity scene, she chose the music, she sang in the choir, she scolded the Sisters, the Brothers, and the Priests, and prepared hundreds of children for their first Holy Communion.

I can't help but think that Mr. Moleres is no doubt quietly tending his sheep in the lush green pastures of heaven, while Mrs. Moleres is cleaning the altars and ordering souls around!

Rafelito

Rafelito was a small man, about 5 feet, 4 inches tall, who weighed about 110 pounds, was fair-skinned and had a balding head. He was always moving—seldom sat down and relaxed. His favorite word was "vamos" ("let's go"). Rafelito worked for many years in the sheep camps of Don Silvestre Mirabal of San Rafael in the 1930s and 1940s. When he came to work at the Peña Ranch, he frequently spoke of his friend and former boss, "Don Pantaleo," one of the most successful sheepmen and businessmen in western New Mexico. Rafelito never married. He got a little nervous around women, but he was always the perfect gentleman. He was the brother of Mateo Martínez, whose father in law, Vicente Otero of San Mateo, homesteaded 160 acres at Milpitas, north of Ambrosio Lake.

One of the most remembered weddings of that period was the marriage of the attractive Florentina Martínez, the oldest daughter of Mateo, to Lizardito Salazar, at Milpitas in the 1920s. People from all over came by car, by wagon, and by horse to join the couple in holy matrimony. The ceremony and dance were held in the immaculately calcimined living room of the ranch house. The whitewash was made from mica chips found in the area. The milk-white walls were artistically highlighted with bluish rosettes, some of which are still visible today on the falling walls of the old homestead.

Lizardito passed away several years ago. He was one of the best auto mechanics in the village. He learned the skills from a blacksmith and was a magician with a screwdriver and a pair of pliers. He and his wife raised a fine family. Florentina is now in her eighties and still as pretty as ever. She told me recently that she had many fond memories of that special day—"We danced till the candles burned out!"

Rafelito, the uncle of the bride, served as camptender to Nicolás Maestas for several years. They were very different personalities, but they liked and respected each other. Nicolás had also worked for Don Silvestre, so they shared a common background. One windy and dusty spring day, they had an argument at Cañada del Camino windmill, where they were watering the herd. Nicolás sent Rafelito ahead to turn the water on and fill the troughs before the sheep, about a thousand head, got there. But he didn't turn the water on; Rafelito could be very stubborn at times. A scuffle resulted, and Nicolás being the bigger man, threw Rafelito to the ground and was pummeling him. At this point my father, Pablo Peña, drove up and broke up the fight. Later when he told the story, he'd say, "Even though he was down on the ground, Rafael was like a feisty bantam rooster —putting up a heck of a fight!" Dad always called him Rafael, his given name. Everyone else called him Rafelito.

After the sheep were sold, the ranch was stocked with cattle, and Rafelito fixed fence and broke ice for them in the winter. He'd ride off on horseback at sunrise and return at sunset. Blackie was his favorite horse, as he went on his appointed rounds from water tank to water tank, breaking ice with an axe day after day. One day I arrived at the ranch house about midday, and he was in bed. He said, "I was breaking ice at La Vega tank, and I guess I passed out. When I came to, I was cold, very cold, and couldn't get on my horse. I walked to the ranch as best I could." I took him to the doctor, who prescribed some pills and plenty of rest.

After that his job was to stay around the headquarters, feeding the chickens and livestock and chopping wood. Mother nature and father time had taken their toll, and it was time for Rafelito to slow down and enjoy his senior years. To the end he preferred the outdoors, the piñon and juniper, the sandstone mesas of western New Mexico.

Dance Halls

"Ten cents please," the collector kept intoning, as he made his rounds among the couples while collecting the fee. After the collection the number continued.

Dance halls in the 1930s were the recreation centers of village
life. The church was the spiritual center. Both were very important in our lives during the Great Depression. There was little or
no money, but we survived through hard work, a song in our
hearts, and yes, the grace of God. Every Hispanic community in
Cíbola County had a dance hall or two. The custom came from
rural Spain through Mexico to New Mexico. Halls were built by
the settlers to celebrate weddings, saint's days, feast days, and
simply for dancing on Saturday nights. Later they were also
used for political rallies. The dance hall was a large, rectangular
building, about 40 feet wide by 100 feet long, with an elevated
platform at one end for the musicians. Some halls instead sported
balconies, where the musicians were literally above the crowd.

One of the most popular dance halls in Grants was the Sunshine. This hall had an adjacent bar, a restaurant next door, a barber shop, and a garage. It was owned by Don Luis McBride,
businessman, rancher, community and political leader. Chavez
Hall gave the Sunshine competition, but they both did a thriving
business. It was owned by Don Pantaleón Chávez and was inherited by his daughter Tillie. Tillie says, "From those 10 cents collected at mid-dance, we had to pay the musicians, the *colector*, the
bastonero, and other expenses. Sometimes there was a little left
over for us!" Tillie's husband, Juan Padilla, remembers that "Los
Natos were the most popular and best-known band. Liberato
Moreno, the leader of Los Natos, played the trumpet like nobody
before and nobody since. He simply was the best." His lips were
puffy and swollen, like the lips of all good trumpet players.

Los Natos played *chotes, polcas, valses, y mucho más.* Some
popular songs of the day were "Adelita," "Las Gaviotas," "Échale
Nicle al Piano," "Senaida," and "El Rancho Grande." Also popular was "You are my Sunshine," which was more or less the
theme song of the Sunshine hall. To go with Liberato's trumpet,
Timoteo Torres played drums, Rosalio Jaramillo the drums and
trumpet, Agapito Moreno the banjo, and the accordionists kept
changing.

There was a story that in the small villages of Cíbola County,
when there was no money to pay the musicians, somebody would

start a fight around midnight. The musicians would have to run for their lives, to save their instruments—so you wouldn't pay them! They returned the following Saturday, to play again; they were musicians and played whether they were paid or not. Of course they preferred to be paid—they had to eat, too.

In the village of San Mateo there were two dance halls. La Sala de Mi Tía Onofre and La Sala de los Michaels. There had been others before, including one owned by my grandfather, which passed on to my grandmother when he died at the age of forty-three, and which was in use for many years.

One of the traditional events before a dance was *sacar el gallo.* In the early days the musicians climbed on a horse-drawn wagon and played up and down the village streets late in the day, announcing the dance. There are stories of musicians celebrating a bit too much, too early, and falling off the wagon! By the late 1930s pickups succeeded wagons, and blaring horns helped the musicians draw attention to the dance.

In San Rafael, Frank Barela remembers, "It was tough sometimes to find one more dime for one more dance. I recall borrowing a dime from a friend to have one more dance; she was a special girl. It took me a while to pay it back, but I paid it back." The late Celito Jaramillo once told me, "I remember coming from San Mateo to a dance at Chavez Hall. A fight started, and I was trying to get closer to see better, when Frutoso's fist came flying out of the pack and struck me right in the mouth. *Hijo de la patada, me dio en la pura música!*" ("Damn, he hit me right in the mouth!")

Some couples in the villages were noted for leading the "La Marcha," the Grand March at wedding dances. After all the lamps had been lit and the hall was full of people, the lead couple led the bride and groom, and the rest followed in a snake dance that got everyone in the mood, as the musicians played with a special flair. Delfinio and Senaida Salazar, and later Vivián and Regina Trujillo, were sought after to lead marches at wedding dances. Celito Jaramillo once remarked, "Don Pedro Silva was a leader, and his daughters Lena and Kela were excellent dancers." Don Pedro, married to Doña Petrita Serna Silva, led the march at the

Sunshine when Celito and his wife, Perla Serna, got married.
Plácido and Sofía Mirabal were the padrinos. Celito and Perla in time also became famous as leaders.

Los López de Pecos orchestra, like Los Natos, always started the dance in high gear. With some high notes on that resonant trumpet, Herminio and his sons, Hermancito and Esequiel López, came to the area with fluorspar mining and added flair to our local dances. So did Las Sopitas, from Cubero. In San Mateo Los Alfredos orchestra came from Albuquerque to play for Fiestas. Word spread very quickly, "Ay vienen los Alfredos!" They usually arrived for the *Vísperas* and played two nights. The women furiously ironed their dresses, as they prepared for two days of dancing and feasting. We men chopped wood, fed the horses, and polished our shoes.

We also had a number of excellent local musicians. Ambrosio Montaño, and later his son Catarino, played the accordion, Willie Montaño the banjo, Serafín Mirabal the guitar, and Justiniano Sandoval the accordion.

Most of the important and colorful characters of the dance hall era who served as colectores, bastoneros, or *chotas* have passed on. Procopio "Copio" Baca, Polinario Montaño, José García, Manuel Saavedra, Francisco Baca, Blas Trujillo, and the notable Sheriff Pablo Gallegos. Fidelino Salazar, a part of that era, has many memories of those days.

The dance hall has been succeeded by the cocktail lounge, and an era has come to an end. To those of us who lived through that period, the memory lingers on.

Seventy Nine Years of Agricultural Enterprise

The New Mexico
FARM & RANCH
Heritage Foundation

Designates

Peña Ranch

Established 1916

A New Mexico
Heritage Ranch

Earl Ray Forehand　　　　10/1/95

Earl Ray Forehand
Foundation President
Date

Figure 13
Farm and Ranch Heritage
Foundation's recognition

Figure 14
Abelicio Peña and son
Antonio, wife Manuelita (left)
and schoolteacher, c. 1911

Figure 15
Watering the sheep,
(on the left) Lydia and
Pablo Peña, c. 1939

Figure 16
Congregational
Mission School pupils,
c. 1919

Figure 17
Eloy Peña (far left) helping
Antonio, Abelicio, and Pablo
Peña with branding, c. 1949

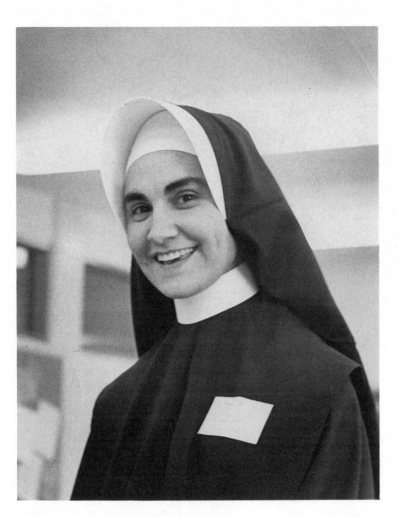

Figure 18
Sister Lydia M. Peña,
Sister of Loretto, 1959

Figure 19
Portrait of Isidoro Solís
by Leona Nellis

Figure 20
Sheep camp in the
Zuni Mountains,
c. 1949

Figure 21
Navajo harvesting carrots
in the Bluewater Valley,
c. 1942

Figure 22
Navajo shearing sheep, c. 1935
(Courtesy the New Mexico State Archives)

Figure 23
Max Miller (right; adopted son of Billy
the Kid?) and Abe Peña, c. 1961

Figure 24
Abe Peña weighing fleece in
the shearing barn, c. 1961

Figure 25
Burros loaded with
sheep camp supplies

Figure 26
Pablo Peña on his favorite
horse Chino, c. 1928

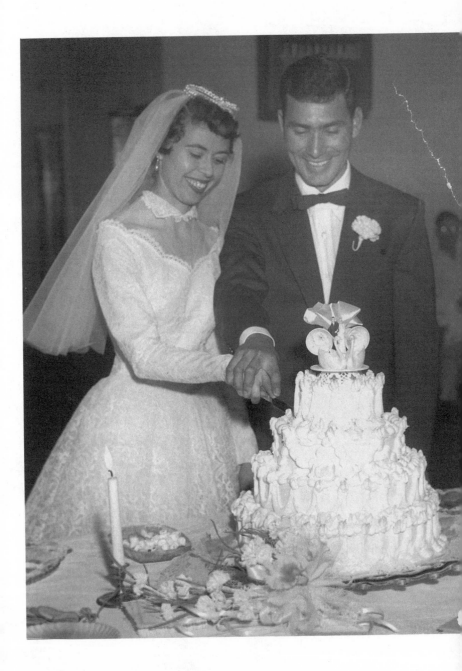

Figure 27
Viola and Abe Peña, 1955

Figure 28
The Peña family—Ramona, Viola, Marco,
Abe, Cecilia, and Paula—in 1962

PART FIVE

Navajoland

The Anasazi, whose name comes from a Navajo word meaning "Enemy Ancestors," are also known as the "Children of Light." They inhabited northwestern New Mexico about a thousand years ago, in much the same area now inhabited by the Navajos. It is generally believed that the disappearance of the Anasazi coincided with the founding of many of the nineteen Indian Pueblos of New Mexico. This sequence in time gives credence to the belief that Pueblo Indians are the descendants of the Anasazi.

The Navajos in the early days were nomadic and built hogans and lean-tos, never using the houses left by the Anasazi. Navajoland has an aura of mystery to it. The Navajo Reservation and the checkerboard lands adjacent to it are so vast that you see little life as you drive through or ride a horse across it. Still every mile you drive or ride is generally a handsome landscape of massive sandstone and rainbow color. I like to say, "From the beautiful Indian country of western New Mexico" when I sign off on voicemail or when I leave a message on someone's answering machine.

Anthropologists tell us that the Navajos are descended from one of the later Asian groups to cross the Bering Sea to the New World. It is believed that the earlier peoples, who settled the territory from northeastern North America on down to Latin America, such as the ancestors of the Incas, Mayas, and Aztecs, crossed over from Asia starting about twenty thousand years ago, while the ancestors of the Navajos probably crossed sometime in the last ten thousand years. The Navajos themselves probably arrived in northwestern New Mexico some time after the Anasazi left Chaco Canyon and Mesa Verde, about seven hundred years ago. So they are relative newcomers.

I was raised close to the Navajos and learned to speak some of their language by mingling and working with them on the Peña Ranch, some three miles from the reservation. I've ridden horseback with them, steam-bathed in miniature hogans, and danced at Yei Bichei ceremonies.

The people you'll meet here are all people I have known. Some of them had impressive credentials, but most of them were simply fine human beings.

Paul Jones

Paul Jones rose to prominence by serving his people and serving them well. He was a singleminded individual pursuing the best interest of the tribe, no matter what the consequences.

Paul Jones, a conservative, was elected the first Navajo tribal chairman when the tribal government was reorganized, in the 1940s. He was presiding over the largest Indian tribe and reservation in the United States—and one of the poorest. World War II saw many Navajos go to war and serve their country with distinction. The most famous were the "code talkers" who were used to confuse the Japanese in the Pacific and the Germans in Europe. The Axis powers simply couldn't decode Navajo. In part our victory in the Pacific, and in Europe, was attributable to these patriotic Americans. They helped shorten the war and save countless casualties on both sides of the conflict. When those soldiers and sailors returned home to the Navajo country, one of the most picturesque in the world, the tribal council, under the direction of Paul Jones, assisted by another great leader, Annie Wanneka, was leasing mineral rights for oil and gas, uranium and coal.

The exploration program, after several false starts, discovered large amounts of minerals and oil and gas. Development and production brought immense royalty wealth to the tribal council. As the fund grew, there was a concerted push by many to divide the wealth and distribute it, in cash, to individual members of the tribe. Paul Jones, their wise leader, proposed a Tribal Development Fund to build factories, roads, schools, and clinics, and probably even more important, to provide scholarships to students who showed promise. He argued that what Navajos needed most were jobs and an education. To his credit he prevailed, and time has proven him right. Today there are qualified professionals in all disciplines taking an interest in what is best for the tribe, rather than what is best for individuals. In the 1970s one of our prestigious national magazines reported that the Navajo tribe was the richest ethnic group in the United States on a per capita basis.

I had the privilege of meeting Mr. Jones when I was a young man managing the Peña Ranch, north of San Mateo. Mr. Enrico (Rico) Menopace introduced us. In 1957 I went to Gallup to buy a pickup at Rico Motor Company, and Rico himself, since everyone else was tied up, attended me. The chemistry was right, and we enjoyed negotiating for the truck. We concluded our negotiating at noon, and he invited me to lunch at the newest and ritziest place in town, the Shalimar Hotel. We drove to the Shalimar and met Paul Jones there. I was a thirty-year-old, sitting in the company of giants, although neither was more than 5 feet 7 inches tall. They were both in their sixties and sharp as tacks, there to transact business. Jones was negotiating for a fleet of twenty-seven pickups for the tribe, and Rico was carefully weighing a price that both could live with. At one point Rico, in his best Italian dramatics, cried "Paul, you're going to break me!" After more skirmishing a deal was concluded, at a good price to the tribe and a fair profit for the dealer.

It would have been so easy for the chairman to pick up a telephone in Window Rock and place an order for twenty-seven pickups, knowing that the Tribal Treasury could easily cover it. His conservative and careful use of tribal funds led him instead to Gallup, to negotiate tooth and nail over a lamb chop—and get a maintenance agreement to boot!

The friendship and respect these two had for each other lasted a lifetime. They are both gone now, but they have both left a legacy. Their spirit lives on. Rico sold GMCs, the most popular pickup in Navajo country for a long time, literally for beans! You could see piles of beans and corn sacks brought in by customers to make a payment on their pickups. And it was not unusual for them to bring in a goat or a sheep, a cow, a sack of wool, or some mohair instead of cash.

Rico put the Navajos on wheels, and Paul Jones built the roads and gave them jobs and a chance at an education to use the pickups wisely. Wherever these two men are now, they are probably negotiating tooth and nail for a "good kind" of GMC pickup!

Hageebah

Hageebah, a tall Navajo woman from the Borrego Pass country, was taking care of a small goat herd on the Peña ranch in 1944. Most of the eighty-five goats in the herd were Angoras, excellent for mohair, and a few Toggenbergs, good for milking. It was the month of May, and she was "kidding" them, taking care of them as the females gave birth, by herself at Mesita del Gato. Many goats have twins, and by the end of May she had more than 120 kids. Her camp was about a mile from the ranch headquarters at Canyon Largo.

Hageebah Hoskie Barbone in her late fifties was strong and in good health. She was honest and reliable and an excellent goatherder. She spoke only Navajo but could understand some Spanish. When you were conversing with her, she kept nodding her head and smiling and sometimes laughed in amusement. Everyone liked Hageebah. I learned some Navajo as a youngster and used to practice with her. She was very patient. She had a white spot in her left eye that made her very attractive.

Her tent was next to the brush corral so she could hear any movement at night. Once in a while a bobcat sneaked in while the herd was sleeping and killed a kid. Hageebah respected bobcats and coyotes, but got very angry when they killed her kids. The losses to predators were small. Hageebah was also shearing the goats with hand shears, and every day during their midday rest, while the herd was "nooning," she sheared 3 or 4 goats and put the mohair in a 6-foot-long burlap bag.

One day she arrived very disturbed at Canyon Largo, looking for my father, Pablo Peña, her employer. In an animated state she spoke and used signs, telling him, "Someone was at my camp today while I was watering the goat herd at Cañada del Camino and stole a sack of mohair!" adding, "There's tracks of two horses, and they head west." My father, a soft-spoken man, told her, "Don't worry, Hageebah, go back to your herd, we'll take care of it." The cook asked her to sit down and gave her a cup of coffee. She gulped it down then hurried back to her herd.

Dad sent for Antonio Sandoval, Hageebah's son-in-law, who was foreman of a sheep herd lambing at another part of the ranch, and told him to take a horse and track the thieves. Antonio, an energetic and hardworking man, was a fine tracker. He returned the next day and said, "The tracks lead to a hogan above Milpitas. I think Jeff was alone and used a pack horse to load and carry the sack. I believe he hid it in the rocks below his hogan, but I couldn't find it."

Dad took Bennie, my older brother, with him and they drove to Jeff's hogan, about eight miles away. When they got there, Jeff came out and greeted them in his usual friendly way and asked what they were doing. Dad said, "Oh, we're on our way to Gallup and wondered if you'd like to go with us." Jeff, a little under the influence of wine, answered in fluent but blurred Spanish, "Sure I'll go with you." When they got to Gallup, they went to the courthouse. Dad went in and Bennie and Jeff stayed in the truck. He told the sheriff the particulars of the theft, and the sheriff came out and asked Jeff, "What did you do with the sack of mohair?" Without hesitation Jeff answered, "I hid it in the rocks near my hogan. I'll show you where it is." Father knew Jeff and his ways, so he told the sheriff he was not filing charges, and they returned Jeff to his hogan, where he helped them load the sack, saying, "I got a little drunk and needed a little money so I took the mohair. I'm sorry."

Hageebah was delighted when she heard the mohair had been found and returned. She said, "I suspected Jeff. He's always getting in trouble, especially when he's drinking."

She had three daughters. Margaret married John Barbone, Mary married Antonio Sandoval, and Mabel married Charlie Morgan. John Barbone and Margaret had fourteen children. Antonio Sandoval and Mary, a very lovely lady who was ill a good part of her adult life, had Portana and Albert.

I recently visited Portana Sandoval Tolth, now a grandmother with five children and nine grandchildren, and she told me her father told her she was born on the east side of the Sandia Mountains. "There was a big piñon crop, and they went to pick piñons during the Depression. It was the month of January and Hageebah delivered me. She was a good midwife."

I asked Portana what she remembered most about her grandmother. "She was my friend. I loved my grandmother and spent a lot of time with her. When she died she willed her land allotment to me. . . . They say I was her favorite." Before I left I asked where Hageebah was buried. "When she died, at age eighty-six, we started a family plot on that sunny slope." She pointed to an enclosure with iron grating around it, about 300 feet from the house. "When Mom and Dad died we buried them there also. I wanted them close to me."

On the way home I kept thinking how fortunate we were to still have connections to the children of people we worked with forty and fifty years ago. The old-timers are gone, and so are most of the horses and wagons, but their children carry on in pickups and run sheep and cattle as well as work at Crownpoint, or off the reservation. School buses come to their door and electricity lights up the new frame houses next to the old but still comfortable hogans. A new chapter is being written in the beautiful earthtone country of northwestern New Mexico, and Hageebah's descendants are helping write it.

Paddy Martinez

Paddy Martinez, the Navajo Indian who discovered uranium in the Grants area in 1950, was inducted into the National Mining Hall of Fame on October 18, 1992. The Navajo Tribal Council declared October 18 Paddy Martinez Day. This remarkable man was trilingual—he spoke Navajo, Spanish, and English. When asked what he was, he sometimes answered, with tongue in cheek, "Half Navajo, half Spanish, and half Mormon!" His Hispanic friends called him by his given name, "Julián."

I remember first seeing Paddy in San Mateo about 1936, where he was riding his horse during the San Juan Fiestas. The fiestas were celebrated annually on June 24, in honor of John the Baptist. Paddy was among a number of horsemen preparing to "correr el gallo," run the rooster pull. He was tall and had an athletic body "a la John Wayne," which was an advantage in the rooster pull and in all other aspects of life in the great outdoors. He and his brothers rode their ponies about fifteen miles from Haystack to join the festivities. Paddy's long arms and riding ability made him very competetive with some of the fine riders from our village, such as Marcelino Jaramillo, Salvador Chávez, Ismael Salazar, Telesfor Gonzales, my uncle Abelicio Peña, Vidal Laure, and others.

In those days it was against the law to sell liquor to Indians. However, Paddy had a lot of friends, and a passing bottle didn't make any judgments! The misguided law was repealed in 1947, the same year the Indians were given the right to vote. Times were tough then. People had to match the times and did what they could to make a living during the Great Depression of the 1930s. Among other things Paddy and his clan picked piñons when there was a crop. He liked the San Mateo Mountains, where they joined hundreds from San Mateo and other villages to harvest the crop. Covered wagons overflowing with families and provisions slowly made their winding way to the top of the mountain, in search of the best area to gather the savory nut. They returned to San Mateo loaded with piñons, usually bagged in 100-pound gunny sacks.

Mr. Merhage Michael and his family had a general merchandise store and bought a lot of piñons. I recall the Michael warehouse stacked to the ceiling with sacks. Later they trucked them to Grants and loaded the nuts in railroad cars for shipping to eastern markets.

Paddy and his clan were also sheep owners and sheep shearers. They contracted with local sheepmen to shear their sheep (see Fig. 22). I remember around 1938 their colorful group arriving by wagon and horseback at el Rancho de la Punta to shear our sheep. My father had leased the ranch from the Fernandez Company. Paddy drove the men hard and was enraged if they didn't shear at least thirty sheep a day each, with their rustic hand shears and bare torsos in the hot days of June. Australians today can shear as many as six hundred, at blinding speed, with electric shears! To feed the shearers and herders we generally butchered a sheep a day and roasted the meat on the open fire, balancing the meal with a pot of chile and breles baked in Dutch ovens and savored with coffee brewed in gallon-sized pots over the fire.

When carrots became big business in the Grants area, in the 1940s, Paddy contracted with the farmers to provide laborers. He played a big part in bringing the Navajo people into the cash economy. He transported men, women, and children by the truckload to work the carrot fields. The vibrant colors of the Navajo velveteen blouses merging with the deep green carrot tops and golden carrots provided a most colorful spectacle during the harvests west of town. Paddy's leadership and influence grew.

In 1950 he picked up a yellow rock near his hogan at Haystack and brought it into town. He had heard that yellow rocks might contain a valuable mineral. At the Bond-Gunderson store, he sought out his friend Carroll Gunderson and showed him the rock. The interesting find drew the attention of some passing geologist friends of the Gundersons, who took it to be assayed. It was uranium, and the rest is well-known history by now.

The discovery of uranium was made on land to which the Santa Fe Railroad held the mineral rights, and the Haystack mine was developed there. The railroad and Anaconda put Paddy on the payroll as a uranium scout and paid him four hundred dollars per month, "for as long as he lived." That was a big paycheck in those days. Prosperity did not change his lifestyle. He did buy a white house in the village of Bluewater, then built a hogan next to it, where he lived for a while, "and the chickens used the house," he told me. Then he moved back home to Haystack, his beloved Navajoland.

In the 1960s Paddy attended a Knights of Columbus picnic at Bluewater Lake, where he sat crosslegged on the ground, grinding out humorous stories for dozens of people gathered around him. He told of the Navajo stopping at an isolated Hispanic homestead late one afternoon. "They sat him by the door while the family ate. Finally the Navajo asked the man of the house, 'Say friend, how much is a ball of gold about this size worth [holding his hands together to indicate about the size of a baseball]? Immediately the family invited him to the table and served him a generous portion. The Hispanic was dying to ask about the gold, but waited until the Navajo was through eating, then asked, 'Where did you find this ball of gold?' The Navajo, grinning sheepishly, answered, 'I haven't found one—I'm asking just in case I find one!'" Paddy slapped his thigh, "The Navajo outsmarted the Mexican!" and bellowed in laughter.

Paddy raised a large family. Most of his surviving children, grandchildren, great grandchildren, and great great grandchildren still live in the Haystack country. In his final years, he spent most of his time on a sheepskin on the earthen floor, "next to mother nature" in his large and comfortable hogan, telling everyone, "Nobody comes to visit me." I used to visit him from time to time, and others did too; and members of his family used to visit quite often. Once I stopped to ask permission to cross a herd of cattle across his land, on the trail to the Zuni Mountains. At that time he could no longer walk, and he told me, "Drive them right by my door so I can see them and hear them and smell them." When I went back later to thank him for letting us cross his land, he said, "I belong out there riding Boots west into the setting sun with the wind in my face." Boots was his favorite horse.

In 1969 Paddy made his last ride. His indomitable spirit rode quietly into the setting sun. His tombstone at Grants Memorial Cemetery simply reads, "Paddy Martinez 1881–1969 Uranium Pioneer." He rests a stones throw from Paddy Martinez Park, where children play.

Wilbur Begay

In 1957 I was looking in the Prewitt area for a ranchhand. I spoke to several Navajos, but none were available. One told me that Wilbur Begay might be available, and that he lived in the

Casimiro Lake country, near Borrego Pass. I didn't know Wilbur Begay, but decided to try and find him.

The Navajo country is big country, and finding someone five miles from a main road, on a twisting wagon track, takes a lot of luck. After several wrong turns, luck was with me. I saw a family of five or six people sitting under the shade of a large but thirsty cottonwood tree, the only one for miles around. As I approached the family group, several barking dogs ran to meet me. Wilbur quieted the dogs and greeted me in Spanish, good Spanish. He was a friendly fellow with a big smile and a pleasant disposition about thirty-five years of age, standing about 5 feet 7 inches tall and weighing about 145 pounds. He introduced his four young sons and his well-dressed and attractive wife, Irene. Her jet-black hair was carefully combed in a *chongo,* and her oval face had two dimples and a Mona Lisa smile. After visiting a while, he told me he was between construction jobs and was expecting word soon, but, "can help you out until word comes." That was alright with me, so he rolled his bedroll and off we went.

The job stretched to more than fifteen years, and Wilbur Begay and the Peña Ranch had a successful relationship over all that time. Although he started as just another ranchhand, very quickly he showed his skills and was given more and more responsibility. He fixed water wells, built fences and corrals, docked lambs, branded and vaccinated cattle, broke and trained horses, drove a 1947 Ford tractor and fixed it when it broke. In less than a year, he was the ranch foreman.

And we became close friends. One day while trailing a herd of cattle to summer pasture in the Zuni Mountains, I asked him where he had learned mechanics and all the other things he could do. He said, "I spent a year in the penitentiary, and I learned many useful things, including mechanics." He went on to say that as a young man, he and an older friend were accused of stealing a horse, and the judge sent them to the penitentiary. "For me it was like going to school." Wilbur could have been a fine doctor, lawyer, teacher, or whatever else he wanted to be, if he had had the opportunity. But he never went to school. He lived a long way from a school and had to work as a boy.

His wife, Irene, lived at the ranch and was the cook. She also wove Navajo rugs from wool produced on the ranch. One of her fine 4 foot by 6 foot rugs was exhibited on a portable loom at the Brown Palace Hotel in Denver, during a National Wool Growers' Convention and received high praise. Over the years her weaving was a good source of additional family income from the sale of rugs and saddle blankets.

In the early 1970s Wilbur and his mother, Emma, leased the uranium rights to an Indian allotment they had near Casimero Lake. The mining company paid them thirty thousand dollars in advance royalties. Before they received the money, we suggested that they buy sheep and go into business for themselves. They thought it was a good idea. However, on the day they received the check, they quietly went to Gallup and bought a brand new pickup, television sets, polaroid cameras, expensive silver and turquoise jewelry, and "booze"—and forgot all about buying sheep.

Six years later, while I was serving in the foreign service in Paraguay, we read in the *Grants Daily Beacon*, which took about a month to get there, that Wilbur Begay had been struck and killed by a truck near the Tomahawk Bar on old Route 66, near Prewitt. It was a sad day for our family; we lost a friend.

With God's grace Irene did a fine job raising her family of boys, and today they are all doing well. She lives in a comfortable home in the Prewitt area. From time to time the boys stop to visit us on their way through Grants.

Max Miller

In the Ramah country west of Grants, there are some old-timers who think that John Miller was Billy the Kid. I first heard the story from Buddy Elkins, in the 1960s. We were trailing a herd of cattle across the Elkins Ranch to summer country in the Zuni Mountains. We stopped the herd for lunch and Buddy came by and had lunch with us.

Among the cowboys eating by the campfire was the old Navajo, Max Miller, whom Buddy knew well. After visiting with

Max for a while, he turned to me and asked if I had heard that, "some people believe that Max Miller is the adopted son of Billy the Kid?" With great interest I answered "no," but recovering quickly, asked him to tell us the story. Buddy said that his uncle Adrian Berryhill had told him that some old-timers in the Ramah country were sure that John Miller, who adopted Max as a young boy, was William Bonney, better known as Billy the Kid.

From several sources, I learned the story of what became of Billy the Kid. He was not shot at Fort Sumner by Sheriff Pat Garrett. Tiny Carter said, "They say the sheriff in the dark of night shot someone else and The Kid went out a window and rode north." Sometime later The Kid showed up in Las Vegas, New Mexico, with the new name of John Miller. He had learned to speak Spanish working with Hispanic cowboys and liked to be with them. Tiny added, "In Las Vegas he took up with a pretty Mexican woman, and they started moving west, eventually winding up in the Quemado country, where fugitives hid from the law near Mangas Coloradas." Miller and his team of horses were hired at a dam site being built. When the day was done, he went to eat with the other teamsters. Looking around carefully, he saw the cook looking him straight in the eye and was sure he had been recognized. He hitched his horses, took his woman, and started north during the night.

They wound up near Ramah and homesteaded a piece of land. They never had children, but adopted a young Navajo boy from the neighboring Navajo country and gave him the name Max. They taught him English and Spanish, and he became fluent in these languages. He also learned to ride a horse all day without tiring him out. That was the mark of a true horseman. During the First World War, Max was drafted into the army and sent to Europe. In 1918 John Miller received a letter from the War Department, telling him that his son Max had been killed in action. By this time John was getting on in years and with his woman left the country and went to Phoenix to live. The old dilapidated house they found there leaked, and John climbed up to fix the roof. He fell through the rotten roofing and died from complications.

When the war was over Max Miller returned, not dead after all. As he told me, "Another Max Miller was killed and they thought it was me." He learned of his father's death in Phoenix and tried to find his mother, but he never was able to locate her.

Max worked for the Crockett Ranch near Fence Lake for years and later came to the Ambrosio Lake country to cowboy for Adrian Berryhill and his brother Duane. He met the young and attractive Navajo widow of John Jones in the Borrego Pass country and married her. They raised several children. When he came to work for the Peña Ranch, he was already in his seventies, but he could still ride a horse all day without tiring and do a full day's work. Max was a man of character, soft-spoken, tall and lanky, and starting to lose his hearing (see Fig. 23).

After returning with the cattle from the Zuni Mountains to the Peña Ranch in the Ambrosio Lake country in the fall one year, we sat quietly, relaxing on the porch of the ranch house, looking toward Mount Taylor to the southeast. I asked him, "Max, was your father Billy the Kid?" He slowly answered, "I don't know, but when we lived near Ramah he spent the night facing the door with a gun across his lap. In the morning he left the cabin and slept among the trees."

Duane Berryhill said that one time when Max had had one cup too many, and they were trying to persuade him to go back to the ranch, he told them, "Leave me alone, I'm the son of Billy the Kid."

Max passed away at Red Rock Daycare Center in Gallup in 1988, at the age of ninety-five and is buried at Sunset Cemetery in Gallup. Was John Miller Billy the Kid? I don't know, but there are some old-timers in western New Mexico who believe he was.

Turquoise Mountain

Majestic Mount Taylor dominates the spectacular landscape of west-central New Mexico. The 11,301-foot peak, an extinct vol-

cano, is known as the Turquoise Mountain or the Sacred Mountain of the South by Navajos who live to the west and northwest
of it. At one time, according to one study, they lived by the thousands on the slopes of Mount Taylor, near San Mateo above El
Rito and at San Lucas Canyon. The mountain is also sacred to
Laguna and Acoma Pueblos, to the south and southwest. The
Spanish called it La Sierra de San Mateo. La Mosca is the north
rim of the volcanic crater, and Los Cerros Pelones the south rim,
highest point on the mountain.

After the Mexican War, the United States claimed New
Mexico. In 1849 Lt. James Simpson, a topographic engineer assigned to the U.S. Geologic Survey, used the name Mount Taylor on his maps, in honor of President Zachary Taylor, the twelfth
president of the United States. General Taylor had commanded
the U.S. forces that led the country to victory against Mexico
and was elected president in 1848.

In the Tertiary period, some four million years ago, the vol-
cano first erupted, sending rivers of lava to the valleys below.
The lava flows created Black Mesa, to the east of Grants, and G
Mesa, to the north of Grants and Milan, as well as miles and
miles of mesa toward Cabezón to the north and Seboyeta to the
southeast. The story of that unimaginably ancient eruption is
best told by a moving Navajo legend narrated by Emma Begay,
which goes something like this:

> For many many moons, the tall mountain puffed white
> smoke from its very top. After many many more moons,
> the mountain exploded with a monumental bang. From its
> fiery bowels spewed red hot embers, turning into black riv-
> ers cascading to the valleys below.

> After many more moons, the mountain suddenly closed
> and swallowed a beautiful Navajo maiden. The mountain
> is holding her captive in its bosom to this very day. Those
> who climb to the top can close their eyes and hear her in
> one of her many moods, sometimes laughing, sometimes
> singing, sometimes humming, sometimes whistling, some-
> times crying, and sometimes eerily silent.

Through the centuries, the mountain has provided many re-
sources to human and beast. It has been the area's primary source
of water, with its many springs radiating in all directions, allow-
ing villages to be built. It has had an abundance of wildlife, especially deer, the principal source of meat and hides for early Native
Americans. The mountain also yielded many roots and herbs,
used for cooking and medicinal purposes. It provided the large
ponderosa *vigas* for San Estevan Mission, at Acoma Sky City.
The church was started in 1629, under the direction of noted
Franciscan Fray Juan Ramírez. Today Acoma is recognized as the
oldest continuously inhabited village in the United States.

With the Spanish settlers came domesticated livestock—
horses, sheep, goats, cattle, and pigs. The mountain provided excellent summer grazing for large herds of sheep and later cattle,
which were the basis for the first commercial industry in the
land of Cíbola. Wool was nonperishable and could be transported
long distances by oxcarts to the textile plants in Mexico and
later by wagons and trucks and trains to the American mills on
the East Coast. Don José Jaramillo, who passed away in his nine-
ties, remembered the story of Eduardo Chávez, a sheepherder
from Seboyeta, taking lunch to another herder on the mountain
and running into a bear cub. The little cub cried out in fright,
and the mama bear coming up from drinking water in El Dado
Canyon attacked and mauled him. His sheepdog kept charging
and nipping at the heels of the enraged beast and cub, until they
ran away and his master was saved.

In San Mateo Nazario Sandoval, Prajeres Candelaria, and
Reymundo Barela had Forest Service grazing permits for their
cattle on Mount Taylor. Other cattlemen and sheepmen, including my father, had permits farther north, in the El Dado and Los
Indios country. The Fernandez Company had private lands on
which it ran sheep and cattle, and Mark Elkins ran cattle on his
ranch. Livestock thrived in the high country and came out fat in
the fall. Over the years logging operations brought logs out of
the mountain to mills in Grants. Stan Hayton, still living in
Grants with his Louisiana bride Jackie, whom he married sixty
years ago, says, "We logged for a mill on Mount Taylor operated

by Jim Childers. We milled the timber on the mountain and brought the lumber to the railhead and railed it east and west to help build a growing America." I remember lumber trucks coming through San Mateo with their heavy loads in the 1930s.

Recreation has also been important on the mountain. Deer and turkeys, and in recent times, elk, have provided excellent hunting. In 1984 a new and exciting race started on the slopes of the mountain—the Mount Taylor Winter Quadrathlon. It's the ultimate challenge for over six hundred athletes, who come from all over the world to bicycle, run, cross-country ski, and snowshoe to the top of the mountain and back to Grants, on President's Day weekend, in February. *Triathlete Magazine* calls the race "One of the toughest endurance races in the world."

My suggestion to competitors, when I was race director, was to pause at the top and listen for the Navajo maiden—then raise their hands to touch the hand of God!

PART SIX

Cíbola

The word Cíbola is Spanish for "female bison" (usually called "buffalo"). It's interesting to note that the buffalo never came west of the Río Grande to the area we generally consider Cíbola. As pointed out before, Professor Rubén Cobos's definition of Cíbola is "sixteenth-century Spanish name for Zuni and all the lands which later (in 1583) became known as Nueba Mexico." Most students of New Mexico history probably first saw or heard the term, as I did myself, in reference to the "Seven Cities of Cíbola." The region of Cíbola includes Cíbola County, which was split off from Valencia County in 1981, and parts of McKinley county, including Zuni Pueblo and the Zuni Mountains. And yet Professor Cobos in his definition includes all of New Mexico. The stories in this book generally conform to the narrower boundaries, and those you'll find in this concluding part deal with topics common to the whole area.

I pray you've found the stories interesting and informative. Hopefully the windows you've opened to the past by reading this book will expand your knowledge of the fascinating land of Cíbola and its even more interesting people.

Sheep

Sheep, the small animals with the golden fleece, were introduced to the Americas by the Spanish conquistadores in the sixteenth century.

Hernando Cortés brought them to Mexico from Spain in 1519, and Francisco Vásquez de Coronado to New Mexico in 1540. Sheep in fact were one important survival advantage the Spanish had over the Pilgrims who landed at Plymouth Rock almost a century later. The Spanish could walk their "groceries" with them across the arid Southwest, whereas the Pilgrims were farmers and needed a full growing season to raise crops. Fortunately for them, the friendly Indians gave them some turkeys to keep them going that first winter.

The hardy churro sheep of Spain were an important part of every expedition. They provided meat for the table and wool for the portable loom to weave into clothing and blankets. They also were given as gifts to the Indians; the Navajos, especially, quickly learned to raise them, to shear, card, spin, dye, and weave wool into rugs, and to roast the meat in an open fire or cook it to a fine stew. And the Navajos developed the craft of rug weaving into an art. Today some of the most beautiful rugs in the world are woven by Navajo women by the side of their hogan, on vertical looms. One of the best is Irene Begay. Her husband, Wilbur, worked as sheep foreman on the Peña Ranch years ago. She was an outstanding artist on the loom and still weaves occasionally in the Prewitt area.

The churro breed, with its coarse wool was followed into the Southwest by the Merino and Rambouillet breeds. They produced a finer wool fiber, which became the principal trade item with Mexico during the early colonization of New Mexico. Oxcarts carried the wool and woolen products down the Camino Real to Chihuahua and brought back spices, small luxuries, and yard goods to the colonists. With the arrival of the railroad in New Mexico in 1879, wool found a market in New England. It was sent by rail to be processed into yarn and then into cloth and bolstered sheep as New Mexico's first commercial industry.

The industry provided jobs to thousands of sheepherders in New Mexico, Arizona, and Colorado. They were the quiet, hardy man of the outdoors, with a cane in their hand, a red bandanna round their necks, a drawstring sack of Dukes Mixture or Bull Durham tobacco in their breast pocket, and a well-trained dog at their side. A good herder could easily manage up to thirteen hundred sheep. One of the best was Felipe Gutiérrez, of San Mateo. They say he could squint his eyes and see a sheep standing still a mile away. He smoked a corncob pipe and wore a straw hat the year round. His friends teased him for wearing his straw hat in the snow in the middle of winter in the Plaza in Santa Fe.

He was taken once or twice a year by Don Lizardo Salazar, his employer and compadre, to visit his three daughters at an orphanage in the state capital. Don Felipe did not mind the teasing. He was a man for all seasons. He always prefaced his comments with "friego" ("botheration"). For example, both he and his compadre Lizardo had some cows running together. One time he found one dead. As he approached very cautiously, he kept telling himself, "Friego, como sea la de mi compadre!" ("Botheration, I hope it's my campadre's!") I knew him in his golden years, when he was in his eighties. Old age took his keen eyesight but not his good humor.

He and my paternal great grandfather, Juan Ortega, who lived to over a hundred, were close friends. They were also in-laws, through the marriage of their children, Maggie Gutiérrez and Tomás Ortega. They frequently reminisced about the past. I remember sitting at a respectful distance, listening to their stories of days gone by. They talked of freighting wool by wagon trains to La Junta in the 1870s. It took three months, and sometimes they had to circle their wagons to ward off Indian attacks, and sometimes they had to tie the wagons together to ford swollen rivers along the way.

By 1900 sheep numbers in America had reached over one hundred million head. Since then the numbers have dwindled to less than fifteen million. In Cíbola County, the only sheep left are on the Navajo, Laguna, and Acoma Reservations. There are some commercial herds left in the northern part of the state and some

in the Vaughn, Roswell, and Picacho areas. Cattle, also introduced to the Americas by the Spaniards, have gradually replaced
sheep in most of the western and southwestern states. Cattlemen came mostly from Texas after the railroad came to New
Mexico. They brought barbwire, which created problems for the
sheepmen used to open range. Hollywood has produced several
movies of the struggle between cattle and sheep. On many
ranches in New Mexico, including ours, we raised both sheep
and cattle. Under proper management, the two species do better
than either alone. In other words sheep and cattle got along fine
but sheepmen and cattlemen sometimes did not! I believe the
attitude in part was brought on by the proud cowboy on a horse,
who felt superior to the sheepherder on foot. Both deserve our
respect, especially sheepherders. They came first and had the
most difficult job.

Although sheep no longer have the prominence they once
had in Cíbola County or throughout New Mexico, they are very
much a part of our economic past. They made exploration and
colonization possible and continue to produce the wool for our
beautiful and unique Navajo rugs (see Fig. 24). Up north, Tierra
Wools at Los Ojos in Río Arriba County uses churro wool to
make shawls, capes, blankets, rugs, and other substantial articles,
which they sell at their own store and also market by catalog.
The one-thousand-head herd owned by the cooperative, Ganados
del Valle, was started in the 1970s to provide employment for
people in northern New Mexico and to maintain some of the
traditions of the past.

María Varela and Antonio Manzanares, both endowed with
vision and commitment, have been the leaders of the cooperative movement. The goals of the cooperative are being met, and
to the credit of cooperative members and their leaders, an old
Hispanic way of life, based on raising sheep and weaving their
wool, is being preserved.

When Columbus discovered the Americas, in 1492, there were no horses in North, Central or South America. Paleontologists have found evidence that small horses began to develop in the Americas over fifty million years ago, and species resembling modern horses died out only about ten thousand years ago.

In 1519 Don Hernando Cortés, the Spanish conqueror of Mexico, brought the first horses ashore off the boats at Vera Cruz, on the Gulf of Mexico. He conquered Mexico with a small horse-mounted troop with metal helmets that struck terror and fear in the hearts of the Aztecs. The horses bred and multiplied in the New World. The original stock was mostly Andaluces with Arabian blood. The Fray Marcos de Niza expedition to Cíbola, in 1539, brought the first horse to New Mexico. The much larger expedition in 1540 of Francisco Vásquez de Coronado gave horses and sheep as gifts to the Indians. Quickly the indigenous people recognized the utility and value of both animals. In time they started raiding and fighting the Spanish settlements for horses and sheep. Their herds grew, and some tribes engaged in more intertribal battles with their new found mobility on horseback.

Indians of all tribes became good herders and riders of horses. Before the horse, their only form of personal transportation was walking or running. They carried their belongings from place to place either by putting them on their person or by dragging them on a travois, sometimes using dogs. Some of the most colorful riders were the Cheyennes, Comanches, and Kiowas from the plains, especially when dressed in full regalia, with feather bonnets flying while riding bareback on painted ponies at full speed—an image Hollywood loves to exaggerate.

The horse made it possible to spend less time hunting for food and more time to fight each other and also harass the Spanish colonists encroaching on their hunting grounds. The Indians were willing to share their lands, but not to abandon them to ownership or exclusive claim. That was a European concept, very foreign to Native Americans philosophy. Even later, when In-

dian reservations were created, the tribes held the land in common. For better or for worse, that is still the case today.

The Navajo had a special love and respect for the horse. The nomadic way of the Navajo kept them on the move. The stamina bred into the Navajo horse through the years was incredible. Their horses were small and wiry and could walk or trot quietly at a fast gait all day. We called them *charravantes* or *charras*. I recall as a young boy riding a charra northwest into the Navajo country alongside Antonio Sandoval, a Navajo, to look for sheepherders and trade sheep pelts for candy and tobacco at Borrego Pass Trading Post.

The Spanish rider's dress and tack have become the dress and tack of the present-day cowboy. The saddle with a horn to pull or restrain anything roped with a lariat is most useful. The stirrups are narrow, to keep the pointed boot from slipping through. The high top of the boot itself was designed for riding through brush, avoiding snakebites and providing a fast slip out for a rider's foot if it became caught in a stirrup. It is also attractive even when the rider is not on a horse. The tight-fitting, narrow-legged pant and form-fitting shirt were also designed to avoid getting caught in brush and to minimize wind resistance. Only one improvement has been made to the shirt through the years—the metal snap button. And a handy zipper has been added to the pants. The wide-legged *chaparreras*, or chaps, also protected the rider's legs from brush, as well as keeping your legs warm in winter and dry in snow or rain.

The wide-brimmed hat, later expanded into a ten-gallon version, protects the head and face from sun, cold, and wind. The bandanna around the neck and the spurs on the heels complete the impressive picture of the cowboy. Every bit of the dress was handed down to us by those intrepid men of Spain. Those were the bold men who dared to cross uncharted oceans and plod across unknown deserts with a few horses, a few sheep, and a handy rosary to found and colonize a new world.

The *burro* is one of the hardiest and certainly one of the most stubborn animals ever domesticated by man. There is just not much one can do when a burro balks and refuses to move. Some say the only answer is a two by four!

Burros played a most important role in the settlement of Cíbola and the rest of west-central New Mexico. Compared to a horse they are smaller, but pound for pound they are stronger. Spanish explorers used them as pack animals. Later the colonists also used them as mounts. Miners and prospectors used them throughout the West and called them donkeys. Burros have been maligned in many sayings: "Eres un burro. Los burros no se acaban" ("You're a jackass and there's no end to jackasses"). "¡Aquí me dejaron teniéndole la jeta al burro!" ("They left me here holding the lip of this ass!") This latter saying is due to the fact that one can, without a rope, cup the lower lip in the palm of one's hand and keep a burro in place for quite a while.

The sheep industry thrived in Cíbola County, in large part because of the burro. Herds of sheep of about a thousand head, herded by one man and assisted by a camptender, could travel a long way to fresh grazing because of burros (see Fig. 25). Generally four burros carried the camp, and they also brought the water every other day, in two 5-gallon barrels, often from long distances, to sustain the herders. Burros could go two days without drinking water. At night they were restrained by cowhide hobbles, and they seldom drifted more than a quarter of a mile from camp. All had names. The one I remember best was El Largo.

He was a stud burro (jack), with a great deal of spirit and a very good gait. He was an average-size burro but also wiry and strong. El Largo was black, with a jet black mane and tail and a lighter grey on his underside. I rode him bareback when I was the camptender with the sheep camps on the north side of Mount Taylor, in the early 1940s. My only problem was that he somehow knew when the *burras* (jennies) of Mi Tío Mariano Ortega were in heat. He sometimes traveled 2 to 3 miles in hobbles during the night to get to one of them. Then I would spend most of the day bringing him back and trying to do my job. One time when my father brought provisions to us, I told him of the problems we were having, and he suggested I find someone in the other camps that knew how to castrate a burro and have him "cut."

Francisco Candelaria, better known as Don Jico, hailed from San Rafael and was herding for Román Sandoval. He told me, "Bring him Sunday, and I'll cut him." The word passed on to the other herds that we were cutting El Largo. When I arrived at Don Jico's, there were several other camptenders there to lend a hand, Jose Gutiérrez, José Largo hijo, a young Navajo, from Haystack, and Eutimio Chávez, from Seboyeta. With ropes and skill we tied down the burro, and Don Jico in fine humor and moving fast on his crippled leg, castrated him. In the tradition of castrating horses, he threw the testicles toward the front, beyond his head, "so he'll run fast." After a lunch of *costillas,* chile, breles, *arroz con pasas,* and friendly talk, I mounted El Largo and started back to our camp. Don Jico said, "Just walk him, don't push him too hard. He'll be alright—he should stay home from now on!" The others added their best wishes also, saying, "your problems are over!"

I rode off whistling, convinced that his meandering days were over. How wrong I was. That night, in spite of his soreness, he hobbled about two miles to the jennies of Mi Tío Mariano. It took him about two weeks to settle down and begin to forget his past!

The sheep herds of four San Mateo sheepmen grazed the U.S. Forest Service permits in common, and some of their camptenders had been a part of the "famous cutting" of El Largo. Each permittee had a more or less defined area he grazed by mutual agreement. Mi Tío Mariano grazed the Tanke de Frésquez country. Mi Primo Román Sandoval Los Cerros de Alejandro, Mi Primo Nabor Márquez Los Cerros de Guadalupe, and Pablo Peña, my father, El Dado and El Cañon de Los Indios. There were seldom any problems except droughts, water shortages, and an occasional coyote. Along with the sheep permits there were several cattle permits grazing the same land. Don Serafín, his son

Luis Jaramillo, and Crescencio López, from Moquino; Merhage Michael and Plácido Mirabal, from San Mateo; and the brothers Rafael and Max Márquez and the brothers Mariano and Enrique Lucero, from Marquez, all had cattle permits.

After the Second World War, herders were hard to find, and we fenced our ranches with woven wire and turned the sheep loose like cattle. The need for burros was over, and most of them were sent to market. Some wound up at dude ranches and others went to dog meat plants. It sounds cruel to send them away for dog food, but a burro eats about the same amount of grass as a cow. A cow raises a calf that brings 85 cents a pound, whereas a burro brings only about 10 cents a pound. Ranching like all other businesses must show a profit to stay in operation. Some years there's enough profit to pay off the bank loans, some years there's only a small profit, but other years there's no profit at all. The family ranch remains a way of life tempered with a lot of hard work, faith, and hope.

On our ranch, as on most of the other commercial sheep ranches in Cíbola County, most of the "retired" burros were turned loose and pastured till they died. The unbroken ones went to market. Another chapter in the history of Cíbola and western New Mexico had come to an end.

Vaqueros

The word *vaquero* (cowboy) comes from the Spanish word *vaca* (cow). Someone who takes care of a number of cows is a vaquero. Hollywood and writers of the dime novel western romanticized the cowboy. That tall, lean, straight-as-an-arrow fellow who's more at home in the saddle than on the street (see Fig. 26). Quite naturally the John Wayne image usually comes to mind when we think of cowboys. He righted what was wrong and was physically and mentally strong—and always a gentleman to the ladies. The legendary Elfego Baca, sheriff of Socorro County, was cut from that same mold.

At the other end of the spectrum was Billy the Kid. His pictures show him as a gangling youth. It is said he had twenty-one notches on his gun by the age of twenty-one, when he was gunned down by Sheriff Pat Garrett at Fort Sumner. However, there are some folks in the Ramah country who believe Garrett shot the wrong man in that dark bedroom, and that Billy the Kid, after picking up a lady in the Las Vegas country, ran for cover to remote Quemado and later the Ramah country, in northwestern New Mexico. He changed his name from William Bonney to John Miller, they say, and adopted a young Navajo and named him Max Miller (see his story, p. 160–162).

One of the most impressive cowboys I ever knew was Salvador Chávez, of San Mateo. He was of medium height and lanky. He sat very easy on his horse. He wore a red bandanna around his neck and well-worn chaps around his legs. He was never boisterous. He had an inner strength that was obvious without demonstration. Salvador had many talents, among them those of a poet, a writer, and a composer. He wrote *corridos*, "ballads," of the cowboy and his life. Probably his best known is "El Rincón de Marcos."

Mi casa es de rama,
No tiene zotea,
Cuando no cae agua,
Pues no se gotea.

Tengo en un sabino
Mi puela colgada,
Porque los ratones
La usan de guitarra.

Cuando me acuesto
Rendido y cansado,
Bajo mi salea
Oigo estar tocando.

Tal vez hacen bailes
Seguido con ella,
Porque entre la arina

Se mira la huella.

Las víboras pasan,
Casi galopeando,
En mi cabecera,
Bailan sus fandangos.

Tambien los coyotes
Que son mis vecinos,
Que bonitas polcas
Tocan en las noches,

Bailan cuadrillas,
Polcas y chotes
También los zorrillos
Valsan al trote.

("My house is of brush,
It has no roof,
As long as it doesn't rain,
Well, it doesn't leak.

I have a juniper tree,
Where my frying pan hangs,
Because the mice
Use it for a guitar.

When I lie down,
Worn-out and tired,
Under my sheepskin
I hear them playing

They often hold dances
With it,
Because in the flour,
You can see their tracks.

Rattlers come by,
Almost galloping,
At the head of my bed
They dance their fandangos.

The coyotes as well,
Who are my neighbors,
What beautiful polkas
They play at night.

They dance polkas,
Squares, and schottisches,
And even the skunks
Waltz by at a trot.")

Salvador's wife, Isabel, is a fascinating lady in her own right. She is now in her eighties and as vibrant as ever. Some years ago she watched the Fourth of July parade in Grants, dressed in bright Spanish colors. She was enjoying the parade and told me, "I haven't missed one since they started." She and Salvador had three sons, who were raised in San Mateo. The memory of Salvador Chávez lives on through his family and through his music.

Another cowboy I remember is Antonio Sandoval, from the Borrego Pass country. We knew him as "El Antonio." He spoke three languages fluently—Navajo, Spanish, and English. He could break a horse to the saddle and give you a good working horse. He could also track a man, a cow, or a sheep for miles. He was the caporal on the Peña Ranch and managed people with sensitivity and respect. His horse never winded; he could pace his mount to ride all day and get the job done—except for one time, in the early 1940s. My father sent him from the ranch to San Mateo, about eighteen miles away, to bring three horses he had purchased. After Antonio found the semiwild horses, he went into the village to visit with friends, of which he had made many over the years. While visiting he was "given" a pint of whiskey; Indians were not allowed to buy liquor until 1947.

He started back after a swig or two. He said, "Along the way the darned horses wanted to turn back to their grazing lands and I was having trouble keeping them on the trail. After a while I decided it was time for another swig. When I uncapped the bottle, the horses bolted into the piñones and I took off after them and accidentally dropped the cap in the brush. With uncapped bottle in hand and at full run, I had to make a decision. Either throw away the bottle to maintain control of the horses, or drink it all and save the liquor! I decided to drink it all, and you guessed it! I lost the horses and lost my senses, but thank God the trusty old buckskin brought me home."

Snakes

"Speaking of snakes," said Celito Jaramillo, "Don Gabriel Romero was bitten by a rattlesnake in the right hand! He recovered, but his index finger remained stiff for the rest of his life." He had been gathering firewood for the sheep camp, and the rattler bit him as he reached down for a piece of wood. Don Gabriel lived in San Mateo and used to warn us, "Chiquitos, tengan mucho cuidao con las víboras!" ("Boys, be very careful with rattlesnakes!")

The people of Cíbola County, beginning with the Native Americans and followed by the Spanish and later the Anglos and others, have learned to live side by side with rattlers and other snakes. The rattler is the most feared and most respected of snakes in west-central New Mexico. There's no question that snakes draw almost everyone's attention, and that most everyone fears snakes. Those of us who were raised in the country instinctively reach for a stick or a rock the moment we see one. Still, in fairness to snakes, most of them are harmless and even beneficial, including the rattlesnake. They're all carnivorous and help to keep the rodent population in balance.

There are over twenty-five hundred species of snakes in the world, but in the Grants area there are only rattlesnakes, which are poisonous, and bull snakes, garter snakes, and water snakes, which are nonpoisonous. In Spanish we generally call the poisonous rattler *víbora* and the nonpoisonous snakes *culebras*. The rattler has a series of loosely attached horny segments at the end of the tail that can be vibrated to produce a rattling or buzzing sound. Once you've heard the rattle, you never forget it. Some people say they have nightmares about them. The prairie rattlers, average about 30 inches in length and an inch in diam-

eter. They are light grey in color, with patterned diamonds on
their backs.

There are also some monstrous rattlers in the area. They seem to be concentrated south of Interstate 40, between Zuni Canyon and Bluewater Canyon. These gigantic snakes are something of a mystery, since they seem to have appeared suddenly in the area. They measure up to 6 feet in length and are about 3 inches in diameter, with a reddish tinge to them. In 1985 Royal Hopper, a rancher near the village of Bluewater, drove into town with one of the big ones in the bed of his pickup. It measured 6 feet long and was bigger around than his arm above the elbow. None of us had seen anything like it before, and several of us were born and raised in the area. One question kept going through our minds: Where did these giant serpents come from?

Clifford Young, born in Bluewater in 1910, remembers seeing a big snake when he was fifteen years old. "It stretched across the road from one wagon wheel track to the other. A few years later we were driving a small herd of cattle to Baca, and we ran into a big one, about 6 feet long in some brush and tall weeds."

Jack Farley, a retired miner who catches rattlers for sport and for sale says, "I don't know their history, but I keep thinking these large coontail rattlesnakes escaped from one of the Snake Gardens on Route 66 near Bluewater and multiplied through the years. I killed one near Bluewater Creek that was 5 feet 8 inches long and weighed 12 pounds after we skinned it. Then we barbecued it and ate it. It was darned good!" adding, "Do you know that they're served as a delicacy in gourmet restaurants, at very high prices?"

Jack Freas remembers hearing of eight-year-old Ruby Chapman, from Bluewater, who was bitten by a rattler in a garden in the village and taken by her mother to the Thigpen campground and store on Route 66, where she died, around 1930. She was a sister of Roy Chapman.

In 1968 four-year-old Wayne, son of Joe and Pauline Gallegos of Grants, was bitten on his upper lip, just below the nose. He was playing in the arroyo near the cemetery, and when he peeked over the bank of the arroyo, a startled rattler bit him. According to his mother, Pauline, "What saved our son was his father taking him immediately to the hospital. Dr. Gutiérrez went to work on him, and there was some concern that the bite so near the brain might seriously affect Wayne. His head swelled enormously, and he was very sick. He recovered completely and our four-year-old boy is now a perfectly healthy man in his thirties. Thanks to God and lots of prayers of family and friends, thanks to Dr. Gilbert Gutiérrez, and thanks to Cíbola General Hospital!"

I had an experience with a rattler when the horse I was riding was bitten by one. In the late 1960s we were moving cattle through some high *chamizo* and tall weeds near the ranch headquarters. I was riding Goldie, a spirited palomino, born and raised on the ranch. On a fast turn, I heard and saw the rattler rise and strike Goldie on the knee. The horse immediately started limping and sweating. I got off him, but the swelling was really puffing up. He could hardly walk and was perspiring severely. He was in great pain. Two fang marks were outlined by drops of blood. I walked him slowly and got him to the corrals nearby. There I unsaddled him, took out my pocket knife, and bled him. The severe swelling had spread to his chest. I made two cuts, one on each fang mark, the way we had been taught by our elders. The horse survived, but it took about three weeks before we could use him again.

At the sheep camps we heard stories about *mamonas* (suckers), snakes that supposedly wrapped themselves around the hind legs of a cow or sheep and suck her udder dry. Then there was the story of *chicoteras* (whippers) that whipped you if you got close to them.

Snakes have always been a part of our lives in Cíbola, and we've learned that, like other wild animals, they want to get away from people as fast as possible. However, when rattlers are startled, they strike at random, and their bite can be very painful and sometimes fatal. Nevertheless, if we give them room to get away, we can coexist with them.

Ambrosio Lake

The Ambrosio Lake area in western New Mexico, twenty-five miles north of Grants, produced more uranium from 1950 to 1980 than any other place in the world. There is ample evidence that dinosaurs ranged the area in prehistoric times, when uranium was possibly laid down. There is also evidence that an inland sea covered the region, as seen in the marine shells and skeletons imprinted on sandstone found in the area. Uranium miners tell of finding large bones—one can be seen at the Mining Museum in Grants, and large dinosaur footprints have been found 635 feet underground, at the Ann Lee Mine. Also discovered nearby—at the same depth, was a forest of crisscrossed tree trunks in a semipetrified state. Erosion and upheavals through millions of years have gradually covered a most interesting distant past—but there is an equally interesting recent past.

From A.D. 750 to A.D. 1250, the Anasazi, forbears of Pueblo Indians, had outlying settlements in the Ambrosio Lake region that provided food and support for Chaco Canyon. When the Anasazi mysteriously abandoned Chaco Canyon, the Navajos gradually moved into the area and settled the whole northwest of New Mexico and Arizona—more or less the same country they inhabit today.

About 1870 Don Ambrosio Trujillo, from nearby San Mateo, homesteaded a section of land in the Ambrosio Lake basin. With ingenuity, a team of horses, and a scraper, he built a low but long dike at the west end of a natural clay bed. It filled with water from run-off during the summer rains and sometimes from snowmelt in the spring, and a lake was born! Through the years tens of thousands of sheep watered there, until the lake disappeared in the dust-bowl years of the 1930s. Everyone knew it as La Laguna de Ambrosio. I remember as a little boy going there with my father, Pablo Peña, and seeing what looked like a vast expanse of water to me. It probably actually covered 2 or 3 acres and had cattails along the southern perimeter. It was a sparkling and beautiful oasis, providing water for humans, livestock, and wildlife.

At the time Don Ambrosio died, the family had a second home in San Mateo, so they sold the old homestead to Don Francisco Sarracino, from Seboyeta. The number of sheep in the area increased rapidly. The Navajos had learned sheepherding from the Spanish, who introduced sheep to the Americas. They and other Indian tribes started building their original herds from gifts and strays of the Coronado expedition in 1540. It has remained a very important activity and even a way of life for the Navajo people, providing mutton, their favorite meat, and wool to spin and weave their colorful and unique Navajo blankets and rugs.

After Don Francisco died, his enterprising wife, Doña Francisquita, managed the enterprise with a firm and knowing hand. My mother, Pablita, remembered her as a very elegant and devout lady, who attended mass every Sunday in Seboyeta until she died.

In the 1860s other homesteaders and sheepmen moved into the area. Among them was Col. Manuel Chávez, of Civil War fame, who built the original ranch house that is now the Floyd Lee home on the Fernandez Ranch, near San Mateo. Nearby at El Rito, his half-brother Don Román Baca built a vast empire of land and sheep. Farther down the draw, at Puertecito, Don Procopio Sandoval established a homestead with a stone house still partially standing today. Still farther down, by Piedra Parada, a homestead was acquired by Don Rudolfo Otero, of San Rafael. He befriended travelers on their way to Grants from San Mateo and left many memorable and humorous sayings, among them, "San Mateo gente, buena gente, son-a-baganes, me robaron mis vacas!" San Mateo people, good people, son-of-a-guns, they stole my cattle! To the north my grandfather, Abelicio Peña bought section 9 and later purchased a township of land from the Santa Fe Pacific Railroad. About that time many sheepmen started adding more cattle to their ranches, and the cattle roamed north to Chaco Canyon before fences appeared. Many of those cattle, along with thousands of sheep, watered at Ambrosio Lake.

With the advent of the railroad came more cattle, barbwire, and windmills, and sheep begin to give way to this new enterprise. Anglo homesteaders also began to arrive, among them

Oscar Carter, who homesteaded section 30, in the middle of the Ambrosio plain. Later this land turned out to contain one of the richest deposits of uranium in the area. Mr. Carter, among other things, was a windmiller. He drilled the first water well and built a wooden windmill tower that rose like a sentinel over the vast plain. I remember in the 1940s stopping to water my horse and drink cool water at "El Rancho del Carter," directly from the flowing pipe.

Other families followed. The Thomases, the Boatmans, and the Berryhills to the west, and the Rooks. Old Man Rook had a taste for life. They say he had a very efficient still in his cellar and bootlegged the spirits, high-quality moonshine, during the infamous Prohibition era. Stella Dysart, the flamboyant grand-daughter of a Missouri Presbyterian minister, arrived on the scene in the late 1920s, drilling for oil on the Ambrosio Lake dome. She never struck oil, but she later made a fortune in ura-nium found in the cuttings of holes drilled years before; she developed them into the appropriately named Rio de Oro, River of Gold, mine. I recall meeting this colorful lady in 1960, in her sumptuous office on the top floor of the Bank of New Mexico, in Albuquerque. On her desk was a well-worn Bible. When I was ready to take my leave, she slowly came around the desk to see me out. She put her hand on the Bible and said, "My favorite is Psalm 23" and graciously escorted me to the door.

Following Paddy Martinez's discovery of uranium, in the early 1950s, prospectors and speculators came in droves in search of the metal. They heard or thought they heard *ambrosia*, the nectar of the gods. The sheer numbers of newcomers using this name overwhelmed the original name, Ambrosio. When a branch of the Grants Post Office located there in 1961, it was named Ambrosio Lake Station, but eventually the contract post office also succumbed to the new name of Ambrosia Lake.

Today the Ambrosio Lake basin is like a graveyard. Some of the A-frames still stand, like giants on a march across the plain, slowly rusting in the sun. They mark the spots where thousands of bold men went down into the bowels of the earth to extract the valuable ore, deposited millions of years ago.

If one listens closely, the quiet of the plain is sometimes broken by the noise of bulldozers covering up tailings. Or by occasional pickups and welding trucks carrying torches to dismantle the A-frames. As the reclamation work continues and the scars are erased, retired miners look across the plain and say with nostalgia, "It's all over."

The Lebanese in Cíbola

With the coming of the railroad to Cíbola, in 1882, people started coming from points east and south to join the Native Americans and Hispanics who were already here. Among others were four immigrant families from Lebanon, in the distant Middle East.

They came to the United States seeking freedom from the political unrest and violence in the region. Moslem Turks had ruled the region for centuries and had imposed restrictions and special taxes, especially on the various Catholic minority groups. And there were struggles among Christian and Moslem Lebanese themselves. But Lebanese Christians also came seeking economic opportunity. They came through Ellis Island, in New York, the historic island that processed hundreds of thousands of immigrants from the Old World around the turn of the century. It sits in the shadows of the colossal Statue of Liberty, engraved with the immortal words of Emma Lazarus:

Give me your tired, your poor,
Your huddled masses, yearning to breathe free,
The wretched refuse of your teeming shore.
Send these, the homeless, tempest-tost to me,
I lift my lamp beside the golden door!

Senator Joe Fidel, the son of one of those families, says, "The word got to Lebanon that there was freedom and opportunity in America, and they came." Elias Francis, Merhage Michael, Abdoo Fidel, and Joseph Hanosh all made their way across the United

States, seeking a place to settle down. Senator Fidel adds, "In Lebanon they lived in mountainous and hilly country, so they sought and found mountains and hilly country in New Mexico." Because of their traditional background in trade and commerce in the Mediterranean, even before the time of Christ, they instinctively started selling and trading goods in their new country. They were known as wagon vendors, selling or trading their merchandise from the back of a wagon.

The first to start a store in Cíbola County was Elias Francis (Abu Hasan). As a result of his vending travels west from the Río Grande, he chose Seboyeta in which to build a store and a home. He then went back to Lebanon to bring his wife and infant son. As his business grew, he expanded into farming and sheep ranching; he employed Abdoo Fidel to help and later sent for Joseph Hanosh and his sister, Fifi, as housekeeper. They were on the same boat that brought Mr. Merhage Michael, who had also gone back to the old country to bring his wife, Tameme, and young son Mike, who was then eleven months old.

Don Francisco, as the Spanish called Elias Francis, was a strong-willed man, and many stories are told about him. They say he liked to "tip the bottle" at times and would climb to the attic and refused to eat or come down. After he had spent a couple of days up there one time, his wife called my grandfather Fermín Márquez, a neighbor and good friend of the Francises, to see if he could convince him to come down. Grandfather Fermín started climbing the stairs, talking to Elias as he slowly ascended. As he reached the top, a shot rang out, and he came tumbling down! Unhurt but shaken, he shouted, "Leave him alone. He'll get hungry sooner or later and come down on his own." A day later he did, and life continued its usual pace.

Elias's son Narciso married Filomena Michael, daughter of Rachid, a brother of Merhage Michael. They had two sons and seven daughters. Narciso managed the business and also served as a state representative for several terms from Valencia County. The oldest son, E. Lee Francis, married Ethel Gottlieb, the daughter of Agnes and Sydney Gottlieb, of Cubero. E. Lee (Elias), as his Hispanic friends called him, served as lieutenant governor of New Mexico for two terms in the 1960s and is now retired in Albuquerque.

Mr. Merhage Michael (actually Merhage Merhage) began his circuit in Lemitar, north of Socorro, and traveled in his wagon vending up along the Río Grande and west to the villages around Mount Taylor. After several trips he chose San Mateo in which to settle and purchased a store from Abelicio Peña, my grandfather. He also expanded into farming and cattle ranching. He and his wife raised five boys and six girls. We were raised together in San Mateo. They spoke Arabic and Spanish and later learned English, as we all did when we started school. The Michaels were our neighbors, and we were close friends. In the 1940s they opened a second store, in Grants, and Mike, now deceased, managed it. Mike married Josephine Barela, and they had two sons. Toby (Tobias), the oldest, is a lawyer and served several terms in the legislature, while Bobby, the youngest, is a soils specialist and works for the Soil Conservation Service.

Another son of Merhage and Tameme was Azize, also now deceased. When he returned from World War II, he married the late Pauline Hanosh, from Bibo, the daughter of José Hanosh, and together they ran a store until he died. Pauline continued to run the store after his death and added Don José's Cocina, a popular restaurant that has attracted customers and publicity from around the area and even the state. The restaurant is located in the original home where all the Hanosh children were born.

The third son of the Michaels, Albert, now deceased, served as mayor of Grants in the 1960s and was co-owner of Michael's Store with his younger brother, Merhage, and their sister-in-law Josephine Michael. Merhage served as a county commissioner. Ernest, the youngest, still farms in San Mateo in the family home, with his wife Mary Martínez Michael.

Mr. Abdoo Fidel (Abdoo Habeeb) tried doing business in the southern United States, where he had an aunt, but did not like the climate and wound up in New Mexico, as an employee of Don Elias Francis. About 1914 he and Lee Hanosh, a brother of José's, started a store in San Fidel, and when the First World War

was over, he sent for Mrs. Fidel, José's sister. She arrived in 1921.
They built a successful business on Route 66 and raised two
boys and one girl, Joe, A. H., and Mary. Joe married Dora Baca,
and they built a successful insurance and real estate business in
Grants. He served on the city council, on the school board, as
county assessor, and currently serves as state senator. A. H.
(Abdoo Habeeb, Jr.) married Irene Baca, Dora's sister. He's now
retired from the grocery business. Mary Fidel is an officer of the
Grants State Bank.

Mr. Fidel embraced his adopted country with all his might.
He never wanted to go back to the "old country" or even visit.
He was an extroverted and exciting man and made many friends
among some of the top political leaders of our state and country.
Senator Joe Fidel says, "One of my father's biggest kicks was
meeting President Dwight Eisenhower in Gallup on a campaign
trip in 1952!" His son also reports that his father "on several
occasions hosted U.S. Senator Dennis Chávez, a favorite, and
Governor Clyde Tingley in San Fidel, when they wanted to get
away from it all."

Joseph Hanosh came to work for Elias Francis, and after he
learned the business, started a store in Seboyetita, now Bibo,
where Pauline, one of the daughters, ran the store and restaurant until she passed away. Her family continues to run the business. The Hanoshes had four sons and two daughters. They, like
all the other Lebanese, learned to speak Spanish fluently. George,
their oldest son, started a Ford dealership in Grants in 1941 and
switched to Chevrolets in 1950. Today George Hanosh, Jr. in
company with his uncle Jimmy, operates Hanosh Motors, a
Chevrolet, Buick, Chrysler, and Plymouth dealership.

In an interview I asked Senator Fidel, Jimmy Hanosh, and
Pauline Hanosh Michael if they considered the decision made
by their parents to come to the United States a good one. In a
resounding voice they all said "yes." I'm certain they were also
speaking for the dozens of others in these four families not mentioned here, who have played equally important roles in the social and economic development of Cíbola County.

Rooster Pull

The *gallo*, a live rooster, was buried to his neck in the middle of the street. Horseman, one at a time, made passes at him from about 30 yards, attempting to grab his head and pull him out while running at full speed. The feisty rooster nervously kept jerking and bobbing his head. It was a tough target to grab.

Eventually someone grabbed him and while on the run, tried to turn him and grasp him by the legs, to use the bird like a club when other riders came at him, trying to take it away. If the rider didn't turn him and instead swung it with the head, he'd yank the head off and someone else would grab the body and use it in turn to protect himself from the onslaught, while trying to reach a designated area. I never saw a rider reach the designated area before the rooster was torn apart. When it was over every rider was bloody, messy, and feathered.

Where did this barbaric sport come from? Well, let's go back to the colonization of the Southwest. Roosters and horses, both central to the Rooster Pull, were introduced to New Mexico by the Spanish colonists, in the sixteenth century. The custom is believed to have been introduced to Spain by the Moors, from Morocco, about A.D. 800, when they invaded Spain. They occupied a large part of the country for seven hundred years. These Arabs were fanciers of fine Arabian horses and were excellent horseman. For entertainment and to test their horsemanship skills, among other games they ran the *Corrido del Gallo*, or Rooster Pull. It became a southern Spanish custom and came to Cíbola with the settlers.

In the village of San Mateo, preparations for the Rooster Pull on June 24, St. John's Feast Day, started in late May. The men would feed their horses a little extra grain and practice short bursts of speed with quick starts. The feasts of Santa Ana, on July 26, and San Mateo, on September 19, were also occasions on which the Corrida del Gallo was generally run. An experienced rooster puller lengthened his left or right stirrup, depending on his preferred side, in order to reach the small, moving rooster head while on the run. The very good ones could sweep

the ground with the palm of their hand while holding on to the
saddle horn, látigos (leather strings holding the saddle together),
or mane with the other hand. The best ones were usually tall
and lanky, with long arms and legs.

From Mesa Redonda, Haystack, some fifteen miles away, came
Paddy Martinez and several of his clan. They were pretty tall.
Paddy in his prime was about 6 feet tall, and his brothers were
no shorter. They arrived mighty thirsty, looking for friends and
drinks, both of which they soon found. Mass was over by noon,
and by one in the afternoon, horsemen started gathering in the
center of the village, in front of El Portalito. Generally a bottle
or two circulated among the riders, as they prepared to make
their runs. Among the horseman were Marcelino Jaramillo, Ray-
mundo Barela, Salvador Apodaca, Tomás Ortega, Vidal Laure,
Plácido Mirabal, Telesfor and Alcario Gonzales, Azize Michael,
Abelicio Peña, Prajeres Candelaria, Ismael Salazar, and Carlos
and Procopio Sandoval. The envy of all was the six-footer Ricardo Salazar, who built a reputation as the best in his day.

About 1942 we ran the last of the Corridas del Gallo in San
Mateo. As far as I can recall, some of the last riders were my
age, among them were Sifredo Sandoval, Pedro Barela, Refugio
Jaramillo, Román Márquez, Albert Michael and his brother
Merhage Michael, Jr., Ben Apodaca, Bennie Sandoval, Reynaldo
Mirabal, Herminio Jaramillo, Tony Ortega, and myself, among
others. Celito Jaramillo says, "It was a dangerous sport. You could
fall off your horse on the run or get trampled by horseman fighting for the rooster."

The custom disappeared in most Hispanic villages by the end
of World War II. Alex Gonzales says they ran the Corrida del
Gallo in Cubero in the 1950s, but instead of burying the rooster,
they tied him on a line and made a run at him. "But I remember
when I was a young boy, Teodoro Arvizo pulled the buried rooster
from the middle of the street and ran for it. It was a mess!" In
some of the Indian pueblos, the custom, learned from the Spanish, continues to this day. In the Pueblo of Zia, they celebrate a
Rooster Pull on San Pedro's feast day. In neighboring Acoma,
they usually have a Rooster Pull on San Estevan's feast day.

There has been concern among animal rights groups about the barbarity of the sport, and demonstrations have been held objecting to the practice. The All Indian Pueblo Council considered the objections and decided that each pueblo should decide for itself whether to abolish the sport or continue to "correr el gallo" as part of their tradition. I believe it's only a matter of time before it disappears altogether.

Barbwire

Barbwire fences. Were they a blessing or a curse? The Spanish explorer Francisco Vásquez de Coronado brought the first sheep to New Mexico in 1540. That started the sheep industry, which flourished on the open range, without fences, for over 350 years. Spanish settlers grazed their herds of sheep and transported their wool and wool products on oxcarts down the Camino Real to markets in Mexico. The meat was consumed locally. Sheep production was the first commercial activity in New Mexico. Our Indian friends learned the husbandry of sheep from the immigrants, and they began to build up their herds also. They learned the art of weaving wool and liked mutton, soon their favorite meat. They also grazed the open range with few problems. Their herds were usually smaller and were tended by members of the family.

After New Mexico became a territory of the United States, in 1846, land surveys were started. In Cibola County the first surveys were made in the 1860s. They were important in the development of an east-west route for a railroad and also in the legal description of lands for tax rolls. The railroad was deeded every other section, one square mile of land, by the government, for a distance of 20 miles in each direction from the roadbed.

Barbwire was invented in 1873. It made its appearance in New Mexico with the coming of the railroad, in 1879 to Las Vegas, and to Grants in 1882. The wire was very heavy and came in rolls in railroad cars. As large cattle herds began to make an appearance, fences were erected to restrict the grazing of sheep. The fences were usually built on section lines. Most of them consisted of four strands of barbwire stapled on *sabina* (juniper) posts about 24 feet apart. Some of those fences built in the 1920s are still standing today.

In the Las Vegas area, fences built during the day were torn down at night by hooded night riders who called themselves Gorras Blancas ("White Hoods") and formed a secret society. There were three Herrera brothers, led by Carlos, who were generally known as the leaders. They had worked in a neighboring state and learned their organizational skills from the Knights of Labor, a labor union. Their goal was to discourage the Anglo cattlemen from fencing the area and putting an end to the centuries-old tradition of sheep herding on the open range. Hollywood has made some exaggerated but dramatic movies on the subject.

In those territorial days, there was an effort to have New Mexico join the Union. According to political observers, eastern congressmen were hearing complaints about the Gorras Blancas, among other things, and didn't trust the loyalty of Hispanic New Mexicans. Congress kept voting down requests for statehood. By 1900 the Gorras Blancas finally put away their hoods, and by 1912 New Mexico was admitted. Hispanics have fought and died bravely for their country in several wars since then and have proven their loyalty by earning more Congressional Medals of Honor than any other minority group in the United States.

By 1940 most of the open range was fenced, and sheep numbers kept declining. Some sheep remained, but now they had to stay fenced in. Homesteaders with one section of land or less had to sell out, since their sheep could no longer roam the open range. Cattle numbers increased, as more and more windmills, the sentinels of the western range, were drilled in areas away from the mountains, where water was scarce.

There was respect for fences, and gates were left unlocked, but during World War II sheepherders were hard to find, and ranchers begin to padlock their gates to protect their livestock. In Cíbola and McKinley Counties, most of the gates were left unlocked until uranium was discovered in the 1950s. Prospectors by the dozens, especially in the Ambrosio Lake area, began to leave gates open, and livestock were going astray. Ranchers were having a difficult time keeping their stock separated by class and grade. Finally we were forced to padlock our gates.

Some sheepmen put woven wire over the barbwire and continued to run sheep in combination with cattle for a while. Eventually it was coyotes that forced the sheepmen out of business. Contrary to popular belief, sheep and cattle, under proper management, get along fine. However, cattlemen and sheepmen sometimes do not. Some ranches had public sections mixed in with private ones. I recall the case of a prospector who took a bulldozer and simply piled up a ramp over the fence, to get to some claims in the Ambrosio Lake area. The rancher put up a sign, "Trespassers will be prosecuted or shot!"

All of that is history now. The Ambrosio plain is now quiet, except for the occasional roar of machinery covering up the scars and reclaiming the land, after thirty-five years of feverish uranium activity. In the end we must ask the question: Were fences a blessing or a curse? I believe that for sheepmen they were a curse, and for cattlemen a blessing. Today the Peña Ranch is stocked with cattle, but we'll never forget that it was built by sheep.

Windmills

"Palo, paparote Nastacio ta querrado" was the cryptic Spanish message scribbled with almagre on the side of the steel storage tank next to the windmill. The message was left by Virginio Alonzo, a Navajo sheepherder at La Lagrimilla Ranch, east of Seboyeta, informing Pablo that Anastacio's windmill was broken. In those days most Indian men of all tribes in the land of Cíbola spoke Spanish, especially the older ones.

It was 1939 and my father, Pablo Peña, had leased the ranch from his brother-in-law, Anastacio Márquez. It was the month of April, and Virginio was afraid he'd run out of water for the sheep under his care. He was watering a thousand ewes bred to drop in May, and each one drank about two gallons a day. Every day the windmill had to pump 2,000 gallons of the precious liq- uid from the bowels of the earth to water the sheep. In May when the sheep started lambing, the wind quit blowing, and the windmill stopped pumping water. My father hired Carasolo Molina, from nearby Piedra Lumbre, to pump water.

Every morning Carasolo, a large man weighing in at close to 300 pounds, drove up to the windmill, jacked up the rear end of his old Model T car, and removed one wheel. He then placed a long belt from the wheel to the pumpjack on the well, disconnected the mill, and started his car in neutral. When he shifted into low gear and slowly released the clutch, water started flowing. When the storage tank was full, he disconnected the belt, hooked up the windmill again, and drove away in a cloud of dust. With luck the wind would blow during the night and keep the tank full. If it didn't, dependable Carasolo assisted the wind with his trusty Model T Ford and a pumpjack.

Windmills, the sentinels of the western range, were introduced into Cíbola County in 1882, with the coming of the railroad. Before their appearance, sheep grazed near the mountains, where springs provided water. In winter, if there was snow, they were herded to fresh and abundant forage away from the waters, since they could obtain water by eating snow.

With the windmill came barbwire and cattle. The open range days were numbered—by 1940 most of the ranges were fenced. That started the decline of the sheep industry and the buildup of the cattle industry in northwestern New Mexico. Cattle needed to drink water every day, and windmills provided the water.

To drill the wells and maintain them, professional well drillers went into business. Lee Hassel says, "Our family came to Bluewater from Mexico after a revolution and my father went into the well drilling business. The original well drilling rig was a spudder. A tall wooden or metal beam, mounted on a wagon or a truck with a pulley and cable. A gasoline engine powered the rig, and a heavy steel head, hanging at the end of the cable, kept pounding and pounding a hole into the ground. It was a slow process, but it was sure, and the holes were always straight and easy to run casing pipe into them."

Another hardworking well driller was Oscar Carter, who homesteaded section 30 at Ambrosio Lake, drilled a well, and put up one of the tallest towers on the broad Ambrosio plain. You could see it for miles, and many of us wet our whistles at the Carter Well. When uranium was discovered, the section 30 mine was one of the richest.

Some water wells were drilled to 500 feet, but most of them averaged 350 feet, depending on the area. And there were some with no water—dry holes. Dry holes were very expensive, but ranchers were willing to take the risk, in order to open more range for grazing. In the Ambrosio Lake area, the average diameter of the windmill wheel was 14 feet.

Long before geologists with knowledge of formations and water-bearing sands were hired to locate well sites, wells were "water witched," with a Y-shaped forked stick. Many still are. Most of us who have drilled wells have taken a forked stick to decide where we should drill. We're not very good at it, but there are individuals who are. Many have built reputations finding water and are in demand. Some water witchers like a green willow stick, while others prefer mountain mahogany. With one branch of the forked stick in each hand, the water witch walks slowly, holding the stick in a horizontal position, pointing forward. The stick bends down in response to water beneath the ground. If after several passes it continues to bend over the same area, there's where the well is drilled. It's not foolproof, but then, neither are geologists.

In the 1950s the spudder began to give way to the rotary drill, which is much faster and is mounted on a large truck for drilling efficiency and for moving from one site to another. In rock, however, it tends to curve, making it harder to run casing pipe. The casing is usually 6 to 8 inches in diameter and keeps the hole from caving in. Inside the casing goes 2- to 3-inch pipe in 20-foot lengths. At the bottom is a brass cylinder with a bottom check. Inside the tubing run sucker rods. They move up and down on a stroke of ten to sixteen inches and pump the water. They were originally wood, because they floated and were a lighter load on the windmill in a light wind. A good well could produce from 3 to 6 gallons per minute.

The original towers were four oil-soaked logs, from 30 to 35
feet high. As is true for many aspects of ranch life, there have
been some accidents around windmills. One of the saddest resulted in the death of prominent rancher Tom Elkins, from Prewitt. He fell from the tower while checking one of his windmills
on January 3, 1949, at the age of fifty-two.

Aermotor windmills, made in Chicago, were the most popular. Bradley's generally serviced shallower wells. Steel towers
came later. Some of the old wooden towers are still in use today,
although the windmills have in large part been replaced by gasoline and electric pumps. Another chapter is closing. The picturesque sentinels of the open range that allowed sheep and cattle
to graze away from the mountains and lulled us to sleep with
their squeaky sounds are disappearing from the landscape.

Laguna Fiestas

The Laguna fiestas are probably the most popular fiestas in
Cíbola County. The patron saint of the pueblo is Saint Joseph,
whose day is traditionally celebrated on March 19 around the
Christian world. The people of Laguna changed it to September
19, exactly six months later, for a very practical reason. The season of harvest, of fat sheep and cattle, is in the late summer and
best for trading. And best for thanking the Lord for his bounty
when your storage bins are full.

I recall from the 1930s through the 1950s, hundreds of Navajo covered wagons hugging the shoulder of old Route 66
through Grants, as they traveled east. They were on their way to
their favorite fiesta, to celebrate and engage in trading. Coming
from the sprawling Navajo Reservation to the west, they brought
their colorful blankets and wool rugs, their beautiful silver and
turquoise jewelry, and their mutton jerky to barter and trade for
fruits and vegetables at the traditional "Fiestas de Laguna."

From the fertile Río Grande Valley came the Isleta Indians
and Hispanic farmers, with apples, chile, melons, pumpkins, on-

ions, and more, to trade with the Lagunas, Navajos, and others. It was a festive time. The fiesta and its unique trading preceded the agricultural fairs and markets of today. The Lagunas danced their festive and elaborate dances. Young men as Eagle Dancers glided gracefully, dominating the skies. Beautiful costumed women danced for most of the day, as did the men. The drum beat could be heard in one plaza or another throughout the village. At the baseball diamond, Pueblos pitted their best against each other and sometimes against neighboring Hispanic villages. The Lagunas were very skilled at the sport and usually the team to beat.

The resplendent white mission church of Saint Joseph stood tall above the village, dominating the landscape as it does today, quietly reminding us of the reason for the celebration. Masses and prayers of thanks were led by Franciscan priests in their brown habits, cinched by the traditional white cotton rope around the waist. Masses were in Latin and the sermon in English. Some priests learned a bit of the Keres language of Laguna and sprinkled their homilies with Indian words, to the silent amusement of the congregation.

From the flat roof of houses that had a family member whose name was José or Joseph, bread and other items were thrown down to the people below, in honor of Saint Joseph's namesake. This unique custom still continues today, although to a lesser degree. The campfires of the visiting Navajos surrounding the village burned day and night. They gave off the pleasant scent of piñon and juniper, mixed with the pleasing smells of green chile pods smoldering in the coals and the distinctive roasting of mutton over the open fires. Those smells sharpened our appetites and no doubt increased the sale of delicious food. Celebrants needed the energy to dance through the night and keep the fiesta going for two days.

Girls from Laguna and other pueblos, as well as other villages and towns, came to dance and to be seen. A huge portable tent served as the dance hall, where many of us learned the Boogie Woogie! Many of our young people met their spouses at Laguna and returned year after year, to celebrate the fiestas and relive the memories of yesteryear.

Following the fiesta, the horses were hitched and the wagons
loaded with their fruits and vegetables, to head back to the Navajo Reservation. The Isletas and Hispanic vendors loaded their
rugs, blankets, jewelry, and jerky and headed back to the Río
Grande. Today pickup trucks have replaced horses and wagons,
and trading has decreased, but the traditional fiesta continues,
on September 19 of every year.

La Nevada

The year was 1931, the year of the Big Snow, "El Año de La
Nevada." Snow covered the land of Cíbola and most of the rest
of New Mexico at an average depth of 30 inches. It was a shared
historic moment for the people who lived through it and for the
generation that followed. I was only five years old, so I don't
remember much. But I do vaguely recall mother being worried
about my father. He was gone most of the winter, taking care of
the sheep. She also worried about running out of firewood, since
that was the only source of heat we had in the village at the time.

The Big Snow fell in only two days. I can remember my father telling us that it started falling the afternoon of October 31
and continued through November 2. "We delivered lambs at the
stockyards in Grants and were loading them on the train when
the snow started. Thank God the storm gave us time to load
them and send them on their way, or we might have lost a whole
bunch." On the way to San Mateo with pack burros and horses,
they made it as far as the Bibo homestead, some ten miles north
of Grants, where they spent the night in their sleeping bags. By
dark there were about 8 inches of snow, and it was still falling.

"We got up before daybreak the following morning. The snow
reached to below our knees and was still falling. We cooked a
hearty breakfast as best we could, then made our way to the
corral in the dark and fed grain to our horses in nosebags. At
daylight we saddled up and started the eight pack burros and
two pack horses ahead, to break the snow. An eerie silence fol-

lowed us, as we slowly made our way home. We were a small party of five, in a sea of snow—and the snow continued to fall. At dark we got to San Mateo and could barely see the yellow light of kerosene lamps through some windows. The snow was still falling. There were about 2 feet on the ground. By the following morning, the snow stopped and there were about 30 inches. The village was literally entombed in snow."

According to Alfredo Barela, "When the snow stopped, all the villagers were shoveling trails from the house to the corrals and chicken coops, where the livestock were penned—and to the escusados (outhouses)."

From the Banco del Rito, where he was gathering cattle for Don Rudolfo Otero, came one of the heroes of the Big Snow, Marcelino Jaramillo. Everyone in San Mateo remembers Don Marcelino and what he did for the village that winter. Alfredo says, "He built a large two-horse driven sled and opened the roads in the village. He hauled wood on the sled to the school and he sometimes carried the children—school continued through the Big Snow."

Ernest Michael told me, "I was born the year of La Nevada, and of course I don't remember anything. But I do remember hearing later that Don Marcelino built a sled. He always had the fattest horses and they say he kept them in good shape, even in the Big Snow."

The early snowfall was followed by very cold temperatures and strong winds, and the snow froze. It stuck to the ground through the months of November, December, January, and into February 1932, before it started thawing and the snow receded. Marcelino kept hauling wood and helping people through the long winter. Celito says, "My father used to say when all the dry wood was gone, he cut a lot of green piñon and sabina trees near the village, in an attempt to keep people warm."

Rosalio Baca told me, "I can't remember much, but I do remember hearing that Don Nazario Sandoval, the mailman, brought the mail from Grants on horseback about once a week." There was a story told about Don Nazario. When he was asked how the snow was in Grants, he answered, "It snowed more over there, but there is more over here!" I believe what he meant was that Grants had more thaw because of its south exposure, while San Mateo had a much slower thaw because of its north exposure. Don Nazario was a colorful and well-respected gentleman in the village; he had homes in Grants and in San Mateo, where he also was a cattle rancher and a notary public.

After some time, the haystacks began to run out, as did the stored grain. The milk cows were growing weak, and milk production was down. The chickens quit laying eggs. Don Miguel Michael and his wife, Doña Meme, the store owners, had a hard time keeping staples in stock. Supplies came from Grants, and the road was nearly impassable. His and Doña Meme's generosity played a big part in helping the village survive the long hard winter, when there was very little or no money to pay the bills.

Reports of large livestock losses started coming back to the village. In some cases some sheepmen lost more than half the herds, especially those that were caught in the open and got weak before they could be moved into protected canyon country. Sheep losses were in the tens of thousands, and cattle losses were heavy also. My father used to say, "I was very lucky. When the snow came, my herd was in canyon country in the Canyon Largo area. The steep south slopes had a lot of brush, and the sheep survived with minor losses."

Stan Hayton lived in the Zuni Mountains at that time and says, "Old Silvestre Mirabal's sheep were in the Tinaja area. He had the men cut trails with a bunch of mules and they got the sheep to cover. He lost a bunch, but they were able to save the larger part of the herds. Old Silvestre was a good man."

During the Big Snow in New Mexico, America was heading into the Great Depression of the 1930s. Money was hard to come by, and times were tough, but people were equally tough. They were survivors. But after the snow melted and things began to get back to normal, the weather changed and the Great Drought of the 1930s began. Catastrophic sandstorms uprooted many of our neighbors from Oklahoma and sent them through Grants, up Santa Fe Avenue to California, seeking a new life. We were all victims of Mother Nature.

John Steinbeck called their sorrowful saga "The Grapes of Wrath." Some of those maligned Okies became oil magnates in California, developing the oil fields of southern California that helped us win the Second World War. But our parents remained in place. Their roots went deep—four centuries into New Mexico soil. We are the children of those remarkable people.

The Dry Years

Returning from his ranch at La Jara, Don Miguel said, "The slopes at La Jara are a little green." Marcelino's response was, "The only thing that's green at La Jara is *lagartijos* (the lizards)!"

Those were the incredibly dry years of the 1950s. Don Miguel, Merhage Michael, Lebanese merchant, farmer, and rancher in San Mateo was attempting to put the best face on a very dry situation. His friend Marcelino Jaramillo, born in San Mateo and raised in the arid Southwest, had lived through the drought of the 1910s and the Great Drought of the 1930s, and was a bit more skeptical.

The average annual precipitation for Cíbola County since records were started is about 9 inches and comes in the form of rain and snow. However, it can get down to 5 inches in the dry years and up to 15 inches in the very wet years. Our Hispanic forebears generally built their villages where canyons coming down from Mount Taylor opened up. Running springwater from the mountain gave life to the villages of Márquez, Seboyeta, Cubero, San José, San Fidel, and San Mateo. San Rafael was founded at the base of the Zuni Mountains, near the very productive El Gallo Spring, and Tinaja was established to the west, at the base of Water Canyon, originating on Oso Ridge on the Continental Divide.

Springwater from the mountains assured a permanent source of water for drinking, household uses, irrigation, and watering livestock. It also provided a habitat for wildlife, an important source of food during the colonial period. Villagers carefully took only the deer they could consume; game laws came much later.

Water was the lifeblood of farming and ranching, the two principal economic activities in colonial and territorial times.

Farmland was measured in strips called *suertes*, about 200 feet by 2,000 feet. Generally all the founding members of a village were granted a suerte by the Spanish crown, with a day or a night of irrigation rights per suerte. When New Mexico became a territory of the United States, in 1848, the Treaty of Guadalupe Hidalgo between the United States and Mexico recognized both the Spanish grants and the Mexican grants. Some discrepancies occurred, but by and large the suertes were recognized by the U.S. courts. Water associations were formed and a *mayordomo* hired to manage the water. He was paid from fees collected from water users. The mayordomo distributed water based on the *tabla* (table of rights) of the association. Water rights were and are still highly respected, and seldom are there any problems. If disputes arise the association resolves them. Suertes and water rights were negotiable, and many were bought and sold or divided and subdivided among heirs.

In San Mateo two reservoirs were built, with horses and scrapers, which stored a night's runoff from the mountain. Later, in the WPA days of the Roosevelt administration, in the 1930s, a large dam was built to store the winter runoff. It's still in use, although it has silted up quite a bit. I recall when the dam was being built. It's an earthen structure, built by dozens of teams with *fresnos* (large scrapers with swivels) and scrapers. Most of the men from the village and some from other villages worked on the structure with their teams.

Usually in the very dry years, the runoff from the mountain declined. The allocation of water was based on time frames of 12 hours—la noche y el día (night and day). The decrease in the flow of water in the dry years affected every user equally, and the increase in wet years helped everyone equally. Besides the irrigated gardens and fields, there was *temporal* farming (dry farming). Those fields were not irrigated and depended on rainfall for production. They were generally planted to corn. A good crop was harvested maybe once every three years. This practice was learned from our Native American neighbors.

The outcome of their farming and herding provided the settlers with a subsistence living. They could live and raise a family by working hard in the spring and summer and harvesting and storing for winter in the fall. Many left the area in the winter to herd sheep in Arizona and other states, bringing outside income to the village.

Orchards were an important source of food, but they also required irrigation. Much of the fruit was eaten fresh and some was dried in the sun to make orejón. Peaches, apricots, plums, pears, apples, and cherries, both in the form of whole fruit and jellies, were preserved in jars. They were an important part of our diet.

Generally the more children you had, the more hands were available to work the farm, and production increased. Family planning or birth control as we know it today were not generally practiced. (However, condoms did make their appearance after World War I.) Large families were considered a blessing. We also took care of our elderly at home and still prefer to do so whenever possible, but our changing lifestyles, where both husband and wife work outside the home, are making it more and more difficult. The extended family is disappearing. In our family there were seven children. All of us worked or did chores and were rewarded with love and appreciation by our parents. That was the case in most families.

Every year in the spring, the mayordomo scheduled about three days for cleaning and working the acequias and *compuertas*. Each adult male had to work a day with the shovel or hire someone to do his turn. An individual with more days of water rights provided more days of labor. Cleaning the acequias minimized the loss of water and gave us a continuing sense of community, as we worked together toward a common goal. It was extremely important to keep the ditch clean, because we all drank water from it, and it supplied all our household needs.

On the range surrounding the village were the *terrenos comunes* (common lands). Almost every villager had a milk cow that grazed on these lands. The milk cows were milked early in the morning and gave about a gallon of milk. Then they were turned out to be herded by a cowboy who was in charge of the whole village herd. The calves were kept in a corral. The herd returned in the late afternoon and was milked again. Later, with the advent of fences, they were turned out without a cowboy. They grazed all day and returned home in the afternoon. The average cow produced about 2 gallons of milk daily, which was about what the average family consumed in the form of fresh milk, *cuajada* (curds), and *queso* (cheese) per day.

Beyond the common lands, sheep herds were grazed. Sheep had an advantage over cattle, because they could live on snow without drinking water in the winter. The herds could graze far from the permanent water of the mountain—in fact, all the way to Chaco Canyon. In the summer they returned to the mountain. Cattle require water every day, winter and summer, and could not go too far from mountain water to graze. When windmills and barbwire were introduced, in 1882, cattle began to move away from the mountain to the plains. Several of the commercial sheep and cattle ranchers got grazing permits on the mountain, when the U.S. Forest Service began to manage these public lands in the 1930s. They grazed the forest in the summer and distant ranches in the winter.

The dry years were tough on livestock, but they were less rigorous for animals on the forest lands. The forests had more sources of water and brush, and livestock did better where they had to walk shorter distances to water. As a rule the forest better utilized the moisture from snow and made more green feed.

Sheep were usually bred on December 10 with one ram to about forty ewes. The lambs started dropping five months later, in early May. The number of lambs saved by ten herders taking care of a thousand sheep depended on how much green feed (grass, weeds, and browse) there was. A ewe on green feed produces more milk, and her mothering instinct increases as her tight udder encourages frequent nursing by her lamb. A dry year on dry feed and no green reduces milk production and lowers the mothering instinct of the ewes, so that fewer lambs can be saved. Lamb crops during wet years could approximate 100 percent, while they could drop to as low as 50 percent in the dry years. In those years ewes would abandon their lambs, and a lot of abandoned lambs, called *pencos,* were given to boys and girls in the village to be raised with the bottle.

Most of us had raised a lamb or two, even before the 4-H Club came into the picture. As they grew the pet males tended to get mean and would butt us on the rump! And sometimes we cried at the loss when they were butchered, as they all inevitably were.

I had often wondered why our ancestors settled in dry and arid New Mexico. The answer came when I visited Spain in 1954 and again with my wife in 1975. Many of our ancestors came from the province of Estremadura, where sheep thrive in relatively dry country. Our ancestors were sheepmen first and farmers second. The dry climate and high elevation of northern New Mexico and the west-central Cíbola country suited their enterprise best.

Most of the commercial sheep are now gone, except for some herds on the neighboring Indian reservations. Acrylic fibers, made in laboratories at a lower cost, have replaced wool in our lives. Lower demand for lamb and mutton, and higher demand for beef, have pretty well ended the sheep industry in Cíbola County, where at one time it was the principal industry. Cattle replaced sheep, and with today's modern cattle auctions, such as the one in Milan, cattlemen can quickly adjust the numbers of cattle to the amount of feed on their ranches. It is now easier to reduce a herd in the dry years and increase it in the wet years, an option not readily available to our sheep-raising ancestors. They didn't have a nearby market for their ewes.

In our semiarid corner of the world, droughts will continue to test the true grit of the people making a living from the land. Despite the uncertainty of the weather, our farmers and ranchers will continue to produce the crops and meat for America's tables. Never in the history of man have a people eaten so well for so little, as Americans have in the past half century.

The Hubbell Ranch

In 1954 when I returned from Australia, where I studied sheep and wool production on a Fulbright scholarship, I went to work for the Frank A. Hubbell Company, in Catron County, in western New Mexico, as the ranch foreman of the Cerro Prieto Ranch. We ran about ten thousand Rambouillet sheep at the ranch near Quemado, on approximately 250,000 acres, in a very traditional but successful way. We used sheepherders instead of netwire fences.

Santiago, Román, and Frank, Jr., the sons of the late Frank A. Hubbell, Sr., and Doña Trinidad García Hubbell, were the owners of Cerro Prieto as well as of the Y Ranch, near Reserve, New Mexico. The three brothers lived and maintained their main office in Albuquerque. The Y Ranch also ran about ten thousand sheep on about 250,000 acres and was managed by Bill Hubbell, the son of Santiago. The Hubbells were known by their Hispanic neighbors as "los Hobles," and the ranches, "los Ranchos de los Hobles." The two ranches represented the largest sheep operation in New Mexico involving over twenty thousand sheep and more than one hundred sheepherders and other workers.

I was single at the time and lived in a small room adjacent to the bunkhouse. When I told Frank Hubbell, Jr., one of the owners and manager of Cerro Prieto, that I was planning to get married, he said, "We can empty and fix the storeroom next to the commissary for you and your bride until we can build a house, if that's okay with you." I told him, "Yes, that's fine." It would give "my bride" a chance to help plan the new house in what her city friends called "the rattlesnake, prairie dog, and coyote country of western New Mexico."

The storeroom was part of an old log building and needed quite a bit of work to get it ready for the "city bride" from Santa Fe. She had earned a bachelor of music in education degree from the College of Mount Saint Joseph, in Cincinnati, Ohio, and had been teaching music in the Santa Fe school system. The night before leaving to get married, I was on my hands and knees scrubbing and polishing the newly laid linoleum floor in the renovated one-room apartment. Mr. Hubbell, whom we called Don Franke, happened to walk by; as he looked in, he said in his deep voice, "Good for you, son. I've lived nearly seventy years, and I've found that it's a lot easier to leave a good impression than to live down a bad one!" Those wise words have been an important part of my life, especially when I am tempted to leave a job unfinished or miss a scheduled appointment.

I met my lovely and talented bride in 1952, while on leave from military service, when I was serving in the army during the Korean War. I went to Santa Fe with my good friend Bony Baca and met Viola on a blind date. She was singing "Granada," and it blinded me for good! Her parents were Ignacio Cisneros (who died in 1933) and Ramona Alarid Cisneros, and she had two sisters, Rose (now deceased) and Lena as well as a brother, Bobby.

Three years later, on August 27, 1955, Father Meldon, a young, friendly, and newly ordained Franciscan priest, married us at St. Francis Cathedral in Santa Fe, amid our families and friends. The organist played "Here Comes the Bride," and her good friend Don Purcell sang a moving song composed by his father especially for our wedding. Even now when I close my eyes and recall that special day, I hear Don's voice floating across that immense cathedral toward the altar, enveloping the bride and the groom.

Wild stories of rattlesnakes, coyotes, and guns peppered the friendly conversation at the reception at St. Michael's College (see Fig. 27). Viola's mother, who raised her children alone after her husband died, was employed as the head cook at the college. That day she was the proud mother of the bride, wearing a happy and contented smile.

After a memorable honeymoon in Carmel-by-the-Sea on the Monterey Peninsula in California, we returned to the ranch, and Viola had her first glimpse of Cerro Prieto and our apartment. Her first comment was, "It's nice, it's very nice. The first thing we'll do is put up curtains!" The men, renovating without a women's touch, had overlooked the curtains! In the planning of the new home, the most important thing for her was "a large

living room where I can put my baby grand piano and a fire-
place." A contractor from Springerville, Arizona, built the house of cinder block, with a flat roof and a spacious living room, including a large fireplace and a big picture window to match the big country.

The year 1955 was a very dry one. The large ranch, which stretched from the malpais south of Grants nearly to the Arizona border, produced very little grass that summer. In the fall, after the lamb crop went to market, the sheep herds were kept in what we called the high summer country, where the grass was a little better than in the lower winter country. A fast-moving snowstorm in January of 1956 dropped nearly 18 inches of snow and forced us to scurry and trail the herds as fast as possible to the low country, where there was only about a foot covering the ground. Some of the sheep became snow-blind, and yearlings got sore mouth on the trail. We normally had from fifty to a hundred sick sheep in the hospital pen. During the snow, we had about four hundred, which led Don Franke to remark, "You know Abe, after seventy years, I'm convinced sheep were born looking for a way to die!"

Sometime after the snow receded, I left one morning before sunrise to check on the fence crew at Los Mireles, a line camp about 8 miles from headquarters. This immense ranch, founded before the turn of the century, had stood the test of time and its owners believed in the old adage that good fences make good neighbors. The ranch had approximately 250 miles of fence, and it took a crew of three working year-round to keep the fence in good repair. Old Tranquilino García, the teamster in the crew, was sitting on the low adobe patio wall, reclining against the house looking east and patiently waiting for the sun to rise. Stopping I rolled down the pickup window and asked, "What are you doing Don Tranquilino?" He answered, "Hijo, estoy esperando la cobija de los pobres!" ("Son, I'm waiting for the blanket of the poor!") He was in his sixties and very much a gentleman and a philosopher.

On August 29, 1956, our first daughter was born in Springerville, Arizona, some 50 miles away. It was the closest hospital,

and Dr. Browning was our family doctor. There were about 20
miles of dirt road to negotiate before reaching the paved highway. It was the rainy season, and Bill Hubbell insisted on escorting us in a 4-wheel drive all the way to Springerville, "to make
sure you don't have any problems with the expectant mother on
the way to the hospital" (see Fig. 28). The baby was born in the
early hours of the morning, shortly after I groggily left the hospital and went to the motel. The motel owner by previous in-
struction banged on my door and yelled, "It's a girl!" At that
very moment, I knew I really wanted a girl, and Ramona was a
charmer! After four days, mother and daughter were released,
and we went home.

Arriving at the ranch, I drove up to our apartment. Several
ranchhands were standing nearby, as if at attention. Grady, who
took care of the chickens and was in charge of the gasoline pump,
never bathed and never took his hat off, no matter what. But he
had bathed and changed clothes, and he was now slowly approaching the car, taking off his hat. He carefully opened the
passenger door, anxious to see the child. Viola opened the blanket, and Grady stood in a reverie, riveted on the baby—and then
a tear came down his cheek. That tender moment will always
live in our hearts. Grady and all those rugged men in a men's
world were prompted by the miracle of creation to a spontaneous showing of love for the first child that had come to that
ranch in recent memory. God touched us all that memorable day
in 1956.

Crypto-Jews

Are some of us descendants of Sephardic Jews? The evidence
indicates that the ancestry of some Hispanics in New Mexico
can be traced back to the Jews who left Spain during the Spanish
Inquisition. Looking at world history, three important events
happened in Spain in 1492. The first was the discovery of the
Americas by Christopher Columbus. The second was the start of

the Spanish Inquisition. And the third was the expulsion of the
Moors to Morocco after seven hundred years in Spain and of the
Jews, to all corners of the globe. All three events, especially the
discovery of the Americas and the start of the Inquisition, had
global implications.

The Inquisition to suppress "heresy" in Spain was earth-shak-
ing to non-Catholics, especially the Jews, who had been in Spain
since the Middle Ages. It was established by the Catholic rulers
of Spain, Queen Isabela and King Ferdinand, in 1480, and was
severely enforced in 1492 by Tomás de Torquemada, the inquisi-
tor general. Anyone who was not Catholic had to leave Spain or
convert to Catholicism. Thousands left Spain and migrated to
other countries. Thousands of others "converted" to Catholicism but secretly practiced their Jewish religion in hiding—hence
the term *crypto-Jew*. They were called *marranos* by the Jews
who left rather than convert, and *conversos* by the Spanish.

The intensity of the Inquisition, including death penalties,
made many conversos nervous, and some found ways to mi-
grate to the Americas, even though it was against the law. The
New World offered remoteness even in Mexico and other Latin
American countries, but most certainly in the frontier region of
New Mexico in the seventeenth and eighteenth centuries.

In the past twenty-five years, more and more has been said
and written about crypto-Jews in New Mexico. The foremost
historian, researcher, and writer on the subject is Dr. Stanley
Hordes, former historian of New Mexico, and now director of
HMS Associates, a historical consulting firm based in Santa Fe.

Some time ago I had breakfast at La Fonda Hotel in Santa Fe
with Dr. Hordes, and he showed me slides of northern New
Mexico gravestones marked with Hebrew inscriptions and others with stars of David carved into the stone. He said, "When I
was historian of New Mexico, some Hispanics slipped into my
office, quietly closed the door, and told me of some family in
their town that didn't eat pork and prayed in a secret room." He
tells of dozens of people he has interviewed who are following
Jewish traditions to some degree, lighting candles on Friday,
carving the menorah on gravestones, placing little stones on the

grave when visiting a loved one's resting place, or even a grandfather telling a grandson in a remote cornfield, "Somos judíos" ("We are Jews").

My first encounter with the subject came as I was drinking coffee with a Costa Rican professor, at a sidewalk cafe in San Jose, Costa Rica, in 1976. During our conversation he paused and said, "Señor Peña, do you know you may be Jewish?" To be honest I was a bit surprised and responded with another question, "What makes you think so?" He said, "Research is finding that many of the conversos in Spain took place names such as Ríos (rivers), Peña (rock), Mesa (mesa), Montaño (mountain) when they discarded their Jewish names."

In 1984 when we returned home from the foreign service in Latin America, where I directed the Peace Corps in a couple of countries and the United States Agency for International Development in several others, we read about some of the research being done on crypto-Jews, especially in the Southwest. Dr. Rowena Rivera and Dr. Tomás Atencio, professors at the University of New Mexico, have collaborated with Dr. Hordes in a research project on the subject at the university's Latin American Institute. Dr. Frances Hernández, professor at the University of Texas at El Paso, is also involved in similar research and has done extensive writing on the subject. Their findings show increasing evidence of a Jewish connection. However, after centuries of secrecy and hiding, the traces are disappearing with every passing generation.

For the past few months, I've been visiting cemeteries in our Hispanic villages in Cíbola County, looking for signs. So far I've found none. The first graveyards in the area date back to 1800, whereas those around Santa Fe date back to the 1600s. The importance of this subject is not whether Hispanics are descendants of Jews or not, but rather, what are our origins? So far history is showing that some of the Spanish who came to colonize the Americas were conversos, or their descendants. They found refuge in northern and central New Mexico, the areas from which they came later to colonize Cíbola County. God only knows to what extremes they may have gone to avoid the severity of the Inquisition; we can only hope that their descendants among New Mexico's Hispanics can recapture some of their heritage before it is completely lost.

Glossary

abrazos	hugs	blanca	white
abuela	grandmother	bonita	pretty
abuelo	grandfather	borrachita	drunken
aceite	oil	botes de cinco	5-pound cans
acequia	irrigation ditch	brasa	live coal
adelante	forward	breles	bread
adorar	adore, worship	brujas	witches
agua	water	bueno/a	good
alabados	hymns	buena mano	gourmet
alaban	praise	burriñates	dish made of baked goat or sheep intestines
almagre	ochre		
altar	altar		
amacha	balk	burra	female donkey
amores	love	burro	male donkey
angelitos	little angels	buques	boats
año	year	buscando	looking for
arroz con pasas	rice pudding	cabecera	head (as of a bed)
		cajete	tub
asada	roast	campo	camp
averiguata	argumentative	cantan	sing
		camino	road
bailále	dance to	campesino	small farmer
bailan	dance	cañada	draw
balcón	balcony	canciones	songs
barejón	pole	cantos	hymns
Bascos	Basques	caporal	foreman
bastonero	dance manager	cariño	gesture
bendito	blessed		

carne	meat
casa	home
casi	almost
casita	small home
cautiva	captive
cerrito	small mountain, hill
cerro	mountain, peak
cesar	cease
chamizo	sagebrush
chaparreras	chaps
charra	small Navajo horse
charravante	small Navajo horse
chicharrones	pork cracklings
chiquitos	small ones (often used of children)
chongo	bun
chota	cop
chote	schottische (dance)
cíbola	female buffalo
cíbolo	male buffalo
colector	collector
colgando	hanging
colorada	red
comadre	female religious cosponsor
compadre	male religious cosponsor
compañero	partner
companía	company
compuerta	irrigation gate
conseguimos	(we) secured
conversos	(Jewish) converts to Catholicism
corridos	ballads
cortar	cut
costillas	ribs
cruz	cross
cuadrilla	square
cuajada	curds
cuaresma	Lent
cuesta	hill
cuatro	four
cuidado	careful
culebra	snake
cunita	cradle
curandera	midwife, healer
derecho	straight, right
diablito	little devil
días	days
Dios	God
dolientes	mourners
Don	Mr.
Doña	Mrs.
dueños	sponsors
el	the
en	in
encerraban (se)	locked (themselves) up
encontrara	meet
enjarradora	plasterer
entrada	entrance
escusado	toilet
fandangos	dances
farol	lantern
fiesta	feast
flores	flowers
fresno	fresno (a large scraper with swivel)
friego	"botheration"
frijolitos	beans
frío	cold
fuella	track, trail
gallo	rooster
gaviotas	seagulls
galletas	biscuits
galopeando	galloping

gloria	glory, heaven	mar	ocean
gorras	hoods	marcha	grand march
gotea	leak	marco	frame
gozo	joy	marranos	hogs, pigs (Jewish converts to Catholicism)
gracias	thanks		
guerra	war	matanza	pig killing
guitarra	guitar	mayor	head, eldest
haciendo	doing	mayordomo	water supervisor
hembra	female	menudo	tripe stew
hermano mayor	Penitente leader	mexicano	Mexican
hermanos	brothers	mi	my
		miedo	fear
hermandad	brotherhood	mil	thousand
hijo	son	militar	military
hija	daughter	milpas	cornfields
hijito	grandson	mochila	bedroll
hijita	granddaughter	mocho	one-armed, one-handed
hostia	host		
huerfano	orphan	morada	chapel
Jesús	Jesus	morado	purple
joven	young	morcillas	blood sausages
judíos	Jews	mosca	fly
la	the	muelas	molars, young boy
Laguna	Indian tribe	mula	mule, moonshine
laguna	lake	música	music, mouth
Lala	grandma	nana	grandmother
látigo	latigo (leather strings)	nazareno	Nazarene
		nevada	big snow
lonjas	strips	nidos	nests
los	the	no	no, does not
luminaria	ritual bonfire	noche	night
luna	moon	nuestros	ours
macho	male	ochá	wild celery
madre	mother	oculto	hidden
mamá	mother	ojo	spring
mamonas	suckers (snakes)	ollas	pots
mano	hand	olvidar	forget
manzana	apple	orejón	dried fruit

orillas	edges
oye	listen
pa'	for
padre	father
padrinos	sponsors
pais	country
pale	grandfather
paloma	dove
panocha	sweet sprouted-wheat pudding
panzona	big belly
papá	dad
parece	looks
partido	shares
pasan	pass
pastorcillos	shepherds
pastor	shepherd
pastorela	nativity
pastores	shepherds
patada	kick
patrón	employer
paye	grandfather
pecados	sins
pechera	bib overalls
pediré	I will ask
pelones	bald
penco	orphaned lamb
penitente	penitent
perdonar	forgive
pie	foot
piñón	pinyon (tree or nuts)
pito	flute
plaza	town
plazuela	patio
poco	a little
poco raro	a bit strange
polca	polka

poleo	mint
pondré	I will put
poquito	a little bit
porque	why
posadas	seek shelter
prima	female cousin
primo	male cousin
provisiones	groceries
pudiera	could
pueblo	village, Indian village
pueblito	small village
puerta	door
puro	pure
que	that
queso	cheese
quiero	want
ramillete	bouquet
rancho	ranch
raro	strange
ratones	mice
reales	money
recen	pray
resolana	sunny side of a building
ricos	rich families
rincón	corner
robar	steal
rodeo	roundup
Roma	Rome
rosa	rose
sábado	saturday
sabe	know
sabino	juniper tree
sabroso	tasty
sacar	take out
sacrístan	altar boy

sala	dance hall	*venir*	come
saludar	greet	*víboras*	poisonous snake
salve	save	*vieja*	old
sea	be, is	*viejo*	old
seguería	follow	*viga*	beam
sestiando	resting at noon	*vienen*	come
solo	alone	*yerba*	herb
somos	we are	*yerba buena*	mint
sopa	soup	*yerba del manso*	plant of the lizard's tail family
sopaipilla	bread-dough fritter		
soy	am	*yo*	me
suerte	plot of farmland	*zotea*	(flat) roof
tabla	table of rights		
tanque	tank		
tápalo	shawl		
tata	grandpa		
taures	card sharks		
te	you		
temporal	dry farming		
tiene	has		
tierra	land		
tía	aunt		
tío	uncle		
tiempo	time		
tinaja	pot or cistern		
todos	all		
torreón	tower		
tren	train		
vallo	buckskin		
valse	waltz		
vamos	let's go		
vapores	steamers, steamships		
velorio	vigil		
vengo	(I) come		
venida	entrance		

Bibliography

Chávez, Fray Angélico.
My Penitente Land: Reflections on Spanish New Mexico.
Albuquerque: University of New Mexico Press, 1974.

Barela, Josephine. *Ojo del Gallo: A Nostalgic Narrative of Historic San Rafael.* Santa Fe: Sleeping Fox Enterprises, 1975.

Chacón, Rafael, and Jacqueline Maketa. *Legacy of Honor: The Life of Rafael Chacón, a Nineteenth-Century New Mexican.* Albuquerque: University of New Mexico Press, 1986.

Cobos, Rubén. *A Dictionary of New Mexico and Southern Colorado Spanish.* Santa Fe: Museum of New Mexico Press, 1983.

Grants Daily Beacon, which in the 1980s became the *Cibola County Beacon.*

Lummis, Charles. *The Land of Poco Tiempo.* Albuquerque: University of New Mexico Press, 1952.

Peterson, C. S. *Representative New Mexicans 1912–14.* Denver: C. S. Peterson, 1912[1914].

Simmons, Marc. *The Little Lion of the Southwest: A Life of Manuel Antonio Chaves.* Chicago: Swallow Press, 1973.

Tietjen, Gary. *Encounter with the Frontier: A History of McKinley County, New Mexico, Part of Valencia County, New Mexico, and the Area around Ft. Defiance, Arizona.* Los Alamos, NM, privately printed, 1969.